The Second Greatest Story Ever Told

THE SECOND GREATEST STORY EVER TOLD

A NOVEL BY

NORMAN BECHARD

A Citadel Press Book

Published by Carol Publishing Group

A Citadel Press Book
Published by Carol Publishing Group
Birch Lane Press is a registered trademark of Carol Communications, Inc.

Editorial Offices: 600 Madison Avenue, New York, N.Y. 10022
Sales & Distribution Offices: 120 Enterprise Avenue, Secaucus, N.J. 07094
In Canada: Musson Book Company, a division of General Publishing Co., Ltd., Don Mills, Ontario M3B 2T6

Queries regarding rights and permissions should be addressed to Carol Publishing Group, 600 Madison Avenue, New York, N.Y. 10022

Carol Publishing Group books are available at special discounts for bulk purchases, for sales promotions, fund raising, or educational purposes. Special editions can be created to specifications. For details contact: Special Sales Department, Carol Publishing Group, 120 Enterprise Avenue, Secaucus, N.J. 07094

Lyrics from "Gloria: In Excelsis Deo" and "Kimberly" reprinted by permission of Patti Smith.

Dialogue from Ingmar Bergman's *The Seventh Seal* from the book *Four Screen Plays of Ingmar Bergman,* Copyright 1960, 1988, by Ingmar Bergman, reprinted by permission of Simon & Schuster, Inc.

Manufactured in the United States of America

10 9 8 7 6 5 4 3 2 1

Library of Congress Cataloging-in-Publication Data

Bechard, Gorman.
    The second greatest story ever told / Gorman Bechard.
      p. cm.
    "A Citadel Press book."
    ISBN 0–8065–1263–6
    I. Title.
PS3552.E238S4   1991
813'.54—dc20   91–20046
                                                    CIP

To the memory of
Claire Roberts

Please Note

The Second Greatest Story Ever Told is a work of fiction that tells the story of the imaginary Daughter of God, Ilona Ann Coggswater. Names, characters, television programs, films, books, songs, places and incidents depicted in *The Second Greatest Story Ever Told* are fictitious or used fictitiously. The events and speeches in this novel are not real, nor are they intended to be so interpreted. For example, the quotes, speeches, thoughts, books and newspaper headlines contained in *The Second Greatest Story Ever Told* are completely the product of the author's imagination and there is no intention to imply that any of the speakers or writers have actually said, thought, delivered, written or published these fictional pieces.

The Second Greatest Story Ever Told

Is it so hard to conceive God with one's senses? Why should He hide in a mist of half-spoken promises? Can we have faith in those who believe when we don't have faith in ourselves? What is going to happen to those of us who want to believe, but aren't able? And what of those who neither want to nor are capable of believing? Why can't I kill God within me? Why does He live on in this painful and humiliating way even though I curse Him and want to tear Him out of my heart? Why, in spite of all, is He a baffling reality that I can't shake off? I want knowledge, not faith, not supposition, but knowledge. I want God to stretch out His hand to me, reveal Himself and speak to me.

—Knight Antonius Block
speaking to Death
in *The Seventh Seal*

Introducing Dudley & Jerry

"What a bunch of fuckups!"

"What was that?"

"What a bunch of fuckups," Dudley said, agitation turning to funk, a consecrated sulk.

"Stop moaning," Jerry said, "and give it up already. You've tried everything."

Dudley nodded. Not a nod of agreement, just a silent nod. A nod for nod's sake.

"There's nothing more you can do."

"Bullshit," Dudley said, the whisper of a brat.

"Look, you're tired, you're drunk, and . . ."

"I have a headache."

"You always have a headache."

"But this is a real bad headache."

"You drank too much."

Dudley looked at his colleague, through his colleague, and spoke slowly, enunciating both syllables. "Bullshit," he said, with extra emphasis on the *t*. Bullshit for everything, about everything, on everything. Bullshit. Bullshit. Bullshit.

"I'm closing up for the night."

Though Dudley thought, Bullshit, the words came out, "What?" then, "You can't."

"But I am." It was Jerry's turn at enunciation, "Now go home. Get some rest."

"I don't want to go home."

"Then go get laid. Try again for all I care."

"And maybe I will."

"Fine. But remember, three strikes and you're out, buddy."

This sobered Dudley up, at least for the moment. "Don't talk baseball," he said, too serious, too straight. "You know I hate baseball."

Jerry shook his head, slightly, sadly. He, too, was tired, not of this, but of everything else. You'll see, he thought, but said, "Mark my words. Just mark my words."

Dudley said nothing. He thought about sighing, but didn't. He thought about crying, but wouldn't. He thought about dying, but couldn't. He just got up and left.

PART ONE

1

The Umbilical Café

> For God did not send His Daughter into the
> world to condemn the world, but that the
> world through Her might be saved.
>   —Updated John 3:17
>   *The Next Testament*

It was a tight squeeze.

And though the safety, comfort, warmth, and humidity of her mother's womb seemed preferable to the glare and rubber gloves that now surrounded her, it was checkout time. And checkout time was as unavoidable as lunch was bland. So bland at the Umbilical Café. So bland. How she longed for a diet soda. That would liven things up, a definite shock to those preborn taste buds. A diet soda. With extra syrup, if possible. And though she wouldn't taste one for one thousand, five hundred and twenty-two days, when that chemical combination known as Tab first passed her lips and trickled down her four-year-old throat—"ahh . . ."—she knew, that this was the taste lacking from the Umbilical Café.

"Ahh . . . ," Tab.

"Ahh . . . ," checkout time.

"Bye, Mom."

And if the glare and rubber gloves weren't enough, the slap was. So rude. Another slap and a reaction. And not exactly the reaction the doctor wanted. No cry, just a stare. An intense, wide-eyed, green-eyed gaze that said, beyond any doubt, "Don't slap me again." And so unnatural, so disturbing was this reaction, this gaze, from a just-born that the doctor issuing the slap gasped and dropped the infant, momentarily forgetting his responsibilities, momentarily awed.

And as that infant floated to the floor of the delivery room in some sort of mock slow motion, that doctor, Dr. Julio Gonzalez, thought of her green eyes, dreamed of her green eyes. Those huge green eyes floating down and away. So large, so delicate, those marvelous green eyes. Greener than any eyes he had seen before or would ever see again. Eyes that knew, eyes that seemed, eyes that could, eyes that—"Ahh . . . ," just "Ahh . . ."

And Gonzalez sighed, much to the horror of the others in the delivery room at the time. Others who felt this was no time to sigh. Others who were watching a just-born fall, not float, to the floor. Others who screamed and panicked while Gonzalez dreamed of those green eyes. Others who watched as a nurse-in-training made a play, a diving catch, that would have made any professional running back proud. Others who watched as that nurse stood, cradling the now smiling infant in her arms, and snapped at Gonzalez.

"Asshole," the nurse snapped.

And Gonzalez stopped dreaming.

"Bravo," said the others, a small round of applause for that nurse. "Why didn't we do that?"

And the just-born was carried to the nursery, and the mother was wheeled to recovery, and Dr. Gonzalez, that nurse-in-training, and the others moved on to the next delivery of the day. It was more or less routine, before the books and talk shows and diet soda commercials. No one knew. Not Gonzalez, not that nurse, not the others.

How could they?

&

STATE OF NEW YORK
DEPARTMENT OF SOCIAL SERVICES

Notice of Registration of Birth

NAME OF CHILD	PLACE OF BIRTH	DATE OF BIRTH
ILONA ANN COGGSWATER	COOPERSTOWN	9-15-70

REGISTRATION NO	FATHER'S NAME
208-33-18126	UNKNOWN

SEX	MOTHER'S MAIDEN NAME
FEMALE	MIRIAM CLARISSA COGGSWATER

The birth of the child named above has been registered
with the New York State Department of Health.

Amas A. Eberhardt

Commissioner of Health

It wasn't that Ilona's father was unknown. It's just that Mariam Clarissa Coggswater never knew how to break the news. It had to be Dave Wiggits. Who else would have raped Mariam?

Well, not rape.

Not exactly.

A keg party. Mariam's first keg party, her last. December. Cold, very cold. Bill Waterworth's house. Captain of the football team Bill, whose parents were in the South of France for the winter, leaving Bill alone in a too large, too empty house.

And, at this keg party, Mariam got wasted. Everyone did. The entire senior class of Cy Young High School, or so it seemed. And six or so beers, Mariam's first beers ever, and about that many shots of Peppermint Schnapps, Mariam's first shots of anything ever, more or less, was all it took.

And somehow, sometime into that keg party, desperately seeking a bathroom, Mariam discovered Bill's parents' bedroom. And Bill's parents' king-size bed discovered Mariam.

"I'll just rest here for a minute," she said to no one, so much for the bathroom.

And rest she did.

First the bed was spinning.

"Woo," she said.

Then nothing.

No spinning. No woos.

And she was out. Not asleep, but unconscious, or so she later figured. Figured, because, when Mariam awoke, Dave Wiggits was fast asleep. Asleep, his head resting on her thigh. Asleep and naked. Stark raving naked. But not Mariam. Her clothing was hardly touched, wrinkled at best.

And Mariam hiccupped.

Uh-oh, she thought, getting up off the bed, quiet, except for the hiccups, mind racing, mind swirling, never mind.

But wait, she thought. Dave Wiggits. Mariam had always had a crush on Dave Wiggits. And Dave Wiggits was asleep. Asleep and naked.

And there *it* was, in all its, well, not glory exactly, but it was there.

Why not?

And so she looked at it, then hiccupped, then laughed, barely.

"Ssshhhh," she said, "you'll wake him up."

"Okay," she answered.

And then she touched it, barely.

"Woo," she said.

No spinning, just a "woo."

And though the situation was fucked up, so was Mariam, and she left Bill's parents' bedroom, smiling and hiccupping, in search of that elusive bathroom, giving what may or may not have happened little thought outside of a damp daydream or two.

Little thought until six weeks later.

"You're pregnant."

And Mariam's mind raced back to Bill Waterworth's keg party

and Bill Waterworth's parents' king-size bed and Dave Wiggits's semi-erect penis in all its, well, not glory exactly, and it all made sense.

Barely.

It had to be Dave. He must have. He had to have. But why? Why not? And what a gyp. Mariam had never even made out with a guy. And as far as she knew she was a virgin.

A virgin, Dr. Gonzalez thought to himself after her first examination. Her boyfriend must have a teeny weeny little pecker, but said, "The test came out positive," and receiving no answer, "You're pregnant."

"Are you sure?" Mariam asked, after a considerable pause.

"The rabbit died," he said, as he so often did, with a chuckle that was more like a snort.

"Huh?"

"Never mind."

And as she walked away teary-eyed, Dr. Gonzalez shook his head ever so slightly. It was baby time and Mariam was just another unwed, pregnant teenage statistic. She didn't know. Gonzalez didn't know.

How could they?

ᖇ

But according to his book, *I Delivered God*, Dr. Gonzalez knew from the start that he "was dealing with a miracle," when, during Mariam's first gynecological exam, he noticed a "heavenly light" shining from deep within her womb.

(Ilona would later explain that it was simply the neon lights from the Umbilical Café.)

"I dropped to my knees and made the sign of the cross when I saw the positive pregnancy test," Gonzalez would write. "And when I called Mariam into my office, I looked deep into her eyes—she, too, had beautiful green eyes—and we both began to cry. I never had to utter the word. She knew. She understood. We hugged and said a rosary."

In a later television interview Mariam would state that she had never, in her life, said a rosary, and now probably never would.

℘

Mariam Clarissa Coggswater was a slightly better than average looking seventeen-year-old girl, a little over five feet, six inches tall, with shoulder-length dirty-blond hair, who possessed two outstanding physical features, those big beautiful green eyes that even a Gonzalez would notice, and a perfect, Playboy centerfold body.

"You've got the most beautiful big green eyes," teachers and bookstore cashiers would say, and stop there.

"She's got great tits," the boys at school would say, or most likely something worse, and stop there.

Stop there, because, more than anything else, Mariam was a loner. And it wasn't because she didn't want friends, or at least acquaintances—she went to the high-school games and had finally attended a party—it's just that those who could have been friends, or at least acquaintances, had so little to say.

Mariam really didn't care who the greatest rock 'n' roll drummer of all time was, or what happened on this soap opera or that sitcom, or who was dating whom, or who was wearing what. It all seemed so trivial. So damned trivial.

She would prefer a film or a ballgame or a lingering sunset on Otsego Lake. And usually she would prefer these alone, more or less, a well-worn paperback her only companion.

"You read too much," the other girls or her mother would say. "That's why none of the guys ever talk to you."

"They're afraid of you," another girl or her father would say.

"Teenagers aren't supposed to read," they all would say. "And they don't watch the evening news."

"But knowledge is preferable to small talk," Mariam would answer, thinking, I've got the best body in school and the only way I can get a guy to touch me is to pass out from drinking Peppermint Schnapps.

But loneliness was also preferable to small talk. And so Mariam kept her "beautiful big green eyes" and "great tits" to herself. She kept her damp daydreams and passing crushes to herself. She kept her knowledge and that loneliness to herself. And for the time being, she would keep the identity of her unborn child's father to herself.

ↂ

Dave Wiggits would not live to see the child that Mariam Coggswater believed was his. But had he, and had he written the inevitable book, he would have told the world how in fact he and his homosexual lover Bill Waterworth made love on one side of Bill's parents' king-size bed while Mariam lay in her unconscious state on the other. And when through with what in his book would have been an extremely graphic depiction of their lovemaking, Bill would excuse himself so that he could get back to his guests while the quite spent and quite naked Dave did the quite natural thing and cuddled up to Mariam's thigh.

But the world would be spared this particular literary miracle when Dave Wiggits would die in a freak bowling accident that summer. During one of his turns, his last turn actually, his fingers would somehow forget to let go of his bowling ball. And that bowling ball, a birthday present from Bill Waterworth, would pull Dave down the oh-so-recently polished lane, smack into the bowling pins, where the restacking machine would proceed to crush his skull quite thoroughly and completely. And though it was a strike, it was most probably not the way Dave Wiggits would have wanted to go.

Mariam cried when she found out about Dave's death. And for once the loneliness stung, the knowledge stung, and lack of it was worse. She wished she had told him about the pregnancy. She wished she had asked him about that night. She wished, she wanted. She didn't know what the fuck she wished or wanted.

Uncertainty wasn't preferable to small talk.

ↂ

In Bill Waterworth's book, *Dave Wiggits Was My Gay Lover*, he would explain how he and Dave made love numerous times that night while "the best body in all of Otsego County lay unconscious and in waiting not twelve inches from where we balled."

Waterworth would also explain that, if he and Dave had indeed not been gay, "We would have done Mariam in a second," adding, "as long as she had been unconscious."

And though Mariam never at this time spoke of her belief that Dave Wiggits was the father of her unborn child, the Cooperstown rumor mill had long since placed the two of them on Bill's parents' king-size bed the night of that keg party.

"It was perfect!" Waterworth would write. "It was the cover Dave and I needed. We would often brag in gym class about taking turns with Mariam the night of the party and how we weren't really sure which of us was the baby's real father."

Mariam would never read Waterworth's book.

Ever.

છ

At one point, early in the pregnancy, Mariam thought about having an abortion. A thought encouraged by her parents, Richard and Lillian.

"It won't hurt," Lillian said.

"That's not what I'm afraid of," Mariam argued.

"So, you're afraid," Lillian said. "I'll go with you and hold your hand."

"No, that's not it," Mariam said.

"What is it then?" Richard asked.

"I think I want to have this baby," Mariam said.

"You're crazy," Richard said. "She's crazy. Fucking nuts."

"You're not ready to have a baby," Lillian said. "You don't even have a boyfriend."

"What does that have to do with anything?" Mariam asked.

"You just want a little friend, don't you?" Lillian said. "She's lonely."

"She's nuts," Richard said, again. "If she wants a friend, she should get a dog."

"She's just confused," Lillian said.

"I'm not confused," Mariam insisted. "And I don't want a dog."

"What have you got against dogs?" Richard asked.

"I haven't got anything against dogs," Mariam said.

"Then what's your problem?" Richard asked.

"Her problem is that she's pregnant," Lillian said.

"I know that, for Christ's sake," Richard yelled.

"I've given this a lot of thought," Mariam said.

"You haven't given it the right thought," Richard said.

"The right thought for whom?" Mariam asked.

"Think of what the neighbors'll think," Lillian said.

"Who cares what the neighbors think?" Mariam said. "It's my baby."

"And who's the father?" Richard demanded.

And Mariam was silent.

"Tell us, dear," Lillian said.

And Mariam was silent.

"Do we know the boy?" Lillian asked.

And Mariam said nothing.

"Oh, so it's an immaculate fucking conception," Richard said. "It's a fucking miracle."

And Mariam began to cry.

"You'll ruin your life,"Richard said.

"What about college?" Lillian asked.

"Your reputation?" Richard asked.

"A career?" Lillian asked.

"What career?" Mariam screamed. "What reputation? This is my baby. And I want it. I have to have it."

"Why?" both Richard and Lillian asked.

And Mariam continued to cry. She continued to scream. She screamed, "I don't know."

And neither did her parents.

How could they?

☙❧

In his book, *From Jesus, Mary, and Joseph to Ilona, Mariam, and Dave*, George Wiggits, Dave's father, would deny his son's homosexuality and insist that Dave was indeed Ilona's natural father and that Dave and Mariam were madly in love and had talked of eloping shortly before Dave's untimely death.

"He told me he was the father, time and time again," the senior Wiggits would write. "He even described most of their sexual encounters in detail. Dave really loved big boobs, and that Coggswater girl certainly delivered in that area," adding, "I was so proud of my boy."

In a later television interview Mariam would say that not only had she not been in love with Dave Wiggits, though she had, at one point, been certain she was carrying his child, they had never spoken of eloping, and in fact, had never spoken at all, period.

"Not even hello?" the television interviewer asked.

"Not even hello."

☙

And during the sixth month of pregnancy, on a particularly lazy midsummer evening, not long after her graduation from Cy Young High, a graduation ceremony her parents would refuse to attend, Mariam, alone, crumpled paperback in hand, napped on a favorite bench overlooking Otsego Lake. And she dreamed. She dreamed a dream that she neither understood nor ever gave much thought to, with one slight exception.

She dreamed of being in the Baseball Hall of Fame. The museum was empty except for her and a man. A strange man, with almost angelic features. And that strange man approached her and introduced himself as Gabe.

And Gabe said, "Rejoice, highly favored one, the Lord is with you; blessed are you among women."

And though Mariam expected to be handed a pamphlet and asked for a donation, she said nothing. And Gabe continued. "Do not be afraid, Mariam," he said, "for you have found favor with God."

How do you know my name, she thought, but again said nothing.

"And behold," Gabe continued, "you have conceived in your womb and shall bring forth a Daughter, and shall call Her name Ilona."

And Mariam was confused, though she sort of liked the name Ilona.

"She will be great, and will be called the Daughter of the Highest."

And Mariam said, finally, "What the hell are you talking about?"

And Gabe said, "The Holy Spirit has come upon you, and the power of the Highest has overshadowed you; therefore, also, the Holy One who is to be born will be called the Daughter of God."

"Oh, that makes it a lot clearer," Mariam said, sarcastically.

And Gabe said, "Just remember, For with God nothing is impossible."

But before Mariam could scream for a security guard, Gabe was gone.

And Mariam awoke to catch the end of what surely must have been the most glorious of sunsets. And she laughed to herself, being pregnant really plays havoc with your system.

"Ilona, huh?" she said.

And she laughed again and watched the sun disappear.

She didn't know.

How could she?

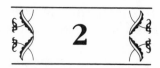

2

Chestnut Street

"How can a baby not change everything?" Mariam Clarissa Coggswater thought, Mariam Clarissa Coggswater said.

"But do you have to move out?" Lillian asked.

"Yes, I have to move out." She had to.

She had to.

And grandmother Lillian looked at the infant Ilona. "She's such a good baby," Lillian said, many times, before starting to cry.

"Is she?" Mariam asked. She didn't know, she couldn't. "Is she really?"

"Absolutely," Lillian answered.

And she was.

And shortly before Thanksgiving, the mother and child moved on.

With her part-time job at the Cooperstown Rexall Pharmacy becoming full time, Mariam found and was able to afford what the real-estate agent, Babs Rothburg, called a "charming" two-bedroom walkup on Chestnut Street, "just four blocks from the Baseball Hall of Fame."

Rothburg would explain in her book, *The New Holy Land*, that Linda Maronne, the apartment's tenant, was looking for a roommate, and when Rothburg first met Mariam and "that divine child" she knew that Maronne's Chestnut Street apartment would be a place "they could call home."

It was.

Linda Maronne was new to Cooperstown. She arrived by way of Waterbury, Connecticut, a loner and lonely. This feisty, dark-haired, dark-eyed, twenty-one-year-old Italian with unpracticed Roman Catholic beliefs had been thrown out of her parents' house only six months earlier. She was pregnant, her cause and their reason. But suffering a miscarriage three months into the pregnancy, Linda left Waterbury, her parents, her past, for good.

Hitchhiking, with a suitcase, a backpack, and what little money she had, Linda was offered a ride by a family of four, an up-and-coming attorney, his wife and two small children, on their way to visit the Baseball Hall of Fame. Why not, she figured, and within a week, early into September's last week, Linda was living in that "charming" two-bedroom walkup on Chestnut Street holding a job as a cocktail waitress at the After Midnight Lounge.

"You're not a Jesus freak, or anything like that?" Linda asked, on that first meeting.

"Nothing like that, at all," Mariam said, "I have very little to do with religion."

"Okay, then get your things."

"That's it? That's all you wanted to know?"

"That's all I need to know."

And the infant Ilona, who until this time had been observing silently from her mother's arms, giggled.

And both women looked at Ilona, then at each other, and they, too, began to laugh.

It was a perfect beginning.

And this trinity of sorts would become a team, the best of friends, three best friends—Mariam's first two best friends, her first two real friends—two single attractive young women and one slightly remarkable baby.

ᏅᏓ

Ilona spoke her first word a few weeks after her first birthday, a birthday that was quietly celebrated with a cake, a candle, and a bevy of presents.

And during one of those many later television interviews, between correcting wrong assumptions, Mariam would joke that that first word was "iconoclast." But after the commercial break, one of many, Mariam would admit that Ilona's first word had really been "Seaver" and was said on a Sunday afternoon while mother and daughter and roommate watched the New York Mets baseball team beat the Los Angeles Dodgers by a score of five to two. During a close-up of the Mets' pitcher Tom Seaver, Ilona pointed at the TV screen and said his name.

"At first I just agreed," Mariam would explain. "Yup, that's Tom Seaver. And then it hit me that Ilona had spoken her first word. 'Seaver.' Linda and I were so excited we popped open a bottle of champagne that Linda had been saving for a special occasion."

That champagne would be Mariam's first drink in quite some time.

❧

In early 1973, Mariam began dating William Smith, who had been courting and urging her on with flowers, notes, and calls for about a month before she finally agreed to "dinner, just dinner," as she explained to Linda.

"It's about time," Linda said.

Smith, a doctor who suffered from what he said were nothing more than bad headaches, met Mariam while having a prescription at the Cooperstown Rexall Pharmacy where she worked.

"Sometimes I feel like I've got the weight of the whole world on my shoulders," Smith told her, popping one of those headache pills.

"Maybe you should see a doctor," Mariam said with a smile.

"I don't believe in doctors." Smith smiled back.

Mariam liked William Smith.

And why not? Smith was a tall, good-looking man of about forty, though at times he seemed ageless, almost timeless, with a rugged face and large hands and a masculine smell that Mariam adored.

"What *is* that cologne?" Linda asked, noticing.

"I don't know," Mariam said, "but it drives me crazy."

And it did.

"He's a good man," Linda added.

And he was.

And kind.

William Smith adored Ilona, treating her as if she were his.

"He's so good with Ilona," Mariam told Linda. "She even calls him Dad."

"He lets her?" Linda asked.

And Mariam nodded.

"Does he have any bad habits?"

"Well, he doesn't really like baseball."

"That's it?"

"Yup."

"Marry him," Linda said.

�''⋅

On Easter morning, Smith arrived at the Chestnut Street apartment with three colorful Easter baskets, one for Mariam, one for Ilona, and one for Linda.

"I didn't want you to feel left out," he told Linda, handing her the basket.

"Thank you," she said.

And Ilona ripped into her basket, exposing the mounds of chocolates and jelly beans, the small stuffed toy rabbit, and an official New York Mets baseball cap.

"The Mets," Ilona said. "Thanks, Dad."

And Mariam smiled as Ilona proudly wore her Mets cap and hugged her rabbit.

"I thought you didn't like baseball," Mariam said.

"But Ilona does," Smith explained.

And Linda discovered similar treats in her basket, including one of those toy rabbits.

"See, I got one, too," Linda said to Ilona.

"That way they won't be lonely," Ilona said.

"That's right, they won't be lonely," Linda said.

"And they can protect each other," Ilona continued. "And they'll never scream."

And Linda smiled. What a wonderful imagination, she thought.

And Mariam opened her basket, and under the mounds of chocolates and jelly beans, instead of yet another rabbit or even an official New York Mets baseball cap, she found a small, perfectly wrapped box. And opening that box she found a simple but elegant gold Rolex watch, a small version of the one William never seemed to take off.

"They last eternities," William said.

"I don't know what to say," Mariam said. "I mean, thank you, but, why? I mean, what's the occasion?"

"Let's just say," William explained, popping one of those headache pills, "Easter has always been very special to me."

☙

Shortly after Ilona's third birthday, a birthday that was heartily celebrated with a cake, three candles, and more than a bevy of presents all in front of a televised Mets game—"I thought you didn't like baseball, Mariam thought at the time, remembering Smith's answer, "But Ilona does"—William Smith left Cooperstown, Ilona, and Mariam, left them to work with the Peace Corps in some remote part of Africa.

"They need me," he explained.

"But, we need you, too," Mariam said. "I need you."

"I'll be back as soon as humanly possible."

But Smith never would return to Cooperstown. Becoming gravely ill in early December, those headaches finally taking their toll, he died in his sleep on Christmas morning, 1973, and was buried in that remote part of Africa.

Mariam was devastated. She would sit silently night after night in the living room of that Chestnut Street apartment. And though the tears would eventually stop, the sadness, the absolute emptiness could not, would not, seem to go away.

"It'll be okay, Mom," Ilona told her. "He's in heaven now."

And Mariam would look up into her daughter's eyes and manage a smile, then a hug.

Mariam didn't know.

How could she?

$$\mathcal{C}\mathcal{O}$$

According to *The Miracle Matinee*, a short book written by Kenneth Arbor, manager of the Cooperstown Cinema 1, 2, 3 & 4 from 1972 to 1978, Mariam Coggswater forgot, or at least tried to forget, that sadness and emptiness at the movies.

"I would see her and little Ilona, and many times Linda, at least twice a week," Arbor would write, "sometimes more, and always on that Sunday matinee."

According to this book, Ilona's favorite film was Charlie Chaplin's *The Kid*, which she first saw in late 1974 during a retrospective of film classics the cinema was sponsoring. Arbor would comment, "Ilona was only four years old, but she fell for Chaplin in a big way. I never knew why at the time, whether it was the baggy suit and big shoes, his cane or his mustache, or maybe his funny walk. It didn't matter. She would say his name over and over again and was just so darn cute about it, I scheduled some of Chaplin's other movies, *The Gold Rush*, *City Lights*, *Modern Times*, and a few of his shorts. And Ilona would arrive early, clutching Mariam's hand, leading her into the theater, always taking her same seat in the third row, and she'd be enthralled, laughing, sometimes crying, as if this little girl understood completely all that was going on."

Ilona would later explain that it was more than the baggy suit and big shoes, more than the cane or mustache, much more than the funny walk. She would explain that it was Chaplin's humaneness.

$$\mathcal{C}\mathcal{O}$$

Ilona began her formal education at Cooperstown's Saint Mary's School just a few days shy of her fifth birthday, a birthday that would be softly celebrated with a cake, six candles ("One for good luck!" Mariam explained), a few rather large presents, and a Chaplin film at the Cooperstown Cinema 1, 2, 3 & 4. Mariam wanted her exceptionally bright child to have the best education she could afford and, at least at the time, Saint Mary's seemed preferable to the Babe Ruth Elementary and Junior High School.

Records verify that Ilona was an exceptional student with a near solid A average from kindergarten right through to eighth grade and graduation. Her only problem subject seemed to be religion, where her various teachers labeled her "disruptive," "argumentative," "impossible," "an atheist," "a pain in the neck," "a troubled child," "possessed by satanic notions," "sarcastic," "a heathen," "disrespectful," "blasphemous," "slightly retarded," "deeply disturbed," "in need of psychiatric counseling," "embarrassing," "a heterodoxy," and "the reason for my early retirement."

But, seeing that religion played no part in Mariam's life, these comments bothered her little, if at all. A solid education was what she wanted for her daughter, and the Bible and the Catholic church with their teachings of Adam and Eve and Noah's Ark had no practical use in today's turbulent world.

"I know all about Noah's Ark," first-grader Ilona told her mother.

"And do you believe that story?" Mariam asked.

"Parts of it," Ilona said.

"What parts?"

"The parts that weren't made up."

"And do you think that God can really make it rain for forty days and forty nights?"

"Yup."

"Well, maybe you're right."

"I am."

"Personally, I don't know."

And it's not that Mariam didn't believe in some supreme being. It's just that she gave that supreme being, that might or might not even exist, little thought. And it's not that she felt that her daughter should likewise give that supreme being, that might or might not even exist, little thought. Mariam, in fact, felt that Ilona should make up her own mind about supreme beings and whatnot. It was, after all, Ilona's life.

Agnostic was the accepted term for what Mariam was. Not that she felt what she was needed a fancy name. She disliked labeling almost as much as she disliked dictionaries, and would never again consciously use either after having to look up *heterodoxy*.

❧

The importance of the New York Mets in Ilona's life would grow and continue well past that first word and her official baseball cap. And while most kids her age were glued to reruns and Saturday morning cartoons, Ilona watched the televised games.

"I've never seen the Mets lose," she would later say.

She never did.

And while many who know major-league baseball might consider that alone some kind of a miracle, Ilona always swore that she never had anything to do with the outcome of any games.

"Never?" amazed interviewers would ask.

"Yup," Ilona would say.

"Yup, never?"

"Yup, never."

Instead Ilona preferred to concentrate on gastronomical miracles, at least at first.

And miracle number one occurred during a second-grade class trip to Cooperstown's Farmers' Museum.

When unable to visit the concession stand for a diet soda, and tired of the stale, lukewarm water in the water coolers that seemed to be located around every corner, Ilona led one of her friends to what she called "a special water cooler."

"Taste the water in that cooler," Ilona said.

"The water here is icky," the other second-grader replied.

"Just taste it."

And she did. And a brown syrupy liquid gushed forth from where water should have come.

|25|

"It tastes like Pepsi," the little girl said.

"Not Pepsi," Ilona explained. "It's Tab."

"What's Tab doin' in the water cooler?"

Ilona shrugged. And her little friend shrugged and took another sip.

And it was Ilona's turn. She stepped up to the cooler and drank its Tab and smiled. How, even at seven, she loved that chemical aftertaste.

"Ahh . . ." she said.

"Ahh . . ." her little friend repeated.

"Ahh . . ."

And they giggled and ran and rejoined the other second-graders.

"Ahh . . ."

$$\mathcal{CO}$$

This was followed by a similar miracle in third grade during lunch.

It seems that the then eight-year-old Ilona was less than thrilled with the scheduled luncheon menu of liver and onions. So, when stepping up to order her food, she firmly requested, "One salad, please."

The stunned cook raised an eyebrow, cocked her head just slightly to one side, and said, "All we got is liver and onions. You want liver and onions, fine. If not, move on."

And Ilona said, "It looks like salad to me."

And the cook glanced down at what should have been a half-filled platter of unappetizing liver and onions and saw neatly arranged rows of reusable plastic bowls each filled with a simple but nutritious mixture of lettuce, cucumbers, tomatoes, grated American cheese, croutons, and one pitted black olive. And looking up at the TODAY'S MENU blackboard the cook read the words, written in her unmistakable handwriting, "Garden Fresh Salad—75 cents," then carefully and slowly, maybe too slowly, placed one of those salad-filled reusable plastic bowls on the tray held in midair by Ilona's outstretched arm.

And Ilona said, "Some creamy Italian dressing, please."

And the cook blindly reached to where the packets of salad dressing would be kept if indeed salad were the food offering of the day, which it appeared to be, and finding the packets, as she was afraid she would, grabbed what she knew to be the creamy Italian and handed it to Ilona.

And Ilona said, "Thank you."

ↁ

Though so much of what would be written about the Chestnut Street years would be filled with hearsay, exaggerations, and lies, there would be two noteworthy exceptions.

The Divine Pupil, a four-thousand-page epic by Sister Hermina Braun, Ilona's fourth-grade teacher, who would write, "Ilona continually criticized the Lord's Prayer, all classic prayers for that matter, insisting that, 'God is sick and tired of the same old thing. It just adds to His headaches. And God has enough headaches.' She was always preaching about God's headaches. I began to believe our Holy Father had a brain tumor."

In *Holy Pediatrics*, Dr. Gerard McKenna, Ilona's pediatrician, would take over nine hundred pages to tell us that Ilona was basically a very healthy child. The doctor would devote nearly half the book to a case of chicken pox Ilona suffered through when she was six, even analyzing the patterns and clusters the disease chose to take, paying special attention to a "crosslike" pattern of severe blotches that erupted on the child's left buttock.

ↁ

Mariam and Ilona would share the Chestnut Street apartment with Linda Maronne for nine years. Nine years of safety, comfort, and warmth, of laughter and tears, of growing up, nine years of love.

And the singular most unbelievable aspect of this living arrangement was that Linda Maronne would never speak or write of her life with Mariam and Ilona. Despite promised advances running into the millions and national exposure on the talk-show circuit, she would never divulge, never give in.

Today Linda runs the Dew Drop Inn, a modest bar on Otsego Lake, earning a more than comfortable living. She has remained single, independent, and a close friend to both Mariam and Ilona.

❧

But that's jumping ahead.

3

Susquehanna Avenue

During the summer of 1979, Babs Rothburg, new owner of a Century 21 real estate franchise, sold Linda what would shortly become the Dew Drop Inn, where customers could, if they so desired, dance, dine, and drink.

In need of minor repairs, this "charming" two story building located on the southwestern edge of Otsego Lake, would give Linda, who had saved many a tip first from waitressing and then from bartending, the freedom and financial security she desired, while its second floor would make a pleasant two-bedroom apartment complete with a balcony overlooking the lake. But both Linda and Mariam knew that this apartment was no place to raise the almost nine-year-old Ilona.

How can a bar not change everything? Mariam and Linda sadly realized.

So, Rothburg found Mariam, who herself had set aside substantial savings after being named manager of the Cooperstown Rexall Pharmacy in late 1975, and Ilona a "charming" six-room white colonial on Susquehanna Avenue, not far from the Susquehanna River, only two and a half blocks from where Susquehanna Avenue crossed Chestnut Street.

This house is where Ilona would spend the next nine years of her life.

୧୨

Ilona's formal education continued with little change. Very little.

Toward the end of her eighth and final year at Saint Mary's, Ilona was sent to the principal's office, an almost daily ritual, one that both Ilona and the school officials had grown tired of.

The principal, Sister Katherine Flaherty, began as she usually did. "What did you do *now*?" Sister Flaherty asked.

"I tried to explain to Sister Barbara that the Old Testament was not to be taken literally."

"Ilona," the nun said, "how many times do I have to ask you not argue with Sister Barbara? I know you disagree with her teachings. We all know. Believe me."

"Then why do I have to sit through her class?"

"Because it's school policy."

"So you expect me to sit there and not voice my opinions?"

"I pray that you sit there and not voice your opinions."

"Well, that's not about to work."

"Then," Sister Flaherty asked, "what do you recommend?"

"That you drop religion class from the school curriculum," Ilona suggested.

"But we're a Catholic school."

"That isn't my problem."

"Can't you just hold your tongue?"

"Not when she's telling me that Eve was made from one of Adam's ribs."

"Well, if Eve wasn't made from one of Adam's ribs, please explain to me then exactly where she came from."

And Ilona looked at the nun with that intense, wide-eyed, green-eyed gaze. A look that made Sister Flaherty gasp slightly.

"This is hopeless," Ilona said.

"For once we agree," Sister Flaherty said.

And hoping for some parental guidance, the principal called Mariam and asked her to stop by the school at her convenience.

"What's wrong?" Mariam asked.

"It's Ilona's attitude."

And Mariam was silent.

"In religion class."

"How's she doing in her other classes?"

"Straight A's, as always."

"That's all I'm concerned with."

"You don't seem to understand."

And Mariam was silent.

"Ilona's upsetting Sister Barbara; she argues with everything Sister Barbara says."

"Then why does she have to sit through her class?"

"Because it's school policy."

"So you expect her to sit there and not voice her opinions?"

"I pray that she sits there and not voice her opinions."

"Well, I doubt that'll work."

"Then," Sister Flaherty asked, "what do you recommend?"

"That you drop religion class from the school curriculum," Mariam suggested.

"But we're a Catholic school."

"That isn't my problem."

"Can't you just tell your daughter to hold her tongue?"

"Not when some teacher is telling her that Eve was made from one of Adam's ribs."

"Well, if Eve wasn't made from one of Adam's ribs, please explain to me then exactly where she came from."

And Mariam laughed. "This is hopeless," she said.

"Apparently so," agreed Sister Flaherty. "Apparently so."

☙

"Saint Ignatius High or Cy Young High?"

It was a question Ilona didn't need to answer, a question Mariam didn't need to ask.

Cooperstown's Cy Young High School had excellent teachers with excellent credentials—Mariam knew this firsthand—and religion was nowhere to be found in the school's curriculum. And without religion to drag her average down, Ilona, whose intelligence and understanding exceeded all practical expectations, would graduate with the highest average in the twenty-seven-year history of Cy Young High.

"Just be careful," Mariam said.

[31]

"Careful?" Ilona asked, confused.

"At keg parties," Mariam explained, wishing she didn't have to.

"Can I ask why?"

And Mariam's mind raced back to Bill Waterworth's keg party and Bill Waterworth's parents' king-size bed and Dave Wiggits's semi-erect penis in all its, well, not glory exactly, and Dr. Gonzalez.

"You're pregnant," he had said, so long ago.

And Mariam looked into her daughter's eyes. My eyes, she thought proudly, smiling slightly, softly saying, "Never mind."

捤

And shortly after her sixteenth birthday, a birthday that was wildly celebrated with a cake, sixteen candles, and one incredibly incredible present, Ilona would get a part-time job at the Cheapskate Record Shop, a cluttered collage of splintered orange crates packed with albums, cardboard boxes jammed with cassettes, shelves lined with compact discs and walls layered with screaming rock posters, located on the second floor over Famous Al's Diner and Baseball Memorabilia Emporium on Main Street in downtown Cooperstown.

This small store, which specialized in used and unusual recordings as well as stocking all the hits, was owned and more or less operated by a sweat-pants-clad, gray-eyed, perpetually unshaven, salt-and-pepper-haired man in his late thirties known as the Professor, just the Professor.

And from three to six every weekday, noon to six on Saturdays, Ilona would help the odd assortment of customers, customers who would journey from the far stretches of Otsego County, find musical answers, musical remedies to their eternal questions, their eternal heartaches.

One evening, a few days before Christmas 1987, Ilona's eighteenth Christmas, just as the Professor was hanging that GO AWAY, WE'RE CLOSED sign on the door, a customer appeared.

"I know exactly what I'm here for," the customer said. "I'll only be a minute."

[32]

And the Professor let him enter with the warning, "Make it snappy."

And the customer walked toward the rear of the store, while Ilona and the Professor counted the day's receipts. He looked through everything but at nothing and finally approached the counter, no records, tapes, or CDs in hand.

"Is there anything I can help you with?" Ilona asked.

"Yes," the customer said, "there is," and he raised the Saturday night special that he held tightly in his left hand from out of his coat pocket and aimed its barrel at her heart.

A lump formed in Ilona's throat, her breathing became hard, as hard as that of the customer who held the gun. And Ilona looked at the customer with that intense, wide-eyed, green-eyed gaze, but he would not return her stare. He would not look into her eyes. Instead, his eyes darted nervously about the store, always drawn back to the glimmering barrel of the gun.

"Let's not do anything foolish," the Professor said.

And the customer turned quickly on the Professor, aiming the gun his way.

"Just put all your money in a bag," he said. "Now!" he screamed. "Now!"

And the Professor did as the customer asked.

"But," Ilona said.

And the customer turned his gun toward her. But before Ilona could speak, the Professor cut her off.

"Be quiet," the Professor told her. "Leave her out of this," he told the customer with the gun. "Leave her alone. I'm putting the money in a bag. All the money. See?"

"Just hurry up," the customer said.

And the Professor handed the customer the bag full of money.

"And don't follow me," the customer said.

"We won't," the Professor assured him. "We won't."

And the customer with the gun left the store.

Stillness for a moment, not a sound, not a breath, not a creak, not a peep. But finally a sigh, an inverted sigh, then another.

"Are you okay?" the Professor asked.

"I guess," Ilona said. "You?"

"Yeah, yeah, I'm fine," he said, leaning against a wall, sliding to the floor. "Jesus Christ."

"You can say that again," Ilona said. "You can say that again."

And after the police and reports and mug shots and necessary phone calls to Mariam and others, the Professor said, "I don't know about you, but I need a drink. Wanna join me?"

"Why, you coming apart?" Ilona said. It was an old joke, one of many used as often as possible at the Cheapskate Record Shop, but still it made the Professor laugh.

"Sure," Ilona said. "But what bar is gonna serve me?"

"Don't worry 'bout it. We'll get a six-pack to go."

"Beer, huh?"

"Don't like beer?"

"Never had one."

"You've never had a beer?"

"My mom doesn't recommend it."

"Moderation. That's the key."

And the Professor picked up a couple of six-packs of ice-cold Rolling Rock and together they sat on the cold floor of his record shop drinking, talking, mostly laughing. A battle of bad jokes, a battle of wits.

And the beer tasted good. Maybe too good, Ilona thought. How it quieted the sounds in her head, how it relaxed, slowed the senses, how it, "Ahh . . ." just "Ahh . . ."

And at half past midnight, the Professor pulled an old black-and-white Zenith television set from the store's storage room and plugged it in.

"Ever watch 'Late Night with David Letterman'?" he asked. And Ilona shook her head.

"Then prepare yourself," the Professor said. "You are about to become a member of a special society, a society of goofy people, goofy people who each and every weeknight spend sixty goofy minutes witnessing a miracle, a miracle from their goofy God."

"What kind of miracle?" Ilona asked.

"The miracle of laughter," the Professor explained.

The most precious and sacred of miracles, Ilona thought, but said nothing. She just sat back and watched.

And sixty goofy minutes later, after the goofy God said his goofy good nights, the Professor walked Ilona home, "just in case," he explained.

"In case what?" she asked. "The gunman's waiting for me around the next corner?"

"Something like that."

And as they turned off Main, south onto Pioneer Street, the Professor asked, "Ever think about heaven?"

"All the time," Ilona said.

"I always wonder what I would be doing there. What my occupation would be."

"Like, is there a Cheapskate Record Shop in heaven?"

And the Professor chuckled slightly, "Something like that," and after a pause added, "or is it just eternal nothingness? I couldn't bear that."

"What purpose would eternal nothingness serve?"

"God's punchline."

"Man's punchline," Ilona said. "Only humankind can be that cruel."

"Then God is kind?"

"I think so."

"And loving?"

"But he doesn't like baseball."

And the Professor laughed.

And at the front door of that "charming" Susquehanna Avenue house, Ilona looked at the Professor, her intense, wide-eyed, green-eyed gaze into his perky, pesky, gray eyes. She had never really looked into the Professor's eyes before, she had never really felt this way before, warm, relaxed, peaceful within, how she wanted to tell him, tell him all, tell him everything, all that she understood, all that there was to do, all.

But all Ilona could say, all Ilona would say, was, "Thanks."

"For what?" asked the Professor.

"That was fun!"

"Getting robbed?"

"No," Ilona said. "The talk, the beer."

"Anytime, kid," the Professor said.

"Good night."

" 'Night."

And, when later asked about Ilona's employment at the Cheapskate Record Shop, the Professor, still just the Professor, would limit his statement to a mere five words. And those five words, uttered to Hazel Testa, a reporter from *People* magazine, would be, "Get the fuck outta here." *Out of* was only one word to this Professor.

❦

Two books would offer a wildly varying book at Ilona's Susquehanna Avenue years, *My Best Friend* by Patti Flogstaff and Robert Cervickas's *Jilted*.

"I'll never forget," Patti would write, "the day Ilona and I saw our first penis. We were twelve at the time. I was looking for a sweater in my older sister's room, and I came across some copies of *Playgirl* magazine and couldn't help but look. I snatched one of the magazines and later showed it to Ilona. She looked and laughed and blushed and looked again, then said, 'So, that's what we have to look forward to,' and rolled those green eyes of hers."

"I'll never forget," Robert would write, "the day Ilona first saw me naked. She laughed. I couldn't believe it. Hell, I was in shape, I was on the track team. But she laughed. And then I saw what those green eyes were staring at. She really knew how to ruin a romantic mood."

Patti would continue, "Ilona had had a crush on Robert Cervickas for years. Not a super severe crush, but enough of one. Since eighth grade I think. I have to admit he was cute. And when he asked her to a school dance at the end of our sophomore year, she freaked. I helped her pick out a really, what should I call it, sophisticated but sexy black dress. She looked great. And they started going steady a few months into our junior year."

"The night I asked Ilona to go steady," Robert would explain, "she dragged me to this Charlie Chaplin movie. 'To celebrate,' she said. It was in black and white and didn't have any sound, just a lot of bad music. It was really stupid but Ilona flipped over it. All night long she kept talking about this Charlie guy. Charlie this. Charlie that. Charlie, Charlie, Charlie. Enough about Charlie, what about me?"

"Chaplin was her magnificent obsession," Patti would say. "She worshipped him, and after her mom bought a video cassette recorder, Ilona spent most of her allowance buying his movies. I remember her excitement the night she first watched *The Great Dictator* at home. We sat through it twice. But I'm still not sure what was more entrancing, Chaplin himself, or Ilona's obsession."

"She was weird," Robert would write. "If she wasn't going off about that Chaplin dude, she was talking about all this punk music crap she listened to. Stuff like Elvis Costello. I tried to turn her onto something good. Get her to listen to some Black Sabbath or Skynyrd or the new Journey album. But no, no way, not Ilona. Then I got tickets for the Van Halen concert in Albany, and she didn't want to go, she wouldn't even discuss it. She just had to be different from everyone else. Now I think back and realize it must have been their song, 'Running with the Devil.' Or maybe because Judas Priest was the opening band. That had to be it. I just wish I had known. Hell, I *should* have known."

"What Ilona didn't spend on Chaplin videos," Patti would recall, "went toward music. She was always searching for something new. She didn't like what was popular. It was as if she knew there had to be something better. And then she discovered Elvis Costello, another obsession. But it was 1985, this was Cooperstown, New York, population 2,327, and our friends had never even heard of Elvis Costello. Then she got that job at the Cheapskate Record Shop and lost all control. I would go to her house and she'd be dancing around her bedroom to some new discovery, the Replacements, Hüsker Dü, the Jesus and Mary Chain, wild stuff. And I'd listen and more than likely love it. Next came a Patti Smith binge. Even though her records were old— they had been released in the late seventies—they were new to Ilona, who would walk around singing, 'Jesus died for somebody's sins, but not mine,' over and over. She got such a kick out of that line."

" 'Jesus died for somebody's sins, but not mine,' " Robert would write. "I didn't know what that meant at the time. And I still don't."

"Then there was the New York Mets," Patti would write. "Night after night all those games on TV, especially during the 1986 season when they won the World Series. We would sit there with a bucket of popcorn and Ilona wearing this old Mets cap, screaming, slamming our fists on the coffee table, just really getting into it. And the funny thing is, I can honestly never remember the Mets losing a game when they had Ilona and me rooting them on."

"Baseball!" Robert would exclaim. "The most boring sport in the world and she couldn't get enough of it. Those damn Mets. And she really had a thing for that pitcher, Bobby Ojeda, especially the year they won the Series. He won eighteen games that year and I swear, she watched every single one on TV. She would have jumped his bones in a second, I'm sure of that."

"I remember when Ilona told me about the time she and Robert made love," Patti would recall. "It was early January of our senior year. They had been going steady for a long time and she loved Robert but I think at this point she was no longer in love with him. And looking back I think maybe she was just curious and knew it would be her last chance, for a long while, anyway. I mean, a woman in her position couldn't exactly be sleeping around, now could she?"

"I waited over a year to have sex with Ilona," Robert would confess. "Sure we made out and stuff like that. But it never got much past a feel. All my friends thought I was getting it regularly. I wish. Anyway, one day, boom."

"School was canceled due to blizzard conditions," Patti would continue. "Robert's parents were at work and he was at home, alone."

"So, I hear a knock at the door and it's Ilona," he would write. "Christ, I thought to myself."

("Wrong as usual," Ilona would later comment, "but close.")

"She walked to his house," Patti would say, "in the freezing cold. He lets her in, she kisses him passionately, throws him down to the living-room floor, right in front of the fireplace, and straddles him."

"Before I could say anything," he would continue, "y'know, offer her a hot chocolate or something, she was all over me, taking off my clothes, taking off her clothes. She was like an animal, except for that brief period where she was laughing at my dick. I thought about it and realized she never said anything to me that afternoon. Not one word."

"Ilona told me they made love all afternoon," Patti would write. "All afternoon! I asked her why and she said because she wanted to know firsthand what all the fuss was about. 'Did you get your answer?' I asked. 'Yup,' she said, as she so often did, and, with this twinkle in her eyes, 'absolutely.' "

Robert would describe the "romp," to use his word, in details that were far too explicit, embarrassing, and unnecessary, summing up the experience with, "I couldn't even walk afterwards," adding, "and then a few nights later we go out, and nothing. Nothing. Just a good-night kiss on the cheek. That afternoon was a one-time thing. I loved this girl but have no idea what was going on in that head of hers."

"They broke up in February," Patti would say.

"And then she deserts me for good on Valentine's Day," he would explain. "She broke my heart and really screwed up my head."

"Ilona explained that she had to move on," Patti would write. "That she and Robert had reached a dead end. She kept saying. 'He won't understand.' "

"I didn't understand," Robert would insist. "I still don't and probably never will."

☙❧

Patti Flogstaff witnessed only one miracle. "And I'm not even sure you'd call it that," she would write. "We were seventeen at the time and at a keg party, Ilona's first, on the banks of the Susquehanna River, just over the Cooperstown town line. It was dark, private, and warm, almost hot, too hot for May. There were lots of kids there, the entire senior class of Cy Young High, or so it seemed. But the beer ran out early and no one wanted to drive into town for a refill, so Ilona asked a couple of the guys to fill the ice chest with water from the river. They did and, sure enough, it became beer. Good beer, too. She told me later it was Rolling Rock. But everyone was so wasted at this point, no one noticed what happened. Except me. It confirmed what I believed all along.

"She seemed sad a lot of the time. I would ask her what was wrong, but she'd only shrug it off, smile, and change the subject. Once, though, she told me she missed her dad, then began to cry. I hugged her, giving her my shoulder to cry on. I wanted to say, 'But you never met your dad,' but I kept my mouth shut. And looking back, I'm damn glad I did.

"Shortly after graduation Ilona tried to explain. She told me she had a mission, a certain destiny, and that she had to move on. I began to cry, it was my turn to be hugged. But she kissed my eyes instead and the tears stopped. Then she told me she loved me and said good-bye."

Anything?

Ilona Ann Coggswater had grown into a very attractive young woman. A head turner, five feet, four inches in height with long but naturally wavy light blond hair. And though she lacked some of her mother's curves, she had a shapely figure, slenderly shapeful, not frail or skinny, but seemingly delicate, as were her arms and hands, especially her hands.

Her face was beautiful, as beautiful as any face could be. Her mouth sensuous, lips full. Lips that would smile and activate a small, hollow dimple in her right cheek and a deep, kidney-shaped dimple in the other. Her teeth were toothpaste-commercial straight, white and perfect. Her nose small, cute, her chin firm, her neck soft and feminine.

And those eyes, those marvelous green eyes, eyes that seemed to know the secrets of the universe, which they did, eyes that could hypnotize, startle, and blind, eyes that could soothe, seduce, and see, see all, see everything, everything that ever was and everything that ever will be. That was the power of Ilona's eyes.

That was the power of Ilona. A remarkable power, a frightening power. A power that had always haunted her, a power that she had only begun to control, to understand, a power that was now coming into full bloom.

A power that magnified her senses, sight, smell, her strength, but mainly her ability to hear.

As a young girl at night she would hide under her pillows hoping the sounds would go away. But they rarely did. The sounds, screams of pain, and not just human screams, screams and cries and howls from creatures she had never heard, creatures she had never seen. Creatures she would be unable to save.

And though she wanted to cry out to her mother for help, to stop the screams, she didn't, she couldn't. Mariam wouldn't understand. How could she?

And as she grew her senses became more acute and the screams persisted and multiplied. Yet Ilona never became immune to them. She didn't want immunity, she wanted the screams to no longer exist. And soon her dreams would give faces to the screams, the cries, the howls. And all those faces, human or otherwise, had one thing in common, and that was innocence.

And then the faces had bodies and hands, little hands, little paws, claws, feet, reaching out, surrounding her, evoking her, enclosing her. But not suffocating her, never suffocating her.

And how she would cry and often rock herself to sleep, imagining she, too, were screaming, she, too, were howling, she, too, were crying out.

"Help me. Please, help me."

❧

Often she felt alone. Abandoned, forgotten, even. And though she loved her mother and she loved her friends dearly, it was all too strange. A strange world at a strange time. Strange and lonely. No one seemed to understand, except maybe the Professor, and of that she wasn't sure. How could he, really? But she would shrug it off, at least for the time being, and move on.

There was so much to do.

❧

Ilona graduated from Cooperstown's Cy Young High on Sunday, June 19, 1988, along with ninety-three classmates. It was a simple ceremony in the school's gym. A ceremony highlighted by Ilona's valedictorian speech, in which she told her fellow classmates to, above everything else—college, success, destiny, even family—always be kind."

"More than cleverness," she said, "we need kindness and gentleness."

And the day after graduation, Ilona reluctantly quit her job at the Cheapskate Record Shop.

"Thanks," she said to the Professor.

"My pleasure, kid," he told her. "Anytime."

And she smiled.

❧

Ilona's destiny, her reason for being, was clear. She had to stop the screaming, the crying, the howling. But first she needed to find the source, cause and effects, to know the every side of every reason, to understand every everything. First she needed knowledge.

And so Ilona would spend her summer reading, watching, learning, everything she could get her hands and ears and eyes on. She became a veritable living, breathing encyclopedia of current events.

The Cable News Network, or CNN as it was more popularly known, was on twenty-four hours a day. And if not CNN then PBS, and if not PBS the Discovery Channel, C-Span, or MTV. And when the cable stations offered nothing new, some video would, Warner Brothers cartoons or *Faces of Death*, hardcore porn or hardcore documentaries, a Swedish drama or *Rambo III*.

Copies of the *New York Times*, the *Washington Post*, and countless other newspapers littered the living room's coffee table and soon stood in ever-growing stacks in every corner of the Susquehanna Avenue house.

And scattered seemingly everywhere were books and pamphlets on physics, science, religion, politics, disease, the arts, sex, money, homosexuality, love, death, the environment, animal rights, drugs, food, pornography, welfare, poverty, sports, psychiatry, the NRA, the NAACP, the ACLU, and MADD.

And then there was the Bible.

The Bible. She read Luke 4:8, "It is written, 'Man shall not live by bread alone, but by every word of God.' "

Every word of God, she thought, smiling. She knew better.

And making herself comfortable in an overstuffed chair, Ilona would curl up with whatever it was she was reading at the moment, glass of Tab by her side, while whatever it was she was watching at the moment blared away on the television. Meals, some cereal or a small salad or a baked potato or a cheese sandwich, would be eaten between pages or during commercial breaks.

"What do you have planned for today," Mariam would ask, before heading off to work.

"More of the same," Ilona would say, nodding toward some newspapers, books, or the TV.

"Are you okay, dear?"

"Yeah, Mom. I'm fine. Why?"

"Just asking."

Yes, Ilona's day would begin early, before eight, and continue well past midnight, when she would usually allow herself a few moments of goofiness via David Letterman's opening monologue, then back to CNN to catch the results of their nonscientific Newsnight 900 poll, and off to bed.

Oh, how she read, watched, and learned.

ᏍᎣ

Ilona took one day off every two weeks, sort of like a baseball team. And on that day she'd catch up with the extracurricular activities that made her life special, music, the Mets, and Charlie Chaplin. And every two weeks, on that day off, after thirteen straight days of reading, watching, and learning, Ilona would schedule a mini-film/sports festival featuring some Chaplin two-reeler, leading directly to the televised Mets game of the day. Her team versus whatever team. It didn't matter, the Mets always triumphed when Ilona was watching.

And dinner would be special, usually shared with her mother and possibly Linda at some favorite restaurant. And the day would be relaxed, as she tried her best to put aside all that she had read, watched, and learned over the past thirteen days to concentrate momentarily on Mariam's dinner conversation, this song or that, and Darryl Strawberry hitting the long ball right out of the stadium.

❧

But the screams and cries and howls became louder, more persistent, at times unbearable, and always as she tried to sleep. The faces and bodies and hands and claws and paws now had names, now seemed to speak her name, as if they were getting closer, or maybe she was getting closer.

How she wanted it all to stop, the screaming to stop, the crying to stop, the howling to stop. How she wanted one of those ice-cold Rolling Rocks. Ahh . . ." she thought, just, Ahh . . . But they were off limits, at least for now. Aspirin, though it didn't stop the screaming, only the pounding that accompanied it, would have to do.

And the days slithered by, toward that destiny, that reason for being. June became July and July became August. A hot, sticky, rain-filled, scream-filled, painful August. And as her eighteenth birthday approached, Ilona became confused. Frightened. All the reading, watching, and learning was taking its toll. Cruelty, ignorance, every word of God.

❧

There was so much to undo. The weekend before turning eighteen, during one of those days off, on a visit to the Cheapskate Record Shop, Ilona's last such day off and last such visit, the Professor asked what she'd be doing with the rest of her life.

"Saving the world, I guess," she said.

"It's about time somebody did," he said.

"You think so?"

"Hell, yeah."

"Where would you start?" she asked. "I mean, if you were going to save the world?"

"New York City," he said, after a short moment's thought.

"Why's that?"

"Might as well start big, if you know what I mean."

And she did.

Besides, she thought, the Mets are there.

"Besides," he said, "the Mets are there."

"But you're not a baseball fan."

"Yeah, but you are."

And as Ilona looked through stacks of the newest releases, the Professor asked, "Remember the man who robbed us?"

"How could I ever forget?"

"He committed suicide in his jail cell last week."

The guy with the gun. His was one of the screams. His was one of the faces. And Ilona closed her eyes for a moment, and a single tear rolled down her cheek.

"How do you feel about that?" she asked the Professor.

And he looked into her eyes. How I'll miss those eyes, he thought, and softly he brushed the tear from her face.

"Like it was my fault," he said, finally, sadly, softly.

"But it wasn't," she said.

"Then who's to blame? Humanity?"

"Inhumanity," she said, thinking, Cruelty, ignorance, every word of God.

And as Ilona was leaving, the Professor handed her a small, badly wrapped package.

"Here. Open it later," he said.

"What is it?" she asked.

"A going-away gift."

"How did you know I was going away?"

"I just did."

"Thank you."

"Anytime, kid," he said. "Now get outta here."

Out of was only one word to this Professor.

And on the walk home Ilona unwrapped that small, badly wrapped package and found it to be a tattered old copy of *Cat's Cradle* by Kurt Vonnegut, Jr. And turning to the inside cover she read the following inscription, "We've all got to follow our destiny. Good luck with yours," and it was signed, "the Professor." Just "the Professor."

And there was a postscript. It read, "P. S. Nothing is impossible."

☙

And on that day off, returning home from the Cheapskate Record Shop and elsewhere, with some cassette tapes and that copy of *Cat's Cradle* under her arm, Ilona flipped to CNN by accident, as she headed toward a Mets game on the television dial, and saw the oil-stained beaches, the oil-stained birds, the oil-stained otters.

Those faces, she thought. Those cries and howls.

"The *Exxon Valdez*," some reporter explained, "went off its course and ran aground in Prince William Sound, Alaska, dropping an estimated ten million gallons of oil into the sound, making it the largest oil spill in world history. Alaskans are in shock."

And so was Ilona.

"I'm sick about it," said some Alaskan.

And so was Ilona.

And the story on the Alaskan oil spill was followed by a report on how hundreds of members of Operation Rescue, including their leader Randall Terry, had been arrested for blocking the entrance to a Planned Parenthood clinic in Seattle, Washington. And when Ilona saw the faces of the women denied entrance to the clinic, she recognized those faces, she had heard their screams.

And that was followed by a report on the burning of the Brazilian tropical rain forests and the global warming process known as the greenhouse effect. And plans for a Japanese-backed highway that would link Brazil's western state of Acre to Peru, providing Acre with a huge outlet for its tropical hardwoods, and destroying yet more forests and wildlife. And Ilona covered her ears with her hands. She had to, so strong was the overwhelming power of these screams, screams for help.

Next came a report on the crack and cocaine epidemic in south-central Los Angeles and the increase in the amount of gang violence and number of drive-by shootings. More familiar faces, more familiar screams.

And that was followed by a report on South Africa and the shooting death of a black teenager.

And then came a report about a new law that allowed Floridians to carry handguns without permits.

And that was followed by a report on how fundamentalist preacher Jimmy Swaggart was being forgiven by his ministry for some scandalous activities and was now back on the air preaching his new message.

And that was followed by a "just in," just-breaking report about a gunman in Stockton, California, who had opened fire in an elementary-school yard, killing at least five children and wounding as many as thirty.

And that was followed by an update on the Alaskan oil spill.

And that was followed by silence.

Silence because Mariam had returned from work to find her daughter sitting on the living-room floor in front of the television set, covering her ears, crying, screaming, rocking back and forth. The screams and cries and howls, the faces and hands and paws and claws had reached out, surrounded her, evoked her, enclosed her. This time suffocating her, Oh, how they suffocated her. And oh, how she screamed.

And shutting off the TV, Mariam placed her arms around Ilona, held her, and rocked with her.

"It's okay," Mariam said.

It wasn't.

It had all come together.

The sources, causes, and effects.

Destiny, and all that.

And the hours passed. And Ilona turned to Mariam and tried to explain. She spoke through the tears as the screams and cries and howls and faces and paws and claws filled her head. And Mariam listened. It was the first time Ilona would have to explain; it would not be the last. The words came, they were carefully chosen. And Ilona watched her mother's reactions, watched as intently as Mariam listened. And as unbelievable as the story was, Mariam never doubted a word of it. Not for a moment. And when Ilona was through they sat together in silence. And more hours passed. And Mariam began to speak but tears preceded her words. And the tears became sobs. And Ilona held her mother, as Mariam had earlier held her. But the words never did come. Mariam didn't know what to say. She didn't know what to feel.

How could she?

❦

Ilona's eighteenth birthday was a quiet one. Dinner, dancing, and drinks at Linda's Dew Drop Inn, and a Sony Walkman, so, as Mariam explained, though she didn't have to, "You can take your music with you no matter where you have to go."

And that night Ilona packed, as Mariam knew she would. She packed only the items that would be necessary. Only the items that would fit into two medium-size suitcases, clothes, accessories, her official New York Mets baseball cap, an old small stuffed toy rabbit, a few books, her favorite tapes, that Walkman, and all her eternal sadness.

And the next morning she was gone.

❦

Ilona Ann Coggswater had grown into a very attractive young woman. With her intelligence, independence, wit, and eminent appeal, she could have gone on to become virtually anything her heart and mind desired. Anything, had she not been immaculately conceived. Anything, had she not been heir apparent to the right to sit at the right hand of God. Anything, had she not been the embodiment of the Second Coming. Anything, had Jesus Christ not been her big Brother. Anything, had she not been the Daughter of God.

Anything.

A Few Moments with Dudley & Jerry

"She's a real sweetheart."

"The apple of my eye."

"Then," Jerry said, with more than just a little bit of outrage, "how in your name can you put her through this?"

"Penance," Dudley said, softly.

"Yours or hers?"

"Ours."

Jerry said nothing.

It was, after all, as much his fault, too. And deep down Jerry found himself rooting for the eighteen-year-old. Maybe she could succeed where so many others had failed. Maybe she could indeed.

He crossed his fingers and said a little prayer.

Dudley twitched, just slightly, and shot his friend a caustic look.

What the *hell* are you doing? that look said.

But Dudley wasn't about to complain. Not really. He knew Ilona could use all the help she could get. Even if it came from the most unlikely of sources.

[51]

 P ART T WO

5

The Destiny Motel

> And the city had no need of the sun or of
> the moon to shine in it, for the glory of Ilona
> illuminated it.
>> —Updated Revelation 21:23
>> *The Next Testament*

A tighter squeeze.

And though the safety, comfort, warmth, and companionship of Cooperstown seemed preferable to the glare and sirens that now surrounded her, it was check-in time, check-in time at the Destiny Motel. We'll leave the lights on, always on, at the Destiny Motel. Eight million locations to serve you best. Clean towels to wipe away your tears, warm blankets under which to hide from your fears, dead bolts, window bars, mace, and kitchen knives. You want it, just ask. All service. Full service. Room service. One Rolling Rock coming up.

"Ahh . . ." Rolling Rock.

"Ahh . . ." check-in time.

"Hello, New York."

And answering a classified ad in the "Apts/Houses to Share" section of the *Village Voice*, Ilona found a "safe," one-bedroom, sixth-floor walkup with working fireplace on East 10th Street, halfway between Second Avenue and Third Avenue in Greenwich Village, that she would share with the apartment's current tenant, Stephanie LaVasseur. And though the apartment was cramped and she'd be sleeping in the living room on a pull-out sofa bed, it was a place Ilona could, and would, call home.

ひつじ

Nineteen-year-old Stephanie LaVasseur was a part-time actress/model, part-time business management student, and part-time bartender at Self-Portrait, a pretentiously trendy restaurant in the TriBeCa district. She was a stunning young woman standing only slightly more than an inch, though she called it two, under six feet, with long, light brown hair that looked perfect no matter what she, the wind, or a night's sleep did or did not do to it. She had shocking blue eyes, not shocking because of their color, but because of the secrets they seemed to hold, sensual secrets full of goosebumps and whispers. Her face, her form, even her feet, seemed chiseled to perfection, as if Rodin's signature itself could be found on or around her ankle. She was so *just so*.

"You're not a born-again Christian or anything like that?" Stephanie asked on that first meeting.

"Nothing like that, at all," Ilona said. "I have very little to do with religion."

"Okay, then get your things."

"That's it? That's all you need to know?"

"That's all I want to know."

And these two young women would become a team, head turners, hair raisers, drop-dead visions, the best of friends. And part-time Stephanie would get Ilona a full-time waitressing position at Self-Portrait, where Ilona, working five nights a week, could witness the cruelty, the ignorance, minus every word of God, firsthand.

And though Stephanie would never speak of her experiences with Ilona, insisting that they were "no one's business but ours," in early March 1989, on the barely watched "Pat Sajak Show," promoting both her flourishing career as, according to Sajak and most who followed the industry, "the hottest new model in the world" and the *Sports Illustrated* swimsuit issue that featured her on its cover, Sajak would be allowed one question about Ilona.

"So, what did you and Ilona do every night after work?" he would ask, raising one eyebrow high, insinuating everything.

"Watch David Letterman," Stephanie would reply, shrugging her shoulders innocently, or at least as innocently as Stephanie could shrug her shoulders, revealing nothing.

Time for a commercial break.

❧

Gone were most of the books, pamphlets, magazines, and videos that had occupied Ilona's summer. And other than an hour or so each afternoon tuned into CNN to catch the headlines and *Exxon Valdez* updates, or a weekly flip through the *Village Voice* and a scan of the daily or Sunday *New York Times*, or her and Stephanie's nightly dose of "Late Night with David Letterman," Ilona's multimedia overdose was over.

There was too much to undo.

❧

And what little free time Ilona allowed herself she used wisely. Music, Chaplin, and the Mets, live, her first time, her first visit to Shea Stadium.

"Wow," she said as she entered the stadium, blinded by the blue, green, and orange.

"Wow?" Stephanie asked, smiling, Ilona's excitement all too contagious.

"Yup." Ilona nodded. "Wow."

It was a Mets game in which Bobby Ojeda would have been pitching if he had not virtually sliced off the middle finger of his pitching hand in a gardening accident the previous evening. And though many felt that he would never pitch again, Ilona was quite sure he would. Positive, in fact, that the finger would heal itself.

"Stephanie sat me down," Ilona would later tell her mother, "and told me something terrible had happened. And I immediately thought of you, but Stephanie explained it was Bobby O. She told me about his finger and the hedge clippers. And I cried. I really loved the team that much. They gave me such a blessed release from everything else, from the screams. The Mets and Rolling Rock, sometimes I felt that was all I needed, all I wanted. I just wish I was able to watch that seventh playoff game with the Dodgers. I feel I really let those guys down, y'know?"

The screams and cries and howls that haunted Ilona so in Cooperstown were nothing compared to the pain she felt in New York City, from New York City, for New York City. Inflicted, unnecessary. Nothing personal, she understood that. This was her trial. Humanity just didn't know any better.

And sleep came hard, if at all, for the same reasons, the same faces. They were close, but not suffocating, not right now. Not just yet.

And late each morning Ilona would walk to a section of the East Village known as Alphabet City to the basement of a run-down brownstone and an establishment known simply as the Soup Kitchen. And here she volunteered to spoon out bowls of that day's soup du jour and hand one of those bowls, along with a roll or some crackers, to any person who needed it, any person who wanted it.

And she would look into the faces, the wrinkled, dirty, bruised, scared, toothless faces. Familiar faces. It sometimes seemed to Ilona as if every face was familiar. And maybe every face was.

And soon she became accepted by the regulars, people who seemingly ate every meal at the Soup Kitchen. "Miss Ilona" they would call her. Or just "miss."

And they would tell her stories, life stories, true stories, exaggerations and half lies. and they would laugh with huge toothless grins. And Ilona would laugh. Laugh to cover the pain she felt, the absolute sorrow. Now the screams not only had faces and hands, they had names and lives and stories. Joe or Billie or Flatcake Al, Lil' Jill and Jerome, Tiny and Indian Jack. And they could also laugh. Why couldn't they *just* laugh? That most precious and sacred of miracles, she thought. Laughter.

And one Sunday morning Ilona said to Stephanie, "Come with me."

"To the Soup Kitchen?"

"Yup."

"Why?"

"There are some people I'd like you to meet."

And soon the regulars were, according to Jerome, "fussin' over Miss Ilona's pretty friend."

"You get roll duty," Ilona told her roommate, introducing her to the regulars as they stepped up for their meal.

"Hey, everybody," said Flatcake Al, "we got us a movie star giving us our daily bread."

"I'm not a movie star," Stephanie explained, embarrassed but flattered.

"But you're as pretty as one," said Flatcake Al.

"An angel and a movie star," Billie said. Billie always called Ilona an "angel."

An angel and a movie star, Stephanie thought, smiling.

The pain, the sorrow wasn't as bad with Stephanie there.

"Miss Ilona here's our savior, y'know?" Tiny explained to Stephanie.

"Does that make me an apostle?" Stephanie asked.

"I guess it does at that," Tiny said. "I guess it does."

❧

As different as the customers at Self-Portrait were from the regulars at the Soup Kitchen, they had a lot in common. The faces were just as familiar to Ilona, as were most of the screams; drugs, unwanted pregnancy, disease. It was just the personalities and pocketbooks that differed.

And the regulars here also had names for Ilona, "babe," "sweetheart" and "hey, waitress" being the most popular.

"Can I get some service here?" someone would yell.

Or, "Get me the check!"

Or, "I've been waiting for almost five minutes."

Or, "What do you mean you're out of the veal?"

And then there was, "What time do you get off work?"

Or, "Sit on my face and let me guess your weight."

Or, "What would you do for a five-hundred-dollar tip?"

Or, "What would I like to eat? How 'bout you, babe."

And Stephanie would ask, "Why do they have to be so rude?" as she filled Ilona's tray with cocktails.

"They don't know any better," Ilona would say.

"Father, forgive them," Stephanie said, "for they do not know what they do."

"Something like that."

෮෮

In his book, *Believe You Me*, Tony Scognamiglio, owner of Self-Portrait, would call Ilona and Stephanie, "two of the hottest babes I've ever seen." And between exaggerations about his lovelife and his overblown theories on running a bar, Scognamiglio would comment that "the customers loved both girls, loved them. And I mean, *loved* them. Especially that Ilona chick. And except for the fact that she was always trying to get the customers to order just the vegetarian dishes, she was a pretty decent waitress. If I only knew then what I know now, we could have made a bundle. Believe you me."

What would follow was a detailed plan of how he would have promoted Ilona's employment at the restaurant if he had indeed at the time known that she was the Daughter of God. His ideas would include renaming the eaterie "Heaven," dressing the staff as angels, and a revamped menu featuring "The Ilona Enchilada," "Jesus Wings," and "The Heavenly Hoagie."

"I couldn't figure it out back then," Scognamiglio would conclude in his final chapter, "but I knew something was fishy. Ilona's working for me for about two months, making a bundle, when one day she comes to me and says she's quitting. I ask her why and she says she can't tell me. So I say to her, 'Babe, you can tell me anything.' She smiled, said, 'I don't think so,' turned, and walked out. At the time I figured, no big deal, the broad's got a screw loose. If only I knew. Believe you me."

☙

And though Stephanie wanted to spend the approaching Thanksgiving holiday frolicking on some remote Caribbean island with her new friend, Ilona had other plans.

"We could go wild," Stephanie pleaded.

"We'd only do things we'd regret in the morning," Ilona said.

"Yeah, but you only live once, right?" said Stephanie.

"Some of us."

Ilona couldn't explain, not just yet anyway, but Stephanie would come to understand, soon enough.

☙

It was convenient certainly, at least for Ilona. Though Pope John Paul II wouldn't consider it as such. Not hardly. But a pontiff visit to New York City on the approaching Thanksgiving holiday—the pontiff mass, the pontiff parade—made Ilona's life just that much easier. She wouldn't have to span the globe to seek him out. He'd come directly to her. She was sure of it.

"Absolutely," she said to herself.

And with the pontiff would travel The Treasures of the Vatican, a collection of excesses that on the fourth Wednesday in November, that day before Thanksgiving, Ilona visited at the Metropolitan Museum of Art.

Outside the museum were dozens of homeless men, women, and children, beggars, shoved aside and ignored by art lovers and security guards alike.

So much to undo.

And one such beggar approached Ilona and asked for some change.

"Please," he said. "Anything would help."

And she looked into his all too familiar face, reached into her pockets, and filled his cupped hands with all the change she had.

"Thank you,' he said, bowing. "And God bless."

And as Ilona walked toward the entrance of the museum, she began to shake, slightly, all over. Beads of sweat began to form on her face, on her chest, she could feel the moisture under her clothes. It was all so close, that destiny and all it entailed.

[61]

"All for the glory of God," she overheard an exiting art lover say.

God, how the word echoed in her head. Why have You forsaken them?

And she didn't even notice her tear, a single, lonely tear, as most tears were, until a security guard asked, "Are you all right, miss?"

"Yes," she said, stammering.

And once inside the museum, in that special Treasures of the Vatican wing, Ilona examined the glory, the excess. And though she knew that this was nothing more, or nothing less, than man's attempt to worship and show reverence and respect, it made her angry, nauseated even, nauseated definitely. Glory, she thought, wanting to cover her face in shame. Glory, and she had had enough.

And Ilona began to walk quickly toward an exit, any exit, the closest exit. *Out*, was all, *Out*, was everything. Out.

And on that way out, a colorful rectangle caught Ilona's eye. A discarded postcard.

She stopped to pick it up.

And she gasped.

Michelangelo's *Creation of Adam*.

God's hand, so strong, so damn large, even in this smallest of reproductions. Hers, small, almost fragile, yet full of life, always moving, touching, giving everything away. And the hand of Adam, so limp-wristed and uninterested. Humankind in general.

Art can be so depressing sometimes, she thought. Humankind can be so depressing sometimes.

છે

But destiny screamed—the faces and those hands and paws and claws, and new cries and howls, and new screams, daily arrivals, of the same pain, of the same suffering, that one true universal language.

And the next morning, after quietly attending the Thanksgiving mass at Saint Patrick's Cathedral, a historic mass in that this

Catholic ritual and the thinking behind it would, within hours, begin a serious and thorough modernization, Ilona took her place on the sidewalk that lines Fifth Avenue to watch the pontiff be driven by in the mighty pope-mobile.

At Ilona's side, waiting patiently for a glimpse of John Paul II, was an elderly Scottish woman named Veronica MacManus, who spoke anxiously to Ilona, telling her that this was the thirty-eighth time she would get to see the pope, that she had visited the Vatican countless times and had witnessed many a pontiff visit many a country.

Ilona listened in a way that made Veronica feel quite at ease, quite appreciated, nodding in agreement that something had to be done about homelessness or smiling at the "such beautiful green eyes" compliments.

And soon the straight line of spectators that lined Fifth Avenue began to whisper, then point, sing, and cheer. And signs were raised along with voices, I NEED A MIRACLE, one such sign said, JUDGMENT DAY IS HERE, said another. The lead automobile in the pontiff's procession could be seen only a few blocks away.

And as the cars drove by, cars filled with this dignitary or that, countless politicians and others of imagined importance, Ilona stepped forward, just slightly, pressing her waist against the blue police barricades. It was the pope-mobile's turn to drive past.

But as the pontiff waved at the sea of faces, waved and smiled, one face, and one face alone, stood out. Stood out so that immediately upon noticing this face—and how could the pontiff *not* notice this face?—Pope John Paul II signaled frantically to the driver of his mighty pope-mobile to stop, to pull over, and to do so pronto. He had to get out.

Aides screamed and rushed to John Paul II's side, only to be pushed away by the dazed pontiff, pushed away as he walked swiftly to that face. What was it about that face?

And soon the pontiff stood before that face, that beautiful young woman's face, Ilona Ann Coggswater's face. And they locked eyes, his warm, tired, deep brown eyes versus her intense, wide-eyed, green-eyed gaze, and his face blanched, turning not the sickly white of a stroke victim but suffering only the momentary loss of color as if one had just seen a God, which in fact he had.

And making a small personal sign of the cross, Pope John Paul II dropped to his knees before Ilona. Dropped to his knees on the sidewalk that lined Fifth Avenue and, bowing obediently, kissed her feet.

He knew. She needed him to.

And as aides continued to scream and rush, scream and rush to the pope to examine more closely what in God's name was going on, and as the followers who had waited behind the blue police barricades gasped and gawked, and as photographers and cameramen and reporters snapped and zoomed and reported away, the pontiff raised his head, so that his eyes would once again lock with Ilona's, and said, "My Lord, what can I do for you?"

And he crossed himself again. But this sign of the cross was different from the one that had preceded it. And though the pontiff wasn't quite sure exactly what made it different, he was positive that no sign of the cross would ever be the same.

And as the screaming, rushing, examining, waiting, gasping, gawking, snapping, zooming, and reporting continued around them, the pope stood and ushered Ilona to his mighty pope-mobile, where she sat patiently amidst the confusion and the confused. And the Pope looked deep into Ilona's gaze and waited for her word. A wait that seemed to last forever, at least to John Paul II, who tried to calm himself by thinking of his favorite biblical passages but couldn't remember one line or verse or word. A wait that was hardly noticeable to Ilona who was more than slightly amused at the unintentional Keystone Kops antics that now surrounded her. She examined the commotion, hoping to spot Veronica MacManus. But not finding her in the blur of the crowd, Ilona turned toward the pontiff, who stared into her intense, wide-eyed, green-eyed gaze and crossed himself yet again, slowly, with hands shaking. And though he would only mouth the words, she could read his lips, "In the name of the Father, the Son . . . ," and his lips stopped moving as he halted the crossing, not knowing how or where to proceed.

And touched, so touched was she by the helplessness of the pope's expression, Ilona said, with just a hint of motherly concern, "Pontiff, we've got to talk."

6

The Papal Transcripts

And talk they did.

Seated in a small, dark, basement office located in the bowels of Saint Patrick's Cathedral—away from the commotion, far from the madding crowds—Pope John Paul II began the conversation.

"Is this the end?" he asked.

"Just a moment," Ilona said, hushing the pontiff and pulling a microcassette recorder from her jacket pocket.

"What's that for?" Pope John Paul asked.

"We don't want to be misquoted this time," she explained.

And pushing the RECORD button, Ilona said, "We can begin."

And the pontiff was silent for a moment before repeating his question, "Is this the end?"

"No," Ilona said, explaining that she was here, "to help."

Though the pontiff didn't understand at first. "We've been following the example set forth by Christ in the Holy Scriptures," he said.

"My Brother."

"Your Brother?"

"Yes, Jesus."

"This is extremely difficult."

And Ilona was silent.

"Are the Scriptures not to be trusted?" he asked.

"They are man's account of what man felt God wanted to say."

"But," the pontiff began.

"Listen," Ilona said, speaking slowly, compassionately. "You have all followed your hearts. I know that. Dad knows that."

"Dad?"

"God."

"I see."

"But now things have to change," she said, "before it's too late."

"Too late?"

"Yes."

"But."

"No buts," Ilona interrupted. "Do you know where you've made your mistakes?"

"I know what my critics have said."

"Sometimes a little criticism is good."

"For the soul?" the pontiff asked.

"For the ego."

"But they aren't mistakes. They're moral decisions."

"They're mistakes as far as I'm concerned," Ilona said, adding, rather abruptly, "and don't forget, you work for me."

"But what about God the Father?" the pontiff asked. "And Christ?"

"It's a family business, and right now I'm the spokesperson."

"I don't know," John Paul II said.

And Ilona shot the pope a look, that intense, wide-eyed, green-eyed gaze, catching him off guard, startling him with its power, making him turn away.

"I," the pontiff began, stopped, then started again, "I think I know what you want, but."

And Ilona was silent.

"It's just that everything is changing so fast," he said. "It's not the same world anymore. Things were simple when I joined the church."

"Things were never simple," Ilona said.

"We live in such a cruel, immoral world," the pope said.

"Let's get to the point," Ilona said.

And the pope cleared his throat and looked around nervously, his eyes clearly avoiding her gaze.

"Birth control?" the pontiff suggested sadly.

And Ilona was silent.

"Homosexuality?" he said, clearing his throat again, as if the word itself had caused some pain. "Divorce?"

And Ilona notice the pontiff's hands shaking, the sweat on his brow.

"Abortion," he said, softly, reluctantly, as if he had never wanted to speak the word.

And Ilona said nothing.

"Sex," Pope John Paul II said. "It all comes down to sex."

And Ilona stood and paced the length and breadth of the room. There were no windows, just a few well-placed desk lamps. Crosses adorned the walls, and photographs of archbishops. Boxes were stacked to the ceiling, hymnals or Bibles, most likely. Odd objects were scattered about, dead plants, candlesticks, Saint Patrick's Day parade paraphernalia and a dirty purple sock. And over in a corner a colorful rectangle caught Ilona's eye. There was no need for further examination. It was a postcard, a familiar postcard. All too familiar. A friendly reminder, shall we say. And the Daughter of God shook her head sadly.

"Welcome to the twentieth century, Pontiff."

ᘓᘔ

And toward the end of their "talk," Ilona said, "Give me your hands."

And the Pope held out his hands, and when Ilona touched them, John Paul II looked up and locked eyes with this young woman, his warm, tired, confused, deep brown eyes versus her intense, wide-eyed, green-eyed gaze.

"Close your eyes," she said.

And as he did, the pontiff heard the screams. And he began to sweat and shake slightly. And the screams grew louder, the cries, the howls. He saw the faces, the bodies, the hands and paws and claws all reaching out, out to him. He felt the pain. How he felt the pain. And John Paul II began to cry, softly at first, then a hard, steady, childlike sob.

And Ilona leaned forward and placed her arms around the pontiff, held and rocked him gently.

"It'll be okay," she promised. "It'll be okay."

ᏟᏏ

The Papal Transcripts, a forty-page booklet sent to every Catholic diocese in the world, was a verbatim transcript of Ilona's "talk" with Pope John Paul II as recorded on that micro-cassette recorder. The booklet was accompanied by a personally signed note from the pontiff to the leaders of each diocese. In it the pontiff explained, "We now know for certain that God is on our side though we might not have been completely on His. We shall accept the teachings of Ilona Ann Coggswater and follow Her wherever She may lead us. Please keep an open mind and try to be understanding."

And there was a postscript. It read, "P. S. Effective imme-diately, we will begin ordaining women."

7

Answering Machines and Stupid Human Tricks

Buzz. What a buzz. That's all it was, but a mighty buzz is was. Divine even, that buzz.

In the days that followed Thanksgiving, the world press sizzled, the world press steamed. They just didn't know what to make of the wild scene at Saint Patrick's. Headlines ranged from "POPE BREAKS DOWN" in the London *Daily Mirror* to "JOHN PAUL'S ILLEGITIMATE CHILD?" in the New York *Daily News* to "PONTIFF LOVE TRYST" in the Chicago *Sun Times* to "PONTIFF OFF ROCKER" in the *New York Post*, all complete with shots of the pontiff on his knees in front of an "unidentified young woman." Pope John Paul II would speak to and see no one, the Vatican was issuing a strict "no comment," and even the most prolific leaks weren't leaking.

Oh, what a buzz it was.

ℭℌ

Stephanie spent her Thanksgiving at a family get-together in southern New Jersey ignoring football, special news reports, and bad jokes from distant, and bound-to-remain-that-way, relatives. She arrived back home on Saturday, November 26, bored and without a clue.

That afternoon Ilona did her best to explain to her roommate what was about to happen. And as Ilona began, Stephanie said without hesitation, "I need a drink." And together they shared "a couple of six-packs of ice-cold Rolling Rock" on a cold Saturday afternoon that turned into a snowy Saturday evening.

"What's he like?" Stephanie asked, as the two roommates sat on their windowsill watching the snow blanket East 10th Street.

"Who?"

"Your Dad. I mean, he's God," Stephanie said, stretching out "God" into at least a couple of syllables. "He's like creator of the universe, right?"

"Yup."

"He knows everything, sees everything?"

And Ilona nodded.

"That must really put a crimp in your sex life," Stephanie said, the thought just sinking into her head. "I mean, whew."

And Ilona started to laugh.

"Aren't you, well, I mean, how do you—" And not finding the rights words, Stephanie said, "Isn't it a trip having him as a Dad?"

"He's just Dad to me."

❦

And as 1 A.M. became 2 A.M. and 2 A.M. became 3, and as Stephanie pulled the last of those "ice-cold Rolling Rocks" from their refrigerator, Ilona watched the snow from her sixth-floor window. The screams were silent, at least in her head, at least for the time being. And the snow was beautiful, large puffy flakes floating to the street below. So calm, so relaxing. And Ilona closed her eyes for a moment and imagined herself lying naked in the middle of East 10th Street, naked except for the flakes. The way they tickled as they landed on her body. How they melted. How goosebumps erupted up, down, sideways, all over, even now, just at the thought. Would Dad be shocked? She laughed to herself. He'd understand. He always did. Always. Ilona really missed her Dad.

"Last call," Stephanie said, handing Ilona a beer, returning to her place on the windowsill.

"Many thousands of years ago," Ilona said, taking a sip of that evening's last beer, those green eyes still closed, "long before civilization, long before man, my Father and the Devil battled, violently, incessantly, needlessly, a battle of showmanship, who could outdo whom, who was better, who was stronger, who would win. It wasn't about good and evil, but simply ego versus ego.

"God would create the most beautiful bird, the Devil would create a creature who could eat nothing but those beautiful birds. The Devil would make a mountain rise out of the Earth, God would create a mountain twice its size, towering over the Devil's work, making it seem small and meaningless. For eons their contests raged, lightning, earthquakes, floods, tidal waves, the wrath of God, the whim of Satan.

"Until they had had enough. The universe wasn't big enough for both of them. And they would fight it out, hand to throat, foot to ass, a barroom brawl to end all.

"It began in Greece, near Athens, long before Greece was Greece and Athens was Athens. And for months and miles it continued, through what is now Yugoslavia, Austria, Germany, and into France, a mighty blow from the Devil's fist, bang, the Adriatic Sea, a slam from God's foot, crash, the Alps. Rivers surged, lakes drained, mountains were formed, mountains crumbled. They made a genuine mess.

"And it was in Paris, or what would someday be Paris, as God stood on one bank of the Seine, and the Devil stood on the other, both exhausted and in pain, bloodied almost beyond recognition, that they stopped. Silence, dead silence, absolute silence. They stood for hours, maybe days. They stood and stared, like statues, never blinking, never turning away.

"And it was my Father who finally, inappropriately, unconsciously, smiled. Just a slight smile at first, a slight smile that grew and beamed and spread its warmth across the Seine, and soon the Devil was smiling, too. And they began to laugh, hearty laughter, a laughter heard around the world, throughout the universe and throughout all of creation, their creation. They laughed because they finally understood, finally saw what they had failed in their infinite wisdom to see, to understand, all along. That their strength was equal and that one really could not, would not, should not, exist without the other. That there could be no winner.

"And so God and Satan called a truce. Not that they would work together, but that their bickering would cease, and they would become, well, I guess you'd call them, drinking buddies."

And there was silence.

And Stephanie asked, softly, "If God and the Devil can coexist peacefully, then why can't we?"

But Ilona didn't answer, she just opened her eyes and turned back toward her view of East 10th Street to watch the snow fall.

And the goosebumps returned.

෪

And on Monday, November 28, 2 P.M., Vatican time, Pope John Paul II, safely back in the confines of Vatican City, held a press conference. Walking solemnly to the bank of microphones, he said, "God has sent His Daughter to save our world. Her name is Ilona Ann Coggswater. She is an American. She has advised me that it is time the Catholic Church updated its thinkings and beliefs."

The Pope spent two hours and twelve minutes outlining the changes that would come about in Catholic practices as ordered by Ilona, answering questions from a confused and startled press corps, and explaining that he believed Ilona to be "beyond any doubt, God incarnate."

And Ilona and Stephanie watched, every clip, every excerpt, every everything from the pope's address, channel hopping from CNN's just-short-of-fanatical coverage to the networks' Special Reports. And it wasn't long before the phone, their phone, began to ring. Oh, how it rang. And those who did call and manage to get through were treated to Stephanie saying "Hello, you've reached Stephanie and Ilona," followed by Ilona's, "We're not here right now," after which Stephanie said, "But leave a real cool message at the beep," to which Ilona added, "And maybe we'll get back to you," followed by Stephanie's sadistically flirtatious closing, "Maybe."

And Stephanie asked Ilona what message Jesus would have had on his answering machine if in fact they had had telephones and answering machines some two thousand years ago and furthermore if in fact Jesus had actually owned one of each.

And giving much thought to the question, Ilona told her roommate that her Brother's message would have probably gone something like this, "Whoever leaves a message for me, receives me; and whoever receives me receives Him who sent me. For he who is least among you all will be great. Please wait for the beep."

℘

Many news organizations knew not what to make of the pope's announcement. Was the pontiff crazy, simply seeing things, or just plain lying? A few even went as far as to suggest that John Paul II was quite possibly telling the truth, maybe. The networks and CNN just told the facts and left the decision up to their viewers, usually adding, "We'll keep you updated." The *New York Times* ran a banner headline that read, "POPE PROCLAIMS SECOND COMING," while the *New York Post* exclaimed, "POPE CRACKS UP," the Chicago *Sun Times* screamed, "ILONA WHO?!?" and the New York *Daily News* said, rather eloquently, "BULLSHIT!"

And that evening, while still avoiding the phone and eating in, Stephanie asked, "So, you bullied the pope, who's next?"

"I didn't bully the pope," Ilona explained. "I was firm, that's all. I had to be."

"For your sake or his?"

"Both."

"So, what's next?"

"I'll show you."

And as soon as the phone stopped ringing, Ilona picked up the receiver and called the NBC news office in Manhattan, explained who she was, and asked to set up an interview with anchorman Tom Brokaw.

Now, while the people at NBC had been receiving similar calls all afternoon from young women claiming to be Ilona Ann Coggswater or "Cobbswater" or "Cockwater" or "Catwaiter" and even a call from a man who claimed the pope had made a mistake and that God had actually sent Jesus back to earth and that he, the caller, was Jesus, the good folks at NBC sensed that this Ilona, our Ilona, *the* Ilona, was in fact, the real thing.

And though getting a call through to Tom Brokaw was no easy task, within minutes Ilona had the anchorman on the phone. He listened, took notes, and thanked her for the opportunity.

The interview would take place at noon the next day in front of an audience of the most respected journalists in the world, journalists who would be able to ask questions, any question, once Brokaw had completed the interview. The entire event would be broadcast live by whoever wished to carry it.

Brokaw would later comment that the phone conversation with Ilona left him both emotionally and mentally drained. "So much was running though my mind as I listened to her instructions. So much, but never any doubt as to who she was. Not a hint of it."

Only hints of confusion and insecurity. "Why me?" Brokaw asked Ilona. "Why not Rather or Koppel or someone else."

"Because," Ilona answered, "you've been kind to, and treated fairly, everyone you've ever interviewed."

And that evening Stephanie helped Ilona pick out what she would wear. They agreed on black as the color, all black, everything black, that much was easy. But as to which piece or pieces of black clothing, that was another story, until finally, after much debate, simplicity won out. Ilona would meet the world dressed in tailored, but not-too-tight pants, a high-neck, long-sleeve, loose-fitting top, and a simple, waist-length, collarless jacket.

And after catching the latest Ilona updates on CNN where the stories now concluded with, "a news conference is scheduled for noon tomorrow," the two friends turned to "Late Night with

David Letterman," a rerun featuring Tony Randall, Tracey Ull-man, and Stupid Human Tricks, and eventually back to CNN to catch the results of the nonscientific Newsnight 900 poll which on this evening asked, "Do you believe the pope's claim that God has sent His Daughter to save the world?" to which nine-teen percent of the CNN viewers responded yes, while eighty-one percent said no, which signaled that it was time to go to bed, and though Ilona knew the screams would prevent sleep, at least from coming easily, she would try to get some rest.

Tomorrow would, after all, be a long, long day.

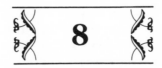

No-Hitter

In his book *The Second Coming*, Tom Brokaw would speak of the anxiety he felt that Monday night after speaking with Ilona.

"First I thought of Dan Rather," he would write, "and how if he hadn't argued with then-Vice President Bush, he might have been chosen to do this interview. Or Ted Koppel, did he blow his chance because of his rude handling of Michael Dukakis? And I remembered how once when speaking with Jim and Tammy Bakker, so many sarcastic and biting comments came to mind but I held them back. It was my place to report the news, not make it.

"Then it hit me. The importance of what was about to happen. I would be interviewing God's Daughter. An all-mighty, all-powerful, all-knowing being. Answers that have plagued human-kind since the birth of modern thought were only questions away. But what questions? What could I ask her aside from the obvious? How's Jesus been? What's the weather like in heaven this time of the year? Would you autograph my Bible?

"How could I not falter somehow? What subjects had to be avoided? What if I said something wrong? Should I be specific or general in my line of questioning? Or should I just sit back and let her have an open forum? What if she doesn't like me? And what should I wear?

"My staff quickly set about getting together the top reporters from the world's news agencies, newspapers, and news bureaus. Only those with spotless reputations for reporting the news without sensationalistic twists would be invited. And everyone agreed to be there, no questions, no doubts. It was as if some outside force were overseeing the event, making sure everything went just so. And when you think about it . . .

"But what surprised me most about that night before the Ilona interview was the peacefulness with which I slept. I would have never believed it, expecting to toss and turn all night. But I put my head to my pillow and was out, dreaming the most wonderfully soothing dream, that I was a pitcher for the New York Mets and we were playing the California Angels and I had just pitched a no-hitter during the seventh game of the World Series. I remember every detail so vividly to this day."

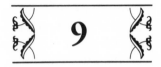

Making a Living

The next morning the roommates slipped out of their apartment unseen. Their answering machine by this point registered thirty messages, its maximum. They walked west on East 10th Street to Third Avenue and caught a cab uptown to Rockefeller Center and the NBC studios.

Stephanie could not believe Ilona's calm. "You look like you're going shopping," she said in the cab.

But this was the prelude to the end of the screaming. And no thought could be more soothing to the Daughter of God.

As they approached their destination, traffic slowed to a bumper-to-bumper, inch-by-inch, crawl. The cabbie, who according to his hack license was named Yakacen Momtaheni, said in a Middle Eastern accent that the traffic was due to "that God girl talking at some news conference."

Ilona just nodded, saying that she had heard something about it on the news.

"Pretty God-damned incredible," Momtaheni added, laying on his horn.

And at 11:22 A.M., Ilona and Stephanie exited the taxi, entered Rockefeller Center, and slipped past the throngs of reporters seemingly looking for a woman wearing long white flowing robes and sporting wings.

"Black was a good idea," Stephanie whispered on their way to the elevators.

"Glad I left the halo at home."

And as the elevator doors closed, the screams, always screams, of "Have you seen her yet?" faded, and Ilona was carried, Stephanie by her side, up toward her destiny on the seventh floor where the news conference would take place.

And calmly entering Studio 6, to loud whispers of "She's here," Ilona and Stephanie marched up to Tom Brokaw and introduced themselves.

"Mr. Brokaw, I'm Ilona Ann Coggswater, the Daughter of God. I believe you're expecting me."

Brokaw, at a loss for words as he looked into that intense, wide-eyed, green-eyed gaze, managed to say, "Hello," just "Hello."

"And I'm Stephanie, Ilona's roommate," that roommate said, taking Brokaw's hand and shaking it firmly.

"Hello," he said again, after a lengthy pause.

"I hope you're going to be more talkative during the interview," Ilona joked.

And Brokaw began to speak but could only manage a nod.

&

The set was simple. Two comfortable officelike dark gray swivel chairs set against a light blue backdrop. No intimidating microphone banks—the sound would be recorded and amplified via sensitive lavaliere mikes pinned to Ilona's and Brokaw's respective lapels.

Five rows of eight chairs were set up for and occupied by the invited press. Video cameramen and photographers lined the walls of the studio.

And Stephanie LaVasseur waited and watched from the wings as Ilona Ann Coggswater and Tom Brokaw took their places and had their lavaliere mikes clipped on by a technician, probably a member of some lavaliere-mike-clipping union, as the big hands on all the Studio 6 clocks inched toward the twelve. That mighty buzz was about to climax.

&

"Hello, this is Tom Brokaw live from Studio Six at the NBC studios in Rockefeller Center in New York City. It is twelve noon, eastern standard time, Tuesday, November twenty-ninth, 1988."

Every camera stayed on a tight shot of Brokaw during his introduction.

"Remember the time and the day and take note of where you are and what you are doing," Brokaw continued. "Because today is a remarkable day, one that will go down in history like so many remarkable days before it. Today is the day that the world meets the Daughter of God, Ilona Ann Coggswater."

And turning to face her, he said, "Ilona."

And Ilona looked up and into the faces and lenses of the reporters and cameramen and photographers present and smiled ever so slightly. But something happened, or more specifically, nothing happened. In that when Ilona looked up and smiled, she was so radiantly beautiful, that wide-eyed, green-eyed gaze never more intense, everything stopped, no reporting, no photographing, even the cameramen ignored their basic instincts to zoom in. Everyone present, including Tom Brokaw, just gasped then gawked helplessly at the Daughter of God, momentarily forgetting their responsibilities, permanently awed.

And, as far as anyone could remember, the entire world populace, or at least the entire world populace with television sets tuned into this press conference, issued a collective gasp along with those reporters and cameramen and photographers. It was all anyone could remember doing the first time they saw Ilona's face and gaze. Even the usually stuffy Bernard Shaw, monitoring and commenting on the event for CNN, couldn't suppress an "Oh, my God" when Ilona first looked up and smiled into the cameras of the world. Her presence was that intoxicating.

And Ilona nodded toward her chosen interviewer. It was time.

And just as Pope John Paul II had five days earlier, Brokaw began by asking "Is this the end?"

And Ilona answered in much the same way, "No," adding, after a short pause, "the end is what I'm here to prevent. Humankind must be forced to open its eyes and put a stop to the cruelty and destruction."

"Cruelty and destruction?"

"Of our planet and to its inhabitants."

"And by inhabitants you mean?"

"All of God's creatures."

"Your creatures?"

"My creatures."

"And the planet?"

"What's left of it."

He let her continue.

"Humankind screwed up," Ilona said, with a shrug. "I wouldn't be here otherwise."

"So, what can we do? What do we do?"

"Follow me. Listen to me. Work with me. Things must change, and so they will."

"What's first on your agenda?"

"To be accepted."

And they discussed the Catholic church and the pontiff, then Brokaw asked, "And what of the Ten Commandments?"

"Why don't we just go through them one at a time?" Ilona suggested.

And gasps of another sort came from the reporters and cameramen and photographers as Brokaw said, "You shall not take the name of the Lord in vain?"

"Believe me, both Jesus and my Dad are used to it by now. How could they not be?" Ilona said. Adding lightly, "And let's be realistic, how long will it really be before my name becomes an expletive deleted?"

"You shall have no other Gods before me?"

"That's a tough one. People need heroes, and people worship their heroes, and whether they be John Lennon or Michael Jordan or Neil Armstrong, God will understand. Just pick your heroes carefully."

"Remember the Sabbath day?"

"Remember, period. We're always there. Just acknowledge God's presence every once in a while. A nod, a smile aimed at the heavens. That's all He asks."

"Honor your father and mother?"

[82]

"That goes without saying," Ilona said. "Speaking of which, Hi, Mom."

And laughter and smiles erupted from the reporters and cameramen and photographers, from everyone, warmth, an overwhelming feeling of love.

"You shall not murder?"

"You shall not murder anything."

"All of God's creatures, right?"

A nod. "Equality amongst the living."

"You shall not commit adultery?"

"No messing around," Ilona said, "especially if you're married." Adding, "That really makes Dad angry."

"You shall not steal?"

"Obviously."

"You shall not bear false witness against your neighbor?"

"Who wrote that?" Ilona asked, smiling.

"According to the Bible, God did."

"Remember, there's no such thing as biblical truth."

"So then, how should the Eighth Commandment read?"

" 'Don't lie.' That's more to the point."

"And what about coveting your neighbor's house or wife?"

"Greed, jealousy, unnecessary evils."

"So the Ten Commandments basically stand?"

"More or less, with a little editing. It's just common sense when you break them down. And they could easily be reduced to one commandment."

"And that being?"

"Be kind."

"Be kind?"

"That's it."

"The Eleventh Commandment?"

"The Only Commandment. We want no misinterpretations this time around."

And Brokaw asked Ilona about her early years, and she spoke candidly about life in Cooperstown, then briefly about her mother and the immaculate conception, her schooling, her passions, and even her relationship with Robert Cervickas.

[83]

"Tell us about Jesus Christ," he asked.

"A typical older Brother," Ilona said. "He's constantly picking on me. Making fun of the way I dress, the music I like. You get the picture. He can be a bit pretentious at times, got a bit of an ego problem. Y'know, he is, after all, Jesus Christ. But I love him, dearly." And after a pause, "He's a big baseball fan, loves the Dodgers, as if that isn't too obvious," referring to their recent upset over the heavily favored Oakland A's in the World Series. "He's the one who turned me on to the game," adding proudly, "but I'm a Mets fan."

"Why did God send you instead of Christ?"

"Jesus already got a second chance and, well, it didn't exactly work out."

"Do you mean to tell us that Christ did return to Earth as he originally prophesized?"

"Yup. And lived for eighty-eight years. He was born April sixteenth 1889—April sixteenth was the date of his first crucifixion—and he died on Christmas day, 1977."

"And yet no one knew?"

"Everyone knew of him. He became the most popular man in the world, but he just never bothered telling anyone he was the Son of God. He was a citizen of the world who wanted to save that world through comedy and kindness. And in the end he was just crucified once more and he lived out his last years in exile. His chosen name was Charles Spencer Chaplin."

"Charlie Chaplin was the Son of God?"

"Jesus Christ, one in the same."

And not knowing what to say, Brokaw said, "I don't know what to say."

"Who would?" Ilona asked, with a shrug.

"But," Brokaw said, regaining, or at least trying to, his train of thought, "you were born before Chaplin's death."

"True. But the world was quickly running out of time, and Dad felt Jesus just didn't get the job done. It was a good try, though. Jesus had concluded that the world couldn't handle a visit from God. So by becoming the most popular person in the world he might be able to influence and lead its people out of their self-destructive path. That he'd be able, through his films, to preach a message of kindness and humanity. But it didn't exactly work out as Jesus expected, so Dad stepped in and sent me."

"But laughter and kindness aside, Chaplin's life was rather scandalous, wasn't it? He was a notorious womanizer, wasn't he?"

"I told you Jesus had an ego problem."

"And what do you think of Chaplin's films?"

"I've never been prouder of my Brother, and though he didn't accomplish what he originally set out to, he made the world a little bit happier through his art. He made us laugh. And laughter is the most precious and sacred of all miracles."

"This is all too fantastic," Brokaw said, shaking his head ever so slightly. "Was Chaplin also immaculately conceived?"

"Of course."

"Then tell me, since you, Chaplin, and Christ were all immaculately conceived, what did God think of Chaplin's womanizing?"

"God created men and women, and if he hadn't meant for them to have sex he wouldn't have made it so much fun. Sex is pleasurable on purpose. The orgasm wasn't a flaw in God's master plan. It's there to be enjoyed. It's just that some people enjoy it more frequently than others. Jesus as Chaplin wanted to see what it was like on the other side of the road and, well, he just got a little carried away. I think Dad was amused by it all."

"You speak frankly about sex?"

"I've already told you I had a boyfriend in high school. I needed to see firsthand what all the fuss was about. So, to be blunt and to end all speculation, I am not a virgin."

"I wouldn't have asked."

"I know, but someone else would have, so let's just get that out of the way."

"What can you tell us about God, the Father?"

"That he is kind and loving and forgiving. He is not to be feared, as many would like us to believe. The vengeful God is a false God, one not to be trusted or believed. And any person who tells you to fear the Lord is likewise not to be trusted or believed. God is love, period."

"And what of the many evangelists preaching God's word?"

"I have nothing nice to say about the Falwells or Swaggerts, or about Jim and Tammy Bakker or Oral Roberts. They have nothing to do with God or Christ and they have nothing to do with me. They don't even begin to understand the Lord, so how can they claim to represent him and preach his word?"

"So you'd advise their followers to stop sending contributions?"

"At the very least."

And Brokaw smiled. "Earlier you mentioned miracles. . . ."

"The miracle of laughter."

"Exactly. Can we expect any miracles from Ilona Ann Coggswater?"

"Other than the miracle of kindness?"

And Brokaw nodded.

And Ilona thought of that Tab-filled water cooler and said, "Only time can answer that one."

"And what of heaven and hell? Do they exist as we have been led to believe?"

"I can only answer that question one way," Ilona said. "I ask everyone to go on believing or not believing as they have. Heaven and hell are exactly what you want them to be. To some, heaven is a place where nothing happens. To me, it's like a spacious white-walled SoHo loft covered with impressionistic masterpieces, flooded with sunlight and smelling of just blossoming roses where Billie Holiday sings 'Body and Soul' on the finest sound system imaginable and every wonderful thought you've ever had materializes into the greatest of literature before your eyes."

"What about hell?"

A laugh. "Hell? Hmm, okay, it's like flying coach with a screaming child behind you, barking dogs in the cargo section directly below your seat, a grossly overweight life-insurance salesman to your left, a grossly overweight shower-curtain-ring salesman to your right, a bad movie that you've already sat through twice but this time your headphones aren't working, where the only available food is microwaved scrambled eggs and the one stewardess is out of ice and suffering through a major bout of PMS."

"Then we've all been to hell at one time or another," Brokaw suggested with a smile.

"And we all dream of heaven."

∽

And Brokaw opened the interview to questions from the invited members of the press starting with Randy Shilts of the *San Francisco Chronicle*, who asked, "What are you going to do about AIDS and AIDS victims?"

"I've heard their screams. I know their pain. A cure for AIDS will be found. I promise you that. But until then its victims must be loved and cared for. And anyone who rejects a victim of this disease, or any disease, will feel the ultimate rejection in the end."

"What do you mean?" some nameless reporter shouted back.

"Be kind."

"Your one Commandment?"

"It's what I'm here to promote."

"That's your only message?"

"Remember, no misinterpretations."

"What about animal protection?" asked Kathleen Milani of the *New York Times*.

"I'm here to save, *to protect*, all of my Father's creatures. All of them."

"Do you plan to meet with the president?" asked Robert Dixon of the *Washington Post*.

"Reagan or President-elect Bush?"

"Either."

"If they'll agree to meet with me. And I hope that they will. There is a lot to do, and they could definitely be of service."

"And what if they refuse to help you?"

"What I plan will happen with or without their help or approval. It is as inevitable as death and taxes."

"Can you outline that plan?" asked Deborah Anderson of the Associated Press.

"I have already answered that question."

"Why are you dressed entirely in black?" asked Junella Wingi of the *New Haven Advocate*.

"My roommate felt it was my best color."

"Have you given any thought to a career in acting?" she asked as a followup.

"No, I haven't. And I doubt seriously that I ever will."

"What kind of music do you like?

"Do you believe in capital punishment?"

"Did you vote for Bush or Dukakis?"

"Why the Mets?"

"Can we trust the Soviets?"

"What are your favorite TV shows?"

"How much gun control?"

"What about child abuse?"

"What about rape?"

"Are you a strict vegetarian?"

"What exactly do you mean by 'Be Kind'?"

"Is your hair naturally blond?"

"Why Tom Brokaw?"

"Can you stop terrorism?"

"Will you help the president balance the budget?"

"You know the NRA will fight you every step of the way?"

"Do you support Star Wars?"

"You mean to tell me you've never eaten meat?"

"Is that jacket linen or cotton?"

The questions came, rapid fire, some serious, some ridiculous, many not even worth mentioning. And Ilona Ann Coggswater, Daughter of God, sat calmly and answered and smiled and won over almost everyone who watched or asked or listened. And three hours after Brokaw's initial introduction, it was over and Ilona had accomplished what she, through this press conference, had set out to do, because aside from all the rave notices, glowing commentaries, and news clips, that night the CNN nonscientific Newsnight 900 poll asked "Do you believe Ilona

Ann Coggswater to be the Daughter of God?" And while eight percent of the viewers said no, a resounding ninety-two percent answered yes.

❦

And that night Ilona sat with Stephanie in their living room drinking Tab and eating a vegetarian Chinese dish out of the carton while a videotape of Charlie Chaplin's *The Kid* played on their television set, with *City Lights* quietly waiting its turn.

Stephanie had never seen a Chaplin film and during the cab ride home she pleaded with her roommate, even offering, "The Chinese food is on me." Stephanie was, shall we say, intrigued by Ilona's big Brother.

And how could Ilona refuse? Chinese and Chaplin seemed like the perfect combination after the events of the day.

❦

And Tom Brokaw sat for many hours in his office on the ninth floor of Rockefeller Center. He sat and thought. I just interviewed the Daughter of God. He thought that line over and over, even saying it out loud a few times, "I just interviewed the Daughter of God, I just interviewed the Daughter of God," but it still didn't seem to sink in. It was too amazing. "I just interviewed the Daughter of God." It was too utterly splendid. "I just interviewed the Daughter of God." It was too damn weird.

But he, Tom Brokaw, *had* just interviewed the Daughter of God.

What a way to make a living.

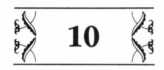

10

In the Name of the Father, Son and Daughter

In his now infamous *The Next Testament*, author Father The-
odore Karkowski would explain a complicated mathematical
equation that he would claim to have devised in the late 1940s,
which, when used in connection with the Old Testament's Book
of Job, predicted the coming of Ilona, the year in which she'd be
born, and the color of her eyes. "I knew her name would be
Ilona Ann Coggswater as early as 1952," Karkowski would write,
"though I believed Ilona to be spelled with two l's."

But, according to Stephen Manzi, an expert on codes, working
in the CIA's espionage division, when trying to apply Karkowski's formula to the Book of Job, the following was revealed,
"The oxen are in heat," along with the date January 8, 1935,
which was Elvis Presley's birthdate, and the French term *total-
isateur*, which roughly translated means "adding machine." In
his report to the U.S. attorney general, Manzi would conclude
that Karkowski was "*un gateau de fruit.*"

"It was September 15, 1970," Karkowski would recall in the
book's introduction. "I was preparing for bed when a star lit up
the eastern sky. That was the sign and I knew my calculations
had been correct." However a check through the Los Angeles
area weather records for that evening would show that portion
of California to be in the midst of "an unending torrential

rainstorm" which lasted from September twelfth until the seven-teenth. Mark Orsini of the National Weather Service would say, "No one saw anything in that sky that night, not a blasted thing. Except clouds, lightning, and rain, that is."

❧❧

The Next Testament would begin much like the Bible, "In the beginning God created the heavens and the earth." But the verbatim quotes would end there.

Karkowski would "update" many sections of both the Old and the New Testament. Most enlightening would be his rewrites of Exodus. For example, the original Exodus 22:1 reads, "If a man steals an ox or a sheep, and slaughters it or sells it, he shall restore five oxen for an ox and four sheep for a sheep." *The Next Testament* version would read, "If a man steals a BMW 325i or a Volvo 740 Turbo Wagon, and sells them whole or for parts, he shall restore one BMW 325i, one Porsche 928, and one Jeep Wagoneer for the BMW 325i and one Volvo 740 Turbo Wagon and one Ferrari Mondial for the Volvo 740 Turbo Wagon."

Or Exodus 22:16, "And if a man entices a virgin who is not betrothed, and lies with her, he shall surely pay the bride-price for her to be his wife," which would become, "And if a man seduces an unengaged virgin, and has sexual relations with her, he shall surely pay the virgin a minimum of two hundred and sixty-five dollars."

Or Exodus 22:25, "If you lend money to any of My people who are poor among you, you shall not be like a moneylender to him; you shall not charge him interest," which would become, "If you lend money to any of My people who are poor among you, you shall not charge him an interest rate that exceeds two points above the current prime lending rate."

❧❧

One point of minor interest in *The Next Testament*, a point actually and factually confirmed time and time again, was that as the infant Ilona slept in the nursery and her mother rested in her

[91]

"semiprivate" room at the Mel Ott Memorial Hospital, Coopers-town was visited by the Mets' Tom Seaver, considered possibly the finest baseball pitcher of the day, visiting the Baseball Hall of Fame between starts, and just for the hell of it, up and coming attorney G. Arthur Evans, his wife and two small children, spend-ing a short and much needed vacation away from Waterbury, Connecticut, and the practice of law, and Dr. Luther Brody, world renowned for his innovative reconstructive heart surgery techniques, who, just down the hall from where the infant Daughter of God slept, saved the life of George Wiggits, who had not been feeling well since the death of his son and had just suffered a major heart attack.

That these "three wise men" should find themselves in Coo-perstown simultaneously and so soon after Ilona's birth was to Karkowski, "a sign from above, a miracle."

"When I first learned," he would write, "that Seaver, Evans, and Brody were all in Cooperstown just after the birth of Ilona, tears came to my eyes. If only they had remembered to bring presents. (Gold, silver, an autographed baseball, maybe?)"

All three men would later comment that their being in Coo-perstown at the same moment in time was purely a coincidence and that while both Evans and Brody had heard of Seaver, they had never heard of each other, just as Seaver had never heard of either of them.

ↂ

Karkowski would cover Ilona's family tree with a collection of *begots*, be the first of too many to analyze her every word and movement, specifically the Brokaw interview and "The Papal Transcripts," and become obsessed with rewriting the sign of the cross and redubbing the "Holy Trinity" the "Holy Quadrity."

Ilona would later comment that O'Donnell's assessment was correct—Karkowski was "a fruitcake." A now very famous "fruit-cake," but a "fruitcake" nonetheless.

ↂ

The Next Testament would be translated into sixty-eight languages and sell close to three hundred million copies worldwide, spending close to a year as a *New York Times Book Review* nonfiction best-seller, before finally being moved to the fiction list, at Ilona's request.

ॐ

But that's jumping ahead.

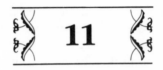

11

And the Fundamentalists Cried

The next morning, shortly after Ilona returned from the Soup Kitchen, a short visit that delighted the regulars who said, "How come you didn't tell us you was God? We'd 'a' believed ya," Stephanie LaVasseur gave Tony Scognamiglio, owner of Self-Portrait, her two-hour notice ("I was pissed. Believe you me!" he would write in his book), and from their "safe," one-bed-room, sixth-floor walkup with working fireplace on East 10th Street in Greenwich Village, assisted Ilona in arranging other necessary interviews and some quality publicity and, though Stephanie didn't know it at the time, putting that eventual but inevitable end to all the screaming, all the crying, all the suffer-ing, all the pain.

And while planning their strategy, CNN's noon offering "Sonya Live," a call-in talk show hosted by Dr. Sonya Friedman, filled their apartment with tears, or at least the sound of tears. Sonya's topic for the day was Ilona; her guests were a panel of experts, so to speak, which included Father Arthur McGoff, head of the theology department at St. Theresa's University, Reverend Patrick West, leader of a group known as Fundamentalists for a Moral America, and Elaine Deaner, president of the American Society of Atheists.

And while Father McGoff admitted having problems with Ilona's ordered changes in Catholic practices, West called Ilona "a blasphemer" and later "a whore," stating that, "Not even God has a right to criticize the Bible." Ms. Deaner was visibly shaken, stating, "The presence of God pushes the atheistic movement back into the Stone Age. How can we claim there's no such thing as God when God is right here staring us in the eye. It's all very upsetting, really."

And then the calls began. And with the calls came the tears. The callers, fundamentalist and born-again Christians. Their tears, tears of shame, tears of sadness, tears of joy, tears of rapture, tears of tears. But not familiar tears, no familiar cries or screams. These tears were new to Ilona, and though they caught her off guard for a moment, she soon saw through them. False tears, hypocritical screams, unnecessary cries, that's all they were.

"We have Percy from Lubbock, Texas, on the line," Sonya said. "What's your question, Percy?"

"I just want Reverend West to know that I love and support him," Percy said, between sobs, "and that together we can defeat this agent of Satan."

And Sonya thanked the caller, shook her head ever so slightly, and moved on.

"I don't know what this world is coming to," said Linda from Waycross, Georgia, sniffling back the tears, "when people can challenge the very word of God and try to change the holy Bible."

But when Sonya tried to explain that it was God himself, or herself, in this miraculous case, that was correcting biblical lore, the logic went well over the heads of Reverend West and the still crying Linda from Waycross, Georgia.

"Is nothing above ridicule?" asked Sandy from Nashua, New Hampshire, breaking down uncontrollably, just managing to spit her question out. "Blasphemer," she screamed before hanging up. "She's a blasphemer."

"A woman can never represent God in my eyes," said Wilma from Los Angeles, California.

"That's such a remarkable statement coming from a woman," said Sonya.

And Wilma from Los Angeles, California, agreed and began to cry.

And Elizabeth from Gunnison, Colorado, called only to say she agreed with Wilma from Los Angeles, California, and she, too, began to cry.

And Ed from Peoria, Illinois, added, "They're right. Just read the Bible. It's all in there."

But when Sonya insisted that it was Ilona's right as God to rewrite the Holy Book, Ed from Peoria, Illinois, muttered some phrase that was mostly "bleeped" by the CNN censor, began to cry, and hung up.

And Ginny from Beaumont, Texas, called and said, between sobs, "As a fundamentalist Christian it is my right to denounce this harlot and devote my life to Jesus."

"But Jesus is Ilona's Brother," Sonya explained.

"Then she's the black sheep of the Holy Family," said Ginny from Beaumont, Texas. "And God should disown her, or something like that."

"If I may interject," said Reverend West, "It is painfully obvious that we fundamentalist Christians believe in the Bible as the holy word of God, and nothing can change that."

"Not even God himself?" asked Sonya.

"No, ma'am, not even God himself."

And Claire from Bartlesville, Oklahoma, said, "Doesn't this Ilona woman want us to accept homosexuals?"

Father McGoff answered, "Yes, it was one of the orders she gave the pope."

"I was askin' Reverend West," interrupted Claire from Bartlesville, Oklahoma.

"Sorry," apologized McGoff.

"Yes, she does. And that, too, goes against biblical teaching," said West.

"It's sickening, added Claire from Bartlesville, Oklahoma, with tears obviously beginning to flow. "I think they should put all those gays and all those people with AIDS in a jail and throw away the key."

"That's what the Bible says to do," said West.

"Hold on there," interrupted Sonya, finally losing some control.

"I love you, Reverend West. I watch your program every morning," concluded Claire from Bartlesville, Oklahoma, before Sonya cut her off, permanently.

"Reverend West, how dare you come on my show and advocate such, such," said Sonya, searching for the right word but choosing the most damaging one, "such fascist tactics? Locking up homosexuals and AIDS victims? C'mon, Reverend West, that is an utterly deplorable statement."

"I'm only quoting biblical fact," West argued.

"You're quoting West fact," said Sonya. "The Bible according to Reverend Patrick West."

Time for a commercial break.

༄

And when "Sonya Live" returned from that commercial break, Reverend West was no longer on the panel of experts, and Ms. Deaner was speaking, "It was backwards thinking like that of West's that made me become an atheist in the first place. I figured that if there was actually a God and if he had spokespeople like that, I wanted nothing to do with him."

"Reverend West could even scare me away from God," added Father McGoff.

"And yet millions of supporters send him and others like him millions of dollars every year," concluded Sonya before taking another caller.

And Joe from Prospect, Connecticut, asked, "Has anyone stopped to question why this Ilona chick wears nothing but black? Me and a bunch of my friends got this theory that she's got nothin' to do with God at all but that she in fact represents the Devil."

And Sonya sighed before passing the question to Father McGoff.

"I honestly doubt that Ilona's fashion statement has anything to do with her divinity," he said.

But Joe from Prospect, Connecticut, pressed on, "But, like,

[97]

shouldn't she have been wearing long, white, flowin' robes with gold and purple trim?"

"Not necessarily," said the priest.

"I would have believed her no matter what she had on and I'm, was, an atheist," said Ms. Deaner.

And Joe from Prospect, Connecticut, hung up and Sonya commented, "At least he wasn't crying, maybe that'll start a trend," before introducing another guest. "And now via satellite from 'Jesus Land' on the Caribbean island of Celeste we welcome televangelist Oral Roberts. Thank you for taking time out to be on our program, Mr. Roberts."

"It's my pleasure, Sonya. But please, call me Oral."

"Very well. Have you been enjoying the Caribbean weather?"

"Oh, definitely, Sonya. And I'd like to take this opportunity to invite believers everywhere to visit our tropical paradise theme park here on Celeste. They won't be disappointed."

"What about nonbelievers?"

"There're invited, too, but I promise them, after a day in Jesus Land they'll accept the Lord God, Jesus Christ, as never before."

"Okay, Oral."

"What about you, Sonya. When are you going to make a pilgrimage to Jesus Land?"

"It's not on my immediate schedule."

"We'll have to do something to change your mind, now won't we?"

"Looks that way," Sonya said. "Now, to get to the subject at hand, Ilona Ann Coggswater, is she the Daughter of God or nothing more than a blasphemer, as Reverend West seems to believe?"

"Oh, definitely a little of both, Sonya. While I don't doubt her divinity for a moment, I also state emphatically that no matter who she is, she has no right to challenge the holy word."

"But if the Bible is indeed the word of God, why then can't God, well, edit those words, rewrite those words."

"Because," Roberts explained, "it just wouldn't be the right thing to do, and God can only do the right thing."

And Sonya, at the end of her patience, took a call. "Hello, Eve from Crump, Tennessee."

"Hello," said a sobbing Eve from Crump, Tennessee. "I'm a fundamentalist Christian, I've been born again twice."

"That doesn't surprise me," said Sonya.

"And I just can't believe how cruel this Ilona is," continued Eve from Crump, Tennessee. "She claims to be the Daughter of God and yet she comes to Earth to disrupt our lives telling us to have abortions and to have sex with everyone and to accept homosexuals and that the Bible is full of lies."

And Oral Roberts began to cry.

"Why can't she leave us alone," said Eve from Crump, Tennessee. "We didn't ask her to come to Earth. She should just go back to where she came from."

"I couldn't agree with your more, Eve," said Roberts as the tears continued to flow. "Ilona Coggswater comes to Earth and expects us to change our ways just because she says so. We live our lives as Jesus lived His. The Bible says to follow Jesus, *not* His sister. And I agree with you when you say she's got some pretty farfetched ideas. If we listen to Ilona Coggswater, women will no longer be allowed to wear fur coats, homosexuals will be teaching sexual education to our children in grade school, we'll have an abortion in every home and no chickens in the pot because we'll all be vegetarians. No one will be able to own guns, there'll be an AIDS clinic in every neighborhood, and women will become priests. This is America, and that is not the American way of life. Who does this Ilona Coggswater think she is?"

"Sounds like you'll be needing another eight million dollars to combat this," commented Sonya.

Time for another commercial break.

And Stephanie, watching and listening and now switching to MTV where she was unconsciously surprised to see an old Elvis Costello video, told Ilona what she thought about the callers and the guests. She said what Sonya would probably have loved to say. She said what both Ms. Deaner and Father McGoff had thought. She said what was on the mind of so many nonfundamentalists and non-born-agains. She said what even Ilona was thinking as the Daughter of God prepared a couple of cheese bagels. What Stephanie said was simple and to the point, as most of what she said usually was.

"They're all so woll aw wghit," was what she said, biting into her cheese bagel three words too early.

"They're all so what?" Ilona asked.

"Woll aw wghit," Stephanie said, still chewing.

"Swallow your food," her roommate advised. And this Stephanie did, following the swallow with a gulp of Tab.

"Now, what are they all?" Ilona asked, laughing and giving it another shot.

"Full of shit," Stephanie said, taking another bite of her cheese bagel.

⁊

And that afternoon, while basically ignoring MTV's strange new play list, an uncomfortable blend of the bands Ilona had so innocently mentioned when asked, "What kind of music do you like?," the Replacements, Patti Smith, Hüsker Dü, Laurie Anderson, and yet more Elvis Costello, with the usual MTV mix of Bon Jovi, Michael Jackson, Def Leppard and Van Halen, Ilona felt it was time to start answering the phone, taking some of the burden off the answering machine, which really had, as of late, been working above and beyond even its call of duty.

And Stephanie became her roommate's *secretaire provocateur*, a title she adored, sitting in an unconsciously sexual pose in the middle of their living-room floor, flipping back her mane, sharpened pencil, datebook, and legal pad in hand, with telephone and telephone book resting comfortably between her long, ripped-jeans-covered legs.

First on the agenda was to raise some much needed pocket cash and rent money. And though money was the furthest thing from Ilona's mind, she knew that the recent revelations prevented her from maintaining her usual means of support. *Usual* meaning waitressing and such. Being the Daughter of God could have its drawbacks, and holding a steady job would definitely be one of them.

So Stephanie suggested that Ilona become the spokesperson for some product. Standing and doing her best to mimic her friend's voice, Stephanie said, "Hi, I'm Ilona Ann Coggswater, the Daughter of God, and I wear Levi's jeans," slapping one of her buttocks to emphasize the word "Levi's."

And though Ilona laughed, the thought was not a bad one, if she could find a product worthy of divine endorsement.

"One day of filming with a few coy looks and some well-chosen phrases will take care of the bills for the next few years," Stephanie said, biting down into her FaberCastell American #2, adding, "easily," with tons of emphasis on the "easily."

"But is that the image I should project?" Ilona asked, biting down on her lower lip, moving restlessly into a restless position on their sofa.

"It's either that or back to waitressing. And you won't get much accomplished if you're bussing tables five nights a week."

"I don't know."

"Well, what did Jesus do for pocket change?"

"He was a carpenter, among other things."

"Oh, yeah," said Stephanie. "What about Chaplin, did he ever do any endorsements?"

And Ilona smiled and nodded and sat up as she remembered the Old Gold cigarette ads and the Liberty Bonds promotional film and said, "Okay, but what can I endorse?"

"Are there any products you absolutely believe in?" asked Stephanie, doing major reconstruction on that FaberCastell.

And while Ilona let up on her lower lip, Stephanie made suggestions, "Why *not* jeans?"

"You wear 501's. You've got the legs. You've got the ass. Not me."

"There's nothing wrong with your ass."

"Thanks, but no."

"I'll put that down in my column then," said Stephanie, scribbling those three digits on the legal pad.

"Your column?"

"Yup," Stephanie said, adding, "as you would say."

Some laughter.

"So, I guess Calvin Klein underwear is out of the question?"

And Ilona tossed a pillow at her roommate in lieu of an answer.

And after Stephanie wrote "Calvin Klein Underwear" in her column, she suggested, "What about Honda? We could use some wheels."

"They sell themselves. They don't need me."

"All right, Chryslers?"

"No."

"Volkswagens?"

"No."

"Fords?"

"I don't want to endorse cars."

"Isuzu? You could strike down Joe Isuzu for telling a lie." And Ilona's use of that intense, wide-eyed, green-eyed gaze indirectly caused even more damage to the FaberCastell, as Stephanie looked beyond the TV and on to another more than obvious possibility. "Budweiser beer?"

"No."

"Rolling Rock maybe?"

"I can't endorse beer."

And Stephanie wrote *beer* in her column. "How 'bout some styling gel or mousse or makeup?"

And Ilona walked to the fridge as Stephanie continued writing in her column. And as the Daughter of God poured some Tab over the three ice cubes that waited patiently at the bottom of her glass, Stephanie yelled out, "Pepsi? What about Pepsi? Or Coke even?"

And Ilona said, ever so quietly, "Tab."

"Tab?"

"Tab."

"At least you drink it."

"I'm hooked on it."

"You don't think Diet Pepsi would be more chic?"

"Tab."

"They could use the help."

"Definitely Tab."

"Then Tab it is." And Stephanie used an unchewed section of the FaberCastell to write the three-letter word in Ilona's column. And as she thumbed through the white pages of the Manhattan phonebook, looking for what, she was not sure, it occurred to her to ask, "Who makes Tab?"

"A product of the Coca-Cola Company, it says here."

And, as Stephanie thumbed through the C's, the telephone rang. Not that this was a seeming spectacular event, it had, after all, been ringing virtually nonstop since Monday afternoon. What made this ring particularly interesting is that the phone had not rung once since being placed between Stephanie's long, ripped-jeans-covered legs. It could have been intimidated, frightened, or simply calculating its next move, who knew? But it was in fact ringing its first ring at this very moment, and though the phone seriously considered changing its mind after seeing the sneer Stephanie aimed its way, it stood firm and continued on bravely to its second ring and then, feeling fearless, damn the torpedoes full speed ahead, to its third. And when Stephanie realized her sneering would not get it to stop, she gave in and answered.

"The Coggswater Corporation," she answered, in a very snitty-snotty type of executive secretarial voice, *secretaire provocateur* to be sure, making Ilona laugh. "How may I help you?"

The call was from a filmmaker. Not a particularly famous filmmaker. Not even a particularly great filmmaker. Just your average ordinary filmmaker. The only thing that really distinguished this filmmaker from all the other filmmakers of the world was that he, Edward Davis Walker, was closest to speaking with the Daughter of God. And this really only distinguished him if in fact any of the other filmmakers of the world were actually trying to get a line through. Which in fact a few were.

What this filmmaker, Edward Davis Walker, suggested was that he be allowed to make a documentary about Ilona Ann Coggswater.

"Why?" asked the *secretaire provocateur*.

"Because," explained the filmmaker, "I really want to." No need for pretentious reasoning.

"Oh," Stephanie said, covering the mouthpiece of the phone and explaining to Ilona. "It's a filmmaker who wants to make a documentary about you."

"Don't need one," Ilona said.

"But he sounds cute," Stephanie said.

"Then let him buy us dinner. We don't have that Tab contract yet."

And clearing her throat, Stephanie made the arrangements to meet with the filmmaker to discuss his proposal over dinner that evening and hung up.

You're enjoying this, Ilona thought, then said.

"Uh huh."

☙

It didn't take long for Stephanie to get through to the people at the Coca-Cola Company regarding Tab. Sales had been suffering since the introductions of Diet Coke and Pepsi and the company executives were more than a little enthused about some divine intervention. A meeting was set up for the following morning.

"But what do we know about contracts?" asked Ilona, but Stephanie, not missing a beat, was already dialing up an author. Not your average ordinary author but a great author, a famous author. And one thing that distinguished this great and famous author from other great and famous authors was that he had recently spent a rollicking few months with the stunning Stephanie LaVasseur. And this author owed her a favor or two, and a recommendation for a good lawyer would be a nice start toward repaying his debt.

"How do you know we can trust this guy?"

"Because if we get screwed, I tell his wife that I was his lover

[104]

last summer while she and the kids were trekking through Europe."

"Did you know he was married?"

"Of course not. And when I found out, I was angry, humiliated, but I wasn't in love and I wasn't about to cause any pain to his wife and children. He was so relieved, he promised, 'If there's ever anything I can do,' blah, blah, blah."

"But would his wife believe you."

"Let's just say there are a few intimate details that his wife would definitely recognize. Get the picture?"

"Yup."

And the great and famous author recommended G. Arthur Evans, renowned as one of the sharpest lawyers in the business, who, to no one's surprise, was thrilled at the chance to represent the Daughter of God.

⸎

And that evening full-time Daughter of God Ilona Ann Coggswater and part-time actress/model, part-time business-management student, and no longer part-time bartender Stephanie LaVasseur met all-the-time filmmaker Edward Davis Walker for dinner at the NoHo Star, a quiet restaurant on Bleecker Street.

Edward Davis Walker was a tall, thin man of twenty-eight with uncombed, short, almost black hair and perpetual whiskers. His eyes were gray, or blue, or green, depending on their surroundings. His voice deep, almost tired, "sexy," Stephanie would say. But his most striking feature were his hands. "Dead hands," he called them, but they were everything but. They reminded Ilona of her own hands, small, almost fragile, yet full of life, always moving, touching. His hands gave everything away. And his style of dress, his manner, his speech, his methods, bohemian, no argument, no doubt. And he was a filmmaker.

And as this filmmaker pitched his documentary, Ilona listened and Stephanie worked overtime on what she would later call "major eye contact."

And though Ilona did have doubts about a documentary,

Ilona, the Movie, she imagined at one point, making herself chuckle out loud, there was one phrase, a thought planted by filmmaker Walker that haunted her, filling the screaming void that a few Rolling Rocks had caused.

And that night as the three continued their conversation over drinks in some Saint Mark's Place bar where word of Ilona's presence quickly spread to the downtown trendies who now packed the place, well beyond all safe or legal or comfortable limits, just to be near the Daughter of God, the thought kept right on haunting.

And as filmmaker Walker walked Ilona and Stephanie safely back to their apartment and Stephanie gave the filmmaker a sweet kiss good night, and Ilona said, regarding the documentary, "I'll think about it," and the roommates walked up the six flights to their "safe," sixth-floor walk up, the haunting continued.

And as Stephanie rambled about her "major crush" on the filmmaker, about this eyes, about his voice, and about his hands, and as the results from this night's nonscientific Newsnight 900 Poll asking whether fundamentalist Christians should be legally forced to accept Ilona's teachings, the thought began to play hide and seek in Ilona's head.

And, as Ilona curled up under her covers on her pull-out sofa bed, the thought crept on. "Damn it," she said to herself, "if it's not the screaming . . ."

It was pessimistic, it was depressing. But it haunted her because the more thought she gave this thought, the more she began to believe that filmmaker Walker might have hit the nail squarely on the proverbial head.

And though sleep finally came it was restless as usual, but not for the same reasons, now, because that blasted thought persisted: Only art survives.

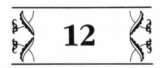

What Kind of Music Do You Like?

And it wasn't long before every word from every song from every album from every musical artist that Ilona Ann Coggswater has so innocently mentioned during Tuesday's Brokaw interview would be examined and evaluated and interpreted to mean this or that or some other thing, and usually a this or that or some other thing that the composer had no intention or thought of meaning. Usually a this or that or some other thing that those doing the interpreting only wanted the word or song or album or rock artist to mean.

It was all very confusing.

C?

And no one was more confused than Paul Westerberg, leader of the Replacements, Ilona's "favorite band." Uncommercial critics' darlings that were, according to *Rolling Stone* magazine, "Hard drinking, notoriously sloppy but always brilliant." This four-member band from Minneapolis just couldn't sell any records despite the glowing press.

They couldn't sell records until Ilona that is. And within two days of the Brokaw press conference the entire Replacements catalogue was sold out.

Everywhere.

And within six weeks, the band's most recent LP, *Pleased to Meet Me*, originally released in 1987, would be number one with a bullet on *Billboard*'s Top 200 albums chart, due mainly to the song "Skyway," which would be released as a single after Buddy Bigtime, a DJ on New York's top-rated WNEW-FM, would explain his theory that Westerberg had written the ballad in anticipation of Ilona's arrival and that the skyway in the song was, "a tramway to heaven." The song, like the album from which it came, would zoom to number one, and would eventually sell over five and a half million copies.

And Ilona fanatics would give new meaning to virtually every Replacements song. "Gary's Got a Boner" would become an anthem for sexual education. "Red Red Wine" would reaffirm the Catholic rite of drinking wine during mass as a symbol of drinking the blood of Christ, "Androgynous" and "We're Coming Out" would become theme songs of sorts for Catholic homosexuals, and "Can't Hardly Wait" with its lines about Jesus Christ's barroom etiquette, would be analyzed in a *Psychology Today* magazine cover story that would call it the "most important rock song of our time."

The Replacements' next album, *Don't Tell a Soul*, which would be released in early February 1989, would debut at number one on the charts and remain there for twenty-three weeks, selling thirty-eight million copies worldwide, making it the biggest-selling album of all time.

In March 1989, when asked by *Musician* magazine for a piece that would be called "Ilona's Favorite Band," about their sudden success, Westerberg, who was being interviewed in some Hollywood bar, would knock over his beer and say, "Fuck you," after which he would stand, fall over, and pass out on the floor. Not missing a beat, bassist Tommy Stinson would say, "He's actually real fuckin' happy about it." Drummer Chris Mars and guitarist Slim Dunlap would nod in agreement, with Dunlap adding, "He cried when *The Replacements Stink* [one of the band's early hardcore punk releases] was certified platinum."

And in June 1989, Westerberg, walking off the stage after playing to over sixty thousand screaming fans at the Astrodome in Houston, Texas, would finally comment, 'I can't write songs anymore. Everything I write I look at and see that it'll be interpreted a hundred and forty-seven different ways and I can't fucking stand it. I just want to write a song that no one understands, that no one analyzes, that no one likes. I just want to be left alone." Stinson, following close behind, would explain, "He's just a little upset 'cause he just found out they don't fuckin' make Lamborghinis in *Ilona green*."

CฦO

The music of Patti Smith, Hüsker Dü, Laurie Anderson, and Elvis Costello would also be interpreted to mean this or that or some other thing. And though no one would know what to make of Smith's "Jesus died for somebody's sins but not mine," her "Pissing in the River" would become a call for baptism, while "Kimberly" from her first album *Horses*, with its chorus of "Little sister the sky is falling," would be construed to be about Ilona as seen through the eyes of Jesus, despite the fact that Smith would insist that it was written about her own kid sister.

The Hüsker Dü song "Green Eyes" would become, like "Skyway," and for all too obvious reasons, a theme song of sorts for Ilona followers, and their song "New Day Rising" would soon become a morning institution on virtually every radio station, where listeners would be asked to call in and explain what the song meant to them, all in spite of the fact that it contained only one lyrical passage, the title, sung over and over and over again.

Laurie Anderson's five-record set, *United States Live*, originally released in late 1984, would zoom into the Top 10 and reach new biblical importance in the eyes of the growing legions of Ilona followers, with its seventy-eight tracks being viewed as modern-day psalms.

And Anderson's next album, *Strange Angels*, whose cover would feature a rather flattering portrait of Anderson by Robert Mapplethorpe, when released in late October 1989, would contain no less than five future number-one hit singles, including

"My Eyes," a song—like most any song from any of Ilona's favorite musical artists to have the word *eyes* in it—that would be interpreted to be not only about the Daughter of God but actually a view of life through her eyes.

With Elvis Costello, whose catalogue of material was as extensive as it was varied, the Ilona fanatics would have a field day. "Brilliant Mistake" would be interpreted as a history of the Catholic Church during the twentieth century, "(What's So Funny 'Bout) Peace, Love And Understanding" would become the Democratic National Committee theme song, while "Blame It on Cain" and "Miracle Man" from his first album, *My Aim Is True*, would be seen as early prophecies that the Bible was incomplete, outdated, and incorrect, and "Waiting For The End Of The World" from that same album, in which Costello longs for a second coming, would have some religious fanatics dubbing him, "rock music's John the Baptist."

And when Costello's latest and long awaited new album *Spike* would be released in late February 1989, it would immediately take its place at number two on the album charts. The more than cynical effort from the "Beloved Entertainer" would be probed, poked, analyzed, dissected, and quite literally ripped apart and left for dead.

And when making a guest appearance on "Late Night with David Letterman" in March 1989, Costello would sarcastically admit that the interpreters were right. "Go out and buy all my records," he would say. "The songs are all about Ilona. Every last one of them."

"Even the ones covered by Linda Ronstadt?" an amused Letterman would ask.

"No. Those are the only exceptions," the Beloved Entertainer would answer with the widest and wildest of smiles.

ℭℑ

The *Billboard* Top 200 albums chart for the week ending March 31, 1989, would list the following as the ten top-selling albums in the country:

1	DON'T TELL A SOUL — Replacements
2	SPIKE — Elvis Costello
3	UNITED STATES LIVE — Laurie Anderson
4	ELECTRIC YOUTH — Debbie Gibson
5	PLEASE TO MEET ME — Replacements
6	NEW DAY RISING — Hüsker Dü
7	KING OF AMERICA — The Costello Show (featuring Elvis Costello)
8	APPETITE FOR DESTRUCTION — Guns N' Roses
9	LET IT BE — Replacements
10	DREAM OF LIFE — Patti Smith

Another Replacements album, *Tim*, would be at number seventeen with a bullet, while the entire Elvis Costello collection along with most of Laurie Anderson's, Husker Dü's, and Patti Smith's other albums, could be found scattered throughout the Top 200 chart along with a half dozen jazz collections containing Billie Holiday's rendition of "Body and Soul."

૨૭

Had God not sent His only daughter to the world, the top ten would have looked like this:

1	ELECTRIC YOUTH — Debbie Gibson
2	APPETITE FOR DESTRUCTION — Guns N' Roses
3	DON'T BE CRUEL — Bobby Brown
4	VOLUME ONE — Traveling Wilburys
5	SHOOTING RUBBERBANDS AT THE STARS — Edie Brickell & The New Bohemians
6	FOREVER YOUR GIRL — Paula Abdul
7	G N' R LIES — Guns N' Roses
8	MYSTERY GIRL — Roy Orbison
9	HYSTERIA — Def Leppard
10	GIVING YOU THE BEST THAT I GOT — Anita Baker

And according to recording-industry experts, the closest any of Ilona's favorite bands would have gotten to the Top 10 during this third week of March, based solely on the sales of their previous efforts, would be *Don't Tell a Soul* and *Spike*, both hovering, give or take a number, somewhere around thirty. And with some luck, *Dream of Life*, might have also been found on the Top 200 chart, most probably in the bottom ten.

≪≫

And the tours would sell as well if not better than the records. Followers seemed to feel they could experience a miraculous healing of sorts at an Elvis Costello or Laurie Anderson or Replacements concert. These artists who once just comfortably filled four- and five-thousand-seat auditoriums would soon be selling out football stadiums.

The Rolling Stones, who would tour during the late summer and fall of 1989, would even ask to be the opening act for an October Laurie Anderson concert at Giants Stadium in East Rutherford, New Jersey, an Anderson concert originally scheduled to take place at the Brooklyn Academy of Music, but moved due to the overwhelming demand for tickets. And after the Stones would present their ninety-minute set featuring a multi-million-dollar light show and special-effects extravaganza to little enthusiasm from the audience, Anderson would walk out onto the empty black stage, violin in hand, to a ten-minute standing ovation. And as the applause died down, as it always must, Anderson would say, "Y'know (pause) I was sitting in my living room one afternoon watching (pause) TV (pause) with the sound off. (pause) And on the TV screen came this 'Special Report' title card, y'know, (pause) the one that always precedes reports about natural disasters, airplane crashes, and (pause) presidential assassinations. (pause) So I grab my remote control to turn up the sound. (pause) 'This better be good,' I say to myself. (pause) And there's anchorman Tom Brokaw, (pause) the cute one, (pause) and he's introducing me to this young woman, the 'Daughter of God,' he calls her. (pause) And I say to myself, 'Hmmm' (pause) 'I wonder if she's a fan.' "

And, also in October 1989, after some talk-show appearance or other where some host or other would ask Ilona what she was listening to now, her answers, Michelle Shocked, Tom Waits, the Pixies, old R.E.M., even older Clash, would soon find themselves zooming to the top of the *Billboard* charts.

Zoom.

And when Ilona was spotted, by a *New York Post* gossip columnist, in a Greenwich Village used-record store purchasing *Catholic Boy*, a 1980 release from the Jim Carroll Band, Atlantic Records was forced, by overwhelming demand, to reissue the now out-of-print LP, which, when reissued, zoomed into the *Billboard* Top 10.

Zoom.

And when Ilona called a local FM radio station requesting to hear XTC's 1986 underground hit "Dear God," a song loaded with questions, criticism, and disbelief, all aimed directly at her dear old Dad, Ilona-ites snatched up copies of all of the band's many albums and the interpreting began all over again.

Zoom, zoom, zoom.

It was all so very very confusing.

ᏬᎧ

But, as usual, that's jumping ahead.

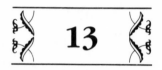

13

Hawaii

And Thursday morning, as Stephanie sat on the sidelines with visions of a filmmaker dancing in her head, attorney G. Arthur Evans guided Ilona through the whereofs, theretos and hereafters of her meeting and contract with the Coca-Cola Company.

His negotiations were based on an inside scoop that Pepsi was about to pay rock star Madonna ten million dollars to represent its soda, which in fact, it shortly would. And that if Pepsi could pay Madonna ten million, then surely the Coca-Cola Company would be compelled to pay Ilona, a far superior representative, twice that much. Ilona was, after all, the Daughter of God, and though she didn't have any hit singles under her belt, she was far more divine than Madonna could ever be.

And when the people from the Coca-Cola Company regained their facial coloring and ability to speak, they asked Evans, through a series of stutters and wipes of sweating brows, how any representative could be worth twenty million dollars, especially when that representative would be representing a diet soda that few people drank.

And Ilona answered this question, letting her intense, wide-eyed, green-eyed gaze meet their tired, doubting, everything-but-green-eyed eyes. She answered the question with a smile. And not even a particularly grand smile, but a simple, relaxed smile. A smile that said, "Trust me. I can help."

A sigh of relief, some laughter. That was the power of Ilona's smile.

And a contract was drawn and signed and the deal was done.

"One other thing," Ilona said before leaving the meeting. "Just a little request."

"Anything," said one of the people from the Coca-Cola Company. "Just name it."

"I'd like the words *Be Kind* printed on every Tab can and bottle, in good-sized letters, just below the Tab logo."

"No problem at all."

"Great idea."

"Why didn't we think of that?"

And that afternoon, sitting in Evans's midtown office, to change the subject at hand from exactly what *was* Stephanie's relationship to his good friend, that great and famous but "married" author, Ilona thanked Evans for his negotiations and suggested that he donate his ten percent fee to some worthy charity or other, since it was all too obvious that he was a man of considerable talent and wealth and what need did he really have for an extra two million dollars. And though he couldn't explain why, and still really wanted an answer to the question he had asked Stephanie, he agreed and shortly would donate the entire amount to AIDS research.

And later when a few nonbelievers in the legal profession heard of Evans donating a two-million-dollar fee to AIDS research, they then knew beyond any and all doubt that Ilona was who she claimed to be, because besides being among the finest in his profession, Evans was also among the stingiest. "Anyone who could make G. Arthur Evans give up two million dollars," an ex-partner would say, "has to be God."

And before leaving Evans's office, Ilona requested that he telephone the people at the Internal Revenue Service and explain to them that she would not be filing an income tax form nor would she be paying twenty-eight percent of her now eighteen-million-dollar fee to them since she was in fact the Daughter of God and really did not have the time nor desire to bother with such forms and payments. But she would gladly donate the five million, forty thousand dollars due to a few select charities on their behalf.

But when Evans explained that the IRS might not buy such logic, Ilona assured him that they would and that if he needed an additional argument, to tell them that she could put the five million, forty thousand dollars to better use than the United States government ever could.

And then she instructed Evans to divide that five million, forty thousand dollars evenly among five organizations.

"Greenpeace," she said. "Handgun Control Incorporated, Planned Parenthood."

"Amnesty International," Stephanie said.

Ilona nodded, adding, "And the Better World Society."

In his book, *Addendums for Ilona*, Evans recalled that immediately after Ilona and Stephanie left his office he dialed up the IRS and, after being connected with Eduardo Carvalho, an agent in the exemption department, he said, "Hello, I'm G. Arthur Evans and I represent Ilona Ann Coggswater."

"Who, sir?" said Agent Carvalho.

"Ilona Ann Coggswater, the Daughter of God."

"Never heard of her, sir."

"Have you looked at a newspaper or turned on a TV in the past couple of days?"

"What I do after I leave this office is none of your business, sir."

"What I mean is, how can you not know who she is?"

"Then say what you mean, sir."

"She's the Daughter of God. Her picture's been everywhere."

"I haven't seen it, sir."

"Are you blind?"

"No, just busy, sir."

"Fine," said Evans, who went on to explain that Ilona would not be paying any taxes.

"And how much would she have owed, sir?"

"Five million, forty thousand."

"Dollars, sir?"

"Dollars, Mr. Carvalho, Dollars."

"Let me connect you with one of my superiors, sir."

And Agent Carvalho did, connecting Evans with Jan Radder,

the branch manager who had at least heard of Ilona.

"She's the real thing, huh?" asked Radder.

"You better believe it."

"Well, I was always instructed that only God came before the Internal Revenue Service. So, I guess I'll take care of it."

Radder explained that there'd be some paperwork and Ilona would have to sign a few forms and that everything would be in the mail to Evan's office in a few weeks. "I just have to do this by the book and there won't be any problems."

"How do you handle a situation like this by the book?" asked a confused Evans.

"Oh, it's covered in our handbook, listed under 'Acts of God' as 'The Second Coming.' Nothing gets past the IRS, remember that."

"I will."

"I'd be able to get the forms to you sooner but we're swamped trying to figure out what we owe the Chaplin estate."

"I beg your pardon," said Evans.

"The Chaplin Estate. If Charlie Chaplin was indeed Jesus Christ, then he never should have paid any taxes. I've spent the past day and a half trying to figure out how much he actually paid in and what the IRS will have to pay back," Radder said, adding, "with interest."

"How big a refund do you expect the estate will get?"

"I figure if we just give them the state of Hawaii, we can call it even."

And Evans thanked Radder, wished him luck and hung up, slightly confused, more than dazed, but still thrilled at the chance to represent the Daughter of God.

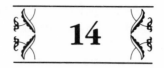

14

How Do You Say "Thank You" to an Answering Machine?

What they heard:

Beep.

"Hello. I'm calling for Ilona Ann Coggswater. My name is Katherine Wellings. I book guests for "Late Night with David Letterman" and we'd love to have you on the show. If you're interested you can reach me at 644-4444."

Beep.

"An answering machine, I should have known. I *was* hoping to speak with you, especially after seeing you on television the other day. I need to get to know you better, to understand your reasons, to understand why. Our destinies are on a collision course. Of that, I am certain."

Beep.

"By the way, my name is John."

Beep.

"Ilona, this is your mother. I just called to say hello. Nothing really important. Just give me a call when you get a chance. If it's busy just keep trying. I seem to be very popular at the moment. Linda sends her best and wanted me to tell you that she's real proud of you. And, well, so am I. So, give me a call. And remember to say hello to your roommate for me."

Beep.

"Hello Stephanie and Ilona, this is Ed Walker and this is kind of a two-part message. Yeah. Well, part one is, would you guys like some dinner company again tonight? And part two is for Stephanie. I was, well, wondering if maybe you might want to take in a movie or something, this weekend, or whenever, really. Give me a call if you get a chance."

Beep.

"My name is Cynthia Goldstein and I represent 'The Morton Downey, Jr., Show.' We're planning a special program on God and we'd very much like for you to be on our panel of experts. Please give me a call at (201) 348-0009."

Beep.

"Yeah, I'm calling for Ilona. I'm a comic-book artist out of Montreal, Canada. My name is Stanlee, that's L-E-E, not L-E-Y, and my number is (514) 756-9301. I've got this great idea for a comic-book series about you. Please call back. Or I'll try later."

Beep.

"Hi. Stephanie, it was really nice to hear your voice yesterday. I hope all went well with Artie Evans. He called and asked how I knew you. I made up some small lie. The reason I'm calling is that I've been thinking a lot about you lately. My wife and I aren't what we used to be, she just doesn't understand me, and I was wondering if maybe you'd like to get together over dinner some night, that little restaurant on the Island you liked so much. Give me a call, huh. Ah, better make it at the office, and don't leave a message with my secretary, she wouldn't understand."

Beep.

"Hey, Ilona and Stephie, this is Tony Scognamiglio. Y'know, your old boss. I'm callin' 'cause I really want you babes to come back an' work for me. And let me tell ya, I've got a big raise in store for both of you, believe you me. So, give me a call when you get this message and I'll give you your hours for the week."

Beep.

"Ilona. Professor here. And I've got just one thing to say to you. Gimme a call, kid, and I'll tell you what it is."

Beep.

[119]

"This is Len Osco. That's Len, L-E-N, Osco, O-S-C-O. I run Crosses R Us. We specialize in religious articles like crosses, Praise the Lord doormats, Stations of the Cross toilet paper, stuff like that. And I want to talk to you about putting out a full line of Ilona bumper stickers, pendants, posters, statues and, well, stuff like that. You can use my eight hundred number, that's 1-800-C-R-U-C-I-F-Y. My name again is Len Osco, that's Len, L-E-N, Osco, O-S-C-O. Look forward to talkin' to you. Be kind!"

Beep.

"Ah, yeah. I'm calling for Ilona. This is Paul Westerberg, of the Replacements. Someone at my record company got me your number. Hope you don't mind me callin' or nothin'. Ah, yeah. I hate these fuckin' machines. Yeah, sorry. Excuse me. It's just that things have gotten real weird for us since you said we were your favorite band. I'm not quite sure what's goin' on. Thanks, I guess. They tell me our records are selling out all over. And, well, I don't understand, why us? I was kinda wondering, that's all. I'll call back later, or, well, in case you wanna call, my number's 612-562-2128. If I'm not home, you can leave a message on the machine. Thank you."

Beep.

"Hello, Ilona, this is Tara Whitehurst at the White House. President and Mrs. Reagan would like to invite you to the annual Christmas dinner on December twenty-second. Please call me back to let me know whether or not you can make it. The number is (202) 456-1414. Look forward to hearing from you."

Beep.

"Stephanie. This is Lance Stryker, remember me from the Palladium, what was it, last April? Was that you I saw with Ilona Coggswater at Club Paradise last night? I wasn't sure and didn't want to make a scene. So, give me a call and maybe we can get together."

Beep.

"Please call Matt Bialer at 586-5100. I'm with the William Morris Agency and I'd like to speak with you about representation."

Beep.

[120]

"Ilona, my name is James Toback. I'm a film director. I made *The Pick-up Artist* with Molly Ringwald and *Exposed* with Nastassia Kinski, and I want you to be in my next film. You'd be perfect. Please call me immediately. My number is 936-0215. Don't hesitate for a moment."

Beep.

"Stephanie, Lance again. Just in case you no longer have my number, it's 565-2750. Ciao."

Beep.

"Hello. I'm looking for Ilona Ann Coggswater. This is Oona Chaplin. Charlie's widow. I would like to speak to you about him. I'm in New York at the moment and can be reached at (212) 555-3720. Please call me."

Beep.

"I'm trying to reach Ilona Ann Coggswater. This is Ariel Pollack, I'm an editor at *Vogue* and we're very interested in doing a photo spread on what you consider fashionable. I'd love to hear from you. My number at the magazine is 880-8800, or you can reach me at home tonight after seven P.M. at 219-0837.

Beep.

"Hello. Hello. Hello. No one's answering. You sure this is the right number?"

Beep.

"This is Dr. Julio Gonzalez. You probably don't remember me, but I delivered you. I just started working on a book about the delivery and was wondering if you'd write an introduction. Please call me. I'm still at the Mel Ott Memorial Hospital, in the new Steve Garvey maternity wing. I'm on duty there till midnight almost every night of the week."

Beep.

"Ilona, this is Veronica MacManus. I met you on Thanksgiving. I was standing next to you on Fifth Avenue waiting to see Pope John Paul. And I just wanted you to know that I saw your interview with Mr. Brokaw and what you said was beautiful. It's about time someone set the world straight. I wish you the best of luck and will pray for you. Bye-bye, now."

Beep.

"Ilona, this is Kathy Pomeroy. I'm an assistant to Larry King and we'd love to have you on our show. Please call me at 404-827-1500. Thanks."

Beep.

"Yes, my name is David Robinson. I've been asked by my publishers to update my biography of Charles Chaplin and was wondering if you could help. Please call me in London at (001) 44-1-60-99-91, or I'll try you later in the week. Thanks very much."

Beep.

"Ilona, this is Bob Guccione at *Penthouse* magazine. I'd be willing to pay you ten million dollars if you'd agree to pose for a photo spread for my magazine. Give me a call and we can talk, or maybe we can discuss it over a drink at my townhouse. The number's 496-6100."

Beep.

"This is John calling back. We need to speak. Destiny, Ilona, Destiny."

Beep.

"Stephanie, this is your mother. How come you never told me your roommate was the Daughter of God. I have to hear it on the TV first. Give me a call when you get home, please."

Beep.

"Hi, Bill Peters from *People* magazine here. I'm trying to reach Ilona Coggswater. We'd like to do a piece on you. Probably not a cover story, but I can promise at least two pages with photos. Give me a ring back at 522-1212."

Beep.

"Ilona, this is Sal Marucci. My friend Tony Scognamiglio told me I should give you a call. I'm an independent talent agent here in the city and I'd like to talk to you about representation. A celebrity like you needs someone to look out for their best interests. Lots of sharks out there, believe you me. And a lot of money can be made off all this attention you're getting. But we gotta jump on it now, you're not getting any younger, y'know. I'm talkin' a recording contract, movies, books, maybe even an Ilona doll. We'll saturate the market. I'd leave my number but I don't really have a phone right now, I'm in a temporary office.

But you can leave a message with Tony and he'll get it to me."

Beep.

"Hello, Please hang up and try your call again. This is a recording, 203-8. Hello. Please hang up and try your call again. This is a recording, 203-8. Hello. Please hang up and try your call again. This is a recording, 203-8. Hello. Please hang up and try your call again. This is a recording, 203-8."

Beep. Beep. Beep.

ᘓᕤ

What they bothered writing down:

Katherine WELLINGS 644-4444
David LETTERMAN Show

CALL MOM

Stephanie → MOVIE!? whenever ED!♥

Stan LEE 514-756 9301
          COMIC BOOK

The Professor?

Paul Westerburg !!!!!! (612) 562-2128   I love him
                                        weirdness?!!

Tara Whitehurst 12/22 X-Mas dinner @ White House
          202 456 1414   ONLY ALL VEGATARIAN DINNER

Stephaine Stryker! Make that Walker — Stephanie? Walker?

Matt Bialer - William Morris 586 5100
          Representation

For Stephanie's ACTING career !

Oona (212) 555 3720 ♀? - DAVID ROBINSON 011-44-1-60-99-91

Aviel Pollack - Vogue Photos
          880 8800 - Mag 219 0837 After 7pm home

Kathy Pomeroy - (404) 827 1500   LARRY KING Show

DESTINY ↑ THAT VOICE — John

Stephanie's MOM

—

· Believe
  you me!!

Ilona SAVES

HONK IF YOU LOVE ILONA

SMILE - Ilona
          loves you ☺ !!!

Ilona will show
          U the way !!

WHEN GUNS are
OUTLAWED
ONLY Ilona will have GUNS

"Ilona IS the ANSWER"
But What was the
          Question?!!

PEOPLE MAGAZINE!
I Ilona ANN Coggswater
—the inside all exclusive SCOOP:
what she eats, where she eats,
          who she eats ...

Charlie
book ↑   203-8

· ONLY
  ART
  SURVIVES "

[123]

15

A Nice Try

"Leave a message."

Beep.

Ilona hadn't expected anything as abrupt.

"This is Ilona Ann Coggswater, the Daughter of God, returning your call," she said, her hands shaking. "I'll be home all night. Please give me a call when you get this message. I'd love to speak with you."

And though Paul Westerberg would, that evening, return Ilona's call, the phone ringing during one of those "Late Night with David Letterman" commercial breaks, what they would say to each other is hardly anyone's business but theirs.

☙

And so after returning all the other calls they planned on returning minus one and scheduling all the events they planned on scheduling, Stephanie stepped out for, as Ilona would put it, "a nice quiet evening of insinuations and eye contact with the filmmaker," while Ilona fixed herself a salad and returned that one last phone call.

Mariam Clarissa Coggswater had herself just finished eating dinner and though she thought seriously about not answering the phone, a thought she had been harboring for days, seriously, she picked up the receiver anyway and responded as she had one hundred thirty-six times, give or take a few, since Tuesday afternoon.

"Hello," Mariam said. That's all, hello.

"Mom, it's Ilona," her Daughter said.

"Prove it," said Mariam, thinking that those damn reporters would sink to any level to get a quote.

"I beg your pardon?"

"Prove it. How do I know you're not a reporter pretending to be my Daughter."

"Okay, how do you want me to prove it?"

"My Daughter has a scar. Where is it?"

"On the left cheek of my behind."

"What's it look like?"

"A cross."

"And how did you get it?"

"Chicken pox."

"Honey, how are you?" said Mariam, her tone suddenly sounding motherly, as motherly, anyway, as Mariam's voice could ever sound.

"Fine. And you?"

"Well, I'm ready to rip this God-damned phone out of the wall, but other than that I'm okay, I guess."

"Sorry about that."

"All this fuss just 'cause you're the Daughter of God."

"I'm also the Daughter of Mariam Coggswater, remember that."

"And not Dave Wiggits?"

"And not Dave Wiggits, Mom."

"Who would have figured?"

"Just me, Mom. Just me," Ilona said, then, thinking, not saying, And Dad.

"How should I deal with all these people?"

"Are they really driving you nuts?"

"Absolutely."

"Do you want to speak to any of them?"

"I've been thinking about going on the Phil Donahue show. I've always liked him. Do you think I should?"

"Why not, it might be fun."

"Morton Downey's people called, but I told them no."

"Yeah, they called me, too."

"Has Oprah called you?"

"Not yet. Why?"

"I like her show. I'm hoping she asks me on."

"I'm sure she'll be calling soon."

"Probably."

"How's Cooperstown?"

"As good as any town could be after discovering it's the birthplace of the Daughter of God."

"A little crazy?"

"A little?" Mariam said. "People kneeling down in the middle of Main Street crying. There are flowers everywhere, on top of everything. Both the Dew Drop Inn and Cheapskate Records are in danger of becoming national shrines."

"Yeah, I just talked to the Professor."

"So, you call him before calling your Mother."

"I was saving the most important call for last."

"Okay. You're forgiven then," Mariam said. Adding, "Listen to me, forgiving God." Then, "What did he have to say?"

"Nothing much. In fact, he forgot what it was exactly that he called about."

"That sounds like the Professor."

"But he recommended a few new bands that he thought I'd like."

"Future Top Ten hits, no doubt?"

"Who knew?"

"I certainly didn't," her mother said, then. "And neither did the Sisters at Saint Mary's obviously!" And Mariam was silent for a moment, suddenly silent, a slight cough, then the inevitable tears.

"Are you okay?" Ilona asked.

"I just miss you, that's all."

"That's a lot. I miss you, too."

"How's the screaming?" Mariam asked, not knowing if she really should.

"Louder," Ilona said, "than ever."

"It hasn't gone away at all?"

"Not yet. It'll take some time."

"I worry about you."

[126]

"Don't worry. I'm half God, remember."

"And half woman."

"Exactly. Invincible."

"I hope so."

And Ilona was silent.

"Are you real busy?" Mariam asked.

"Real busy," Ilona said, explaining the Tab commercial and her far too great salary, part of which she would be sending to Mariam.

"I'm doing fine. I don't need any money."

"I have over twelve million dollars left. I don't need that much to survive," Ilona insisted, changing subjects quickly, to the *Vogue* shoot that would feature her and Stephanie, next week's appearance on the Letterman show, and all the other events so recently scheduled.

And Mariam said, "Two questions," not sure.

"Ask away."

"I keep thinking about your first word, 'Seaver,' and I find myself wondering if what you actually said might have been 'savior,' and you were trying to tell me something. But I was just too stupid to realize it."

"Mom," Ilona said, slowly, lovingly, "you aren't stupid. We were watching a Mets game. I said 'Seaver.' Tom Seaver. I wasn't trying to tell you anything."

"Really?"

"Really. Now what's the other question?"

"William Smith?"

And Ilona was silent.

"Well, is he up there? Is he okay?"

"I didn't expect that question."

"He's the only man I ever bothered to fall in love with," Mariam said, sounding so eternally sad.

"Mom," Ilona said, trying to console.

"I'm sorry."

"Don't be."

"Just tell me, is he in heaven? Will I see him again?"

"Yes, of course you'll see him again."

"Are you sure?"

"Absolutely. I promise."

"Thank you."

And both mother and daughter were silent.

"I miss him, too, y'know?"

"You do?"

"Yup."

"He was like a father to you, at least for a little while. The father you never had."

"I know."

"You used to call him Dad"

"And I still would."

And when the conversation was over, and it seemed as if it was over much too soon, Mariam began to cry. Not the tears of self-pity she cried when Ilona first left home. But tears of fear and sadness, fear and sadness not for herself but for her Daughter. Because the more Mariam thought about what it was Ilona had set out to do, the more she believed her Daughter had set out to do the impossible. Not that anything should really be impossible for God, but on this Earth with these People at this Time, most anything based in Kindness surely seemed impossible and most likely was.

She wanted so badly for Ilona to succeed, as any parent would want for their child. It's just that most children aren't immaculately conceived, or so Mariam believed, and most parents aren't faced with the proposition of a child intending absolutely on single-handedly saving the planet. Somehow Mariam couldn't imagine one day having to tell her Daughter that, "Hey, you didn't save the planet and now humankind is doomed, but you gave it your best shot. It was a nice try."

Mariam laughed to herself as this last thought ran through her head: A nice try. And clearing the dinner dishes from the table, she put them in the dishwasher. And as that dishwasher started up and made those loud *gurgle, gurgle, gurgle* sounds, Mariam laughed again, shook her head slightly, and unconsciously went to find that old *American Heritage Dictionary* where she just as unconsciously looked up *heterodoxy*, for old times' sake.

[128]

In the days that followed, Mariam would learn that her parents, Richard and Lillian, had begun work on a book, Mariam's life as seen through their eyes.

But problems would shortly arise when Richard and Lillian could not decide on an angle for their book. And having had enough, of what he would never specifically say, Richard would announce that he was writing his own book and that Lillian could go to hell. They would divorce shortly thereafter.

Richard's book, *Mariam, You Slut*, would paint a picture of Mariam as, "a drunk who slept with everyone she could get her hands on."

"I can name twenty-five guys in our neighborhood alone who could have been the father of that child," Richard would say in the book's opening paragraph. And he would proceed to name them, in alphabetical order, listing their names, addresses, ages, and occupations. When he hit upon three plumbers in a row he would add the aside, "Mariam really liked plumbers."

In a later television interview, one of many, Mariam would claim to have never even heard of the people mentioned in her father's book, and "I didn't sleep with them either." Adding, just before a commercial break, that she had a particular distaste for men in the plumbing field.

In Lillian's book, *Saint Mariam*, Mariam's mother would speak of how she always knew her daughter had "a special calling" and how as a child Mariam spoke of becoming a nun and devoting her life to Christianity, and of quoted biblical passages and speaking in tongues.

In that same television interview Mariam would just shake her head sadly and say no.

Just no.

When Richard's book would outsell Lillian's by four million copies, including a serialization in the *National Enquirer*, Lillian would sue Richard, claiming that since they were each telling one side of the same story, their books should have sold equally well.

But while on the witness stand during the trial, Richard would suffer a massive coronary seizure when Lillian's attorney, Alfred Stein, would inform him that Bill Waterworth's book, *Dave Wiggits Was My Gay Lover*, was in its seventeenth printing and had outsold *Mariam, You Slut* by two and a half million copies. Richard would die that evening, causing readers worldwide to rush to their bookshops in search of additional copies of his already best-selling book, eventually pushing its sales figures well above those for Waterworth's book.

Shortly after Richard's death, Lillian would become Mrs. Alfred Stein, and together they would write *Richard Was Right, Mariam Was a Slut After All*, which would top the *New York Times Book Review*'s nonfiction list and actually outsell both *Dave Wiggits Was My Gay Lover* and *Mariam, You Slut*.

In her second to last television interview, Mariam would claim that she unfortunately had stopped reading altogether and was in the process of looking for a good hobby.

❧

In the weeks and months that followed, Mariam would become a celebrity in her own right, appearing in December on both "The Phil Donahue Show" and "The Oprah Winfrey Show."

And though the questions were as predictable as the calls from the crying fundamentalist Christians, Mariam would enjoy her initial moment in the spotlight. And though she would get tired of explaining that she really had no idea what an immaculate conception felt like if indeed it felt like anything at all, she would enjoy speaking with the members of the studio audience, people who seemed to admire and love her Daughter almost as much as she did.

But as the weeks and months passed, and as book after book after book was published, Mariam would grow weary of the talk-show circuit, program after program after program devoted to denying what her parents, Dr. Gonzalez, Bill Waterworth, George Wiggits, and so many others had been writing. And finally she would get fed up.

Being interviewed by Bryant Gumbel on the "Today" show on June 15, 1989, Mariam, when asked by Gumbel, "Were you as big a slut as your father implies in his book?" would turn to the unlikable host, slap him in the face, and tell him in very exacting terms, "Go fuck yourself." After which she would get up and walk calmly off the set. Jane Pauley, the show's co-host, would quickly intercede and cut to a commercial break.

And seeing that the "Today" show was being broadcast live across the country without any tape delay, some twelve million people would hear and see what Mariam said and did. While the remaining two hundred fourteen million Americans would catch the highlights replayed ad nauseam on the evening news, many of whom would be voting on the issue when that evening's CNN's nonscientific Newsnight 900 Poll would ask, "Did Mariam Coggswater act appropriately by slapping Bryant Gumbel?" A full one hundred percent of those who called in would answer yes.

And while many television viewers were voting on CNN's nonscientific Newsnight 900 Poll, others would be watching "Late Night with David Letterman," where Letterman would read that evening's Top Ten list, "Bryant Gumbel's Top Ten Fears." According to Letterman and his writers, Gumbel's number-one fear would be, "Spending eternity burning in hell because of one stupid mistake."

Gumbel, who refused to comment on the incident, would take an immediate "leave of absence" from the program and would not rejoin the popular morning show until late August.

❦

That would be Mariam's final television appearance. It would also be the last time she would ever intentionally speak to any member of the media.

"I've had enough," she would explain to Ilona.

"I can understand that,"Ilona would say.

"You're not mad at me for slapping that Gumbel guy, are you?" Mariam would ask.

"Of course not. He was being rude," Ilona would answer.

"I miss you." Mariam would say.

"I miss you, too," Ilona would say. Adding, "I love you, Mom."

ℭℜ

And so, that summer, the summer of 1989, with part of the money Ilona had given her, Mariam and her oldest, closest friend Linda Maronne, would take the vacation both women had only dreamed of. The two ex-roommates would spend four months visiting most of the capitals of Western Europe, Moscow, Tokyo, Hong Kong, Australia, the Egyptian pyramids and, because Mariam would insist upon returning, Hawaii, which the United States government had decided against giving to Charlie Chaplin's heirs.

And in November, Mariam would return to her management position at the Cooperstown Rexall Pharmacy, not that she really needed to, but because she wanted to, and Linda would return to her beloved Dew Drop Inn, both women rested, happy, and exceedingly well tanned.

ℭℜ

But that's jumping ahead.

16

Just So

Ilona was pouring her first Friday morning Tab and catching the CNN "Newsday" updates as Stephanie attempted to sneak into their apartment.

"I didn't think you'd be up this early."

"It's almost nine o'clock," said Ilona, unable to hold back a grin.

"Oh," said Stephanie, eying the kitchen wall clock, "right."

"So how was your nice quiet evening of insinuations and eye contact?"

And Stephanie kicked off her shoes, threw her coat into any neutral corner, and sank down in a chair before sighing her answer.

"Oh, really?"

Another sigh.

"I don't want to hear about it."

"Yes, you do."

"All right, I do."

"But not right now," Stephanie said. "I've got to get some sleep."

"And I've got to meet with the advertising people at the Coca-Cola Company about the commercial shoot tomorrow."

"That's right. I forgot, I'm sorry. Do you want me to go with you?"

"Don't worry about it," Ilona said. "Get some sleep and we'll go over the commercial ideas when I get back."

❧

The meeting with the people from the Coca-Cola Company was exactly what Ilona expected the meeting with the people from the Coca-Cola Company to be, boring.

She was informed that the director of the commercials would be Adrian Lyne, best known for his feature films, *Fatal Attraction, 9½ Weeks* and *Flashdance.*

"Not Woody Allen?" Ilona said.

"Would you have preferred Woody Allen?" And the people from the Coca-Cola Company began to panic.

"Yes," Ilona said, smiling, "but Adrian Lyne will be just fine."

"Are you sure?"

And Ilona nodded.

Next she was given a choice of six possible scripts and asked to choose her two favorites, which she did, to their cries of "good choice" and "bravo" and to her amusement.

And the people from the Coca-Cola Company smiled and nodded and thanked her again for becoming the new Tab representative.

"Be kind," they all seemed to say as she left the meeting.

What have I started? Ilona though, shaking her head slightly as she smiled and answered their "be kind's" with one of her own.

God, did she feel silly.

☙

And looking over the scripts while munching on "the usual" on that Friday afternoon, Stephanie was quite surprised to see that she was cast in one of the two commercials.

"Why do they want to use me?" she asked, flustered, excited, delighted.

"They thought it would be cute."

"You didn't insist?"

"Not at all. They showed me six different scripts, and I liked these two best."

"And they agreed?"

"Yup."

"You didn't use your eyes to convince them, or anything like that?"

"No," Ilona said, laughing.

"I can't believe it."

"Now you know how I felt," the Daughter of God said, between bites of the "usual," "when Paul Westerberg called."

$$\infty$$

The scripts for the two Tab commercials read as follows:

Tab Commercial #1/Ilona:

We see a beautiful sunlit close-up of Ilona's face. She is looking down to her right. She looks up and directly into the camera, smiling only slightly. The camera dollies back very slowly and slightly as Ilona brings a clear sparkling glass straw to her lips. She begins to sip as the dolly back continues. An hourglass-shaped glass with the Tab logo is seen as the dolly back continues. The dolly stops just as Ilona has emptied the glass of the Tab. She pulls her mouth from the straw and smiles at the camera. The shot fades to black and the Tab logo in yellow fades up on the black background with the words BE KIND in white, centered under the logo.

THE END

Commercial #2/Ilona & Stephanie:

(series of shots)

A. We hear hot rock music throughout the commercial. It is shot in a photo studio and in 16mm, giving it a very grainy, contrasty look. We see a medium-shot of Ilona. She is dressed as she was during the Tom Brokaw interview. She is leaning against a wall. We see a shaky zoom to her face as she turns and says:

ILONA

I'm Ilona.

B. We see a series of six very quick jump cuts of Ilona. The first is a long-shot, she has her hands on her hips.

C. The second is a medium close-up of her leaning over slightly, laughing.

D. The third is an extreme close-up of her eyes. She winks.

E. The fourth is a shaky zoom backward beginning in a medium close-up and ending in a medium long-shot as she turns around slightly.

F. The fifth is a medium shot where the camera spins around Ilona while she spins in the opposite direction.

G. The sixth is a close up of her face as she smiles and says:

ILONA

And that's my friend, Stephanie.

H. We see a series of six very quick jump cuts of Stephanie beginning with a swish pan to a long shot of Stephanie, who is dressed to show off her perfect form.

I. The second is a close-up of Stephanie smiling, then laughing.

J. The third is a medium shot where the camera does a shaky spin around Stephanie while she stands still but turns her head with the camera.

K. The fourth is an jumpy extreme close-up pan up Stephanie's body beginning at her feet and ending at the back of her head, she turns and smiles at the camera.

L. The fifth is a long shot of Stephanie with her right hand on her right hip and her left hand extended outward as if asking, "What?"

M. The sixth shot is an extreme close-up of her smile.

N. We see a swish pan to a medium close-up of Ilona who looks at the camera and says:

ILONA

And we drink Tab.

[136]

O. We see a close-up of Stephanie's hands popping opening a Tab can. We hear the fresh-sounding snap as the can is opened.

P. We see a close-up of Ilona's hands opening a Tab can as above.

Q. We see a long shot of Ilona as she sips. Stephanie, laughing, enters the frame from the viewer's frame right.

R. We see a close-up of Stephanie smiling after taking a sip of Tab.

S. We see a close-up of Ilona smiling.

T. We see a medium-shot of the two girls clicking their Tab cans together as if in a toast.

U. We see a freeze-frame close-up of the two Tab cans being clicked together. The words BE KIND in white letters, fade up, centered at the bottom of the screen, superimposed over the freeze-frame.

THE END

ℭℌ

Two days were scheduled for the filming of the two Tab commercials, and those two days were used thoroughly, surprising both Ilona and Stephanie at what a long, boring process it was to get an image on film.

"Walker warned us," Ilona said.

And he had.

And arriving early on Saturday, the two roommates waited and observed as the twenty-four-person crew including director Lyne, set lights, ran electrical cords, took readings, dollied this, boomed that, adjusted this, changed that, and got everything just so only to have to start all over again because the just so was not the just so the director had envisioned.

"And all this for two thirty-second commercials," Ilona said to her roommate, overheard by some Coca-Cola Company representative.

"Two very expensive thirty-second commercials," said the

Coca-Cola Company representative, with extreme emphasis on the "very expensive."

"Sorry," she said, not really sure why.

And after everything was the just so that it was just so supposed to be and after Ilona suffered though makeup, hair dressing, and costuming, she was ready to shoot *Tab Commercial #1/Ilona*. The lights were set, the camera was set, Ilona was set, the Tab was set.

"Action," whispered director Lyne.

And Ilona looked up and directly into the camera and smiled ever so slightly, just as called for in the script. But something happened on this first take, or more specifically nothing happened. In that when Ilona looked up she was so radiantly beautiful, that wide-eyed, green-eyed gaze as intense as ever, everything stopped. The dolly back that was supposed to begin at the smile didn't. The entire twenty-four-person crew including directory Lyne and every Coca-Cola Company representative present just gasped then gawked helplessly at the new Tab spokesperson, momentarily forgetting their responsibilities, permanently awed.

"She's so beautiful," Stephanie heard that "very expensive" Coca-Cola Company representative whisper to no one. It was the thought on everyone's mind, on everyone's lips.

And as Ilona looked from gaffer to director to best boy to Coca-Cola Company representative, she thought to herself, Give me a break already, but smiled and said, "Is something wrong?"

And the twenty-four-person crew including director Lyne and every Coca-Cola Company representative present snapped to.

"Our fault," director Lyne explained, and the shot was once again set up just so and this time the commercial was filmed just so. Perfectly just so. And though this perfect take should have been to everyone's surprise, everyone's except Ilona's that is, it wasn't. And an additional two takes were filmed, "safeties," they were called, both perfect. Perfectly just so.

"How will he ever choose which take is best?" that "very expensive" Coca-Cola Company representative asked another Coca-Cola Company representative about director Lyne.

A sigh was the only answer that question ever received.

And a break was called and director Lyne approached Ilona and Stephanie to discuss his vision of *Tab Commercial #2/Ilona & Stephanie*, as it was then known.

In his book, *My Vision*, Lyne would describe the conversation, "Ilona and Stephanie seemed enthralled as I explained the importance of each and every shot of this second commercial. How a simple look to the right meant something completely different from a look to the left. How a hair out of place could give the piece an entirely different meaning. They understood my vision, completely."

And Ilona and Stephanie listened and nodded politely, an occasional "of course" or a "that's fascinating," and as director Lyne turned, finally, to speak to some crew member or other, the Daughter of God thought, "Maybe I should have insisted on Woody Allen."

And the roommates waited and observed once again as the twenty-four-person crew including director Lyne, set lights, ran electrical cords, took readings, dollied this, boomed that, adjusted this, changed that, and got everything just so only to have to start all over again because the just so was close to, but not exactly, the just so the director had envisioned.

But eventually the set for *Tab Commercial #2/Ilona & Stephanie*, was ready. A set that looked very much like a messed-up, overused photo studio with a large roll of ripped seamless background paper and lots of light stands everywhere. A set that looked very much like the studio originally looked when Ilona and Stephanie had arrived so much earlier that day.

"What a visionary," commented the "very expensive" Coca-Cola Company representative about director Lyne. "Sheer genius."

Ilona and Stephanie just nodded and smiled. Politely, of course.

And when everything was the just so that it was just so supposed to be and after Ilona and Stephanie suffered through makeup, hair dressing, and costuming, they were ready to shoot *Tab Commercial #2/Ilona & Stephanie*. The lights were set, the camera was set, Ilona was set, Stephanie was set, and yes, the Tab was set.

But before director Lyne could whisper "action," some member of the twenty-four-person crew pointed out that according to their union the work day had reached its end. And thus it had, despite the fact that they were shooting a commercial starring the Daughter of God and her roommate. Film unions, unlike the IRS made no exceptions.

And someone yelled, "It's a wrap," and it was for that day.

"I didn't want to stop shooting," director Lyne would write in his book. "I never wanted to stop looking at her. Those green eyes had cast a spell over me as they had the rest of the world. But alas, I couldn't argue with the unions. No one can argue with unions. It's one of those unwritten laws, along the lines of, 'Nothing gets past the IRS.' "

☙

The second day of shooting was much like the first with a lot of waiting and observing along with more than the usual amount, whatever that usual amount was, of setting, running, taking, dollying, booming, adjusting, changing, and getting. And the just sos were always just so as envisioned.

And once again each of Ilona's takes was perfect. "Divine," some Coca-Cola Company representative, not the "very expensive" one, called them. And not that Stephanie's takes weren't damn good. They were in fact nothing short of excellent. But she was, after all, only human. Mind you, a just so sublime young female human with a sensuality factor of infinity to the umpteenth power, whose smile—that mouth inviting like the insides of a slice of hot cherry pie, teeth glistening like the scoop of vanilla ice cream melting over its sides—sent blood rushing south. Mind you, a just so young female human, with legs that Jesus Christ himself would be recrucified for, dressed to show off her just so young female human who was, in the eyes of most any straight male human that bothered looking and most did, as just so as any young female human could be. But, mind you, she wasn't the Daughter of God.

And once again everything came to a standstill the first time Ilona looked into the camera. The gawks, the gasps, the "Is something wrong?" And though nothing specifically happened or failed to happen when just so Stephanie took her turn at looking into the camera, as called for in the script, crazed, lustful thoughts did manage to creep into the minds of many of those on that twenty-four-person crew including director Lyne and every Coca-Cola Company representative present. And by the end of the second day of shooting slightly less than half of that twenty-four-person crew, including director Lyne and every Coca-Cola Company representative present, had approached Ilona's just so roommate in one way or other requesting or suggesting, among other things, a phone number, a kiss, a date, sex, dinner, more sex, a weekend in the Caribbean, yet more sex, and even marriage. But just-so Stephanie brushed off the requests and suggestions with a few flips of her long light brown hair. "Not interested," those flips said.

And as the last "It's a wrap" was called, just so Stephanie turned to her roommate and summed up those requests and suggestions. "With you they just want to stare into your eyes and sigh," she said. "Me, they just wanna fuck."

"We're both divine in our own way," Ilona said, adding, "And admit it, you'd look a hell of a lot sexier romping in the Caribbean sun wearing one of those thong-back bikinis."

"I guess so," Stephanie said. "But do you have any idea how uncomfortable thong-backs are?"

"Wanna switch places?"

"Not in a million years."

And it was over. *Tab Commercial #1/Ilona* and *Tab Commercial #2/Ilona & Stephanie* were, as they say, in the can.

Just so.

17

The God That Got Away

"Only art survives."

Ilona didn't know. But Charlie did. Jesus did. He was one up on her. Two, if you count the Dodgers winning the 1988 World Series.

"If film is the great art form of this century, and I believe it is," Ilona would tell Stephanie and filmmaker Walker, "and Charlie was the greatest of all filmmakers, and I know he was, then maybe my Brother knew what he was doing after all."

ↅↄ

During his cinematic prime Charles Spencer Chaplin was the most popular man in the world, worshipped and loved as a veritable Everyman, worshipped and loved as a comic genius, worshipped and loved as an artistic god, at least figuratively. But when Chaplin's character in *The Great Dictator* said, "More than cleverness, we need kindness and gentleness," did anyone really bother to listen, other than George Bush who, when running for president in 1988 would cleverly beat the kinder, gentler part into the ground?

They didn't know.

George Bush didn't know.

How could they?

And nothing was more confusing to the masses.

Believers rushed to get whatever information they could about the God that had made them laugh, the God who made them cry, the God who became the world's most famous homeless person, the God who wanted to spread his good will by being a "citizen of the world," the God they had once again crucified.

The God that got away.

And no one was more confused than Chaplin's widow, Oona. When Ilona called, Lady Oona spoke of how Charlie confessed to being Jesus Christ shortly before his death, and knowing the end was near, Oona listened and told her dying husband she believed what he said, though in reality she felt his mind was just leaving a few days ahead of his body.

"I feel so guilty for not believing him," Oona said. "He tried to tell me everything. He asked me if I had any questions. I just began to cry because I felt so sad for him, not just because he was so ill, but because I thought he had lost his mind. And to discover that he was telling me the truth after all."

And though a massive Chaplin retrospective was already being planned by film historians for the centennial of his birth, on April 16, 1989, the public couldn't wait. And by January, Chaplin films would be seen theatrically, everywhere. That month *The Gold Rush*, playing at just over sixteen hundred screens across the United States and Canada, would gross $114,887,263, outperforming *Rainman, Working Girl,* and *Mississippi Burning* combined. *City Lights* would run for a record-breaking forty-seven weeks at the Paris Theater in New York City. And for the week ending February 17, 1989, Chaplin videotapes would occupy eleven places, including the entire top five, on *Billboard*'s Top 20 video rentals listing.

And how Chaplin's art would be evaluated, reevaluated, and evaluated again. Every frame, every gesture, every look, line, title card, every everything. During many screenings the film, whatever film, would be stopped whenever Charlie stretched out his arms in anything resembling a crosslike position, and the audience members would ooh and ahh and applaud and cry. It was all so helplessly pathetic. All so hopelessly confusing.

Even the old Chaplin studios on North LaBrea in Hollywood would be declared a national, historical, and religious monument and be turned into the Chaplin Museum, forcing the studios' long-time owner and occupant, A & M Records, to find new headquarters.

And as the centennial approached, the world would be swept by Charlie-mania. Books, books, and more books, posters, little Chaplin crucifixes, statues, and dolls. Crosses R Us would make a fortune.

The most noteworthy of the books, books, and more books, would be David Robinson's massive reworking of *Chaplin, His Life and Art* now titled, simply, *Chaplin*. Close to twenty-six hundred pages, including a lengthy introduction written by Ilona at Robinson's request, containing seven hundred sixty-one photographs, numerous charts and drawings, and weighing over twenty pounds, the book left no Chaplin stone upturned. And Robinson, with the help of his new co-author, film historian Kevin Brownlow, evaluated Chaplin's message, religious, humanitarian, or otherwise, reevaluated every aspect of the performer's life from birth to death to Ilona, and evaluated again every Chaplin film cut by cut.

When asked about *Chaplin*, Ilona would say, "It's a New Testament we're very proud of."

Though, despite or quite possibly because of Ilona's praise, when the authors would appear on CNN's "Sonya Live," the usual barrage of sobbing fundamentalists and born-agains would provide the usual barrage of calls and the usual barrage of tears and shouts of "blasphemy."

"Do you people have an in at the phone company?" Robinson would ask, wishing, hoping, praying for an intelligent caller.

Not that the crying fundamentalists would matter, *Chaplin* would be considered a literary masterwork, capturing the Nobel Prize, the Pulitzer Prize, and the National Book Award for nonfiction, and would outsell even *Richard Was Right, Mariam Was a Slut After All.*

Among the ninety-three other books about Charlie Chaplin that would invade bookseller's shelves over the next year, most noteworthy would be, *Our Lord, the Tramp* by Walter Hyde-Eaton, a relatively witty, very British look at what would happen if Christ actually looked, dressed, and acted as Chaplin's Tramp character back in those days of Roman emperors, crucifixions, and parables. In Hyde-Eaton's version of the Last Supper, instead of breaking the bread and passing it to the apostles, the Tramp performs the dance of the rolls and passes around his boiled boot, saying, through title cards of course, "Take, eat; this is My boot."

Charlie's Angels, by Claire DeCarlo and Rosa Vigario, would examine each of Chaplin's relationships and then some, his girlfriends and wives and then some, his reputed sexual likes and dislikes and then some, all in all-too-vivid details. The authors would devote a large portion of the book to criticizing Chaplin's lust for young women and would attribute the following quote to the comic God, "Women, unlike wine, do not improve with age."

Jesus Chaplin, by Reverend Perry Henderson, would compare in exacting detail, the life, words, crucifixion, and death of Jesus Christ to the life, films, crucifixion, and death of Charlie Chaplin. Most interesting would be Henderson's theory that Chaplin's films were based on Christ's words, the Beatitudes becoming *City Lights* and *The Immigrant* and so many others, cinematic versions of the "Blessed Ares."

Charlie on the Cross, by ex-FBI agent Carl Wilke, would give us a lengthy analysis of over fifty years' worth of files the Federal Bureau of Investigation maintained on Chaplin with special emphasis being paid to the McCarthy era rumors that Chaplin was a member of and contributor to the Communist Party.

Grave Decision, a short book by Gantcho Ganev and Roman Wardas, the two men convicted of stealing Chaplin's corpse from its burial place in Vevey Cemetery in March 1978, would be an outlandish stretch of both truth and imagination in which the two authors, who originally demanded six hundred thousand Swiss francs for the return of the body, would claim to have known of Chaplin's divinity, and to have acted in the hopes that Chaplin would "rise from the dead."

And a reissue of Chaplin's own, *My Autobiography*, first published in 1964 and dedicated to Oona, the book was Charlie's version of his life, art, and crucifixion. ("If only he hadn't left out one important detail," Ilona would comment.)

And shortly before the centennial, the United States government would return to the Chaplin estate the amount the comedian had paid in taxes, including interest, compounded daily. And when Oona Chaplin would receive that check for just over seven hundred million dollars she would donate it to the charity she felt her dear Charlie would have most liked and respected, the charity that had taken care of so many so like the character Charlie had made famous, the charity known for kindness and gentleness. She would donate that just over seven hundred million dollars to the Salvation Army.

And when Ilona would hear of this donation, she would send her sister-in-law a note reading, quite simply, "My Brother approves and sends his eternal love."

But that's jumping ahead.

18

Magazine Monday

Ilona Ann Coggswater awoke that Monday morning to find her photograph on the covers of *Time, Newsweek, U.S. News & World Report*, and virtually every infotainment weekly with the lone exception of *People*, which chose instead to run a cover story of Mark David Chapman, assassin of John Lennon. According to *People*'s managing editor, Leonard Knight, "Religious covers just don't sell." But during this first week of December 1989, it was magazines that glamorized murderers that didn't seem to be selling.

And though the *Time* article, titled "Promoting Kindness," made Ilona most proud because of how it focused on her message instead of on her fashion statement, it bothered her greatly to find a full-page ad from the National Rifle Association littering the back pages of the magazine. And she wasted no time writing the newsweekly a letter stating so.

Among other things her letter asked, "How could you accept advertising from an organization that so fully represents the backward thinking I am here to triumph against? Next time think with your hearts and not your wallets." The letter was signed, "Ilona Ann Coggswater, Daughter of God," and would be printed in the following week's issue along with a promise from the magazine's editors and publishers to no longer accept advertising from the NRA.

સ્ટ

And that afternoon full-time Daughter of God Ilona Ann Coggswater and part-time actress/model and part-time business management student Stephanie LaVasseur along with all-the-time filmmaker Edward Davis Walker searched for a new apartment, one somewhat larger and more suitable, preferably with an elevator.

But when Ilona, with her friends in tow, visited the offices of Rothburg Reality, she never in her wildest expected to find Babs Rothburg seated behind a "charming" mahogany desk with a name plaque reading, BABS ROTHBURG, PRESIDENT. Not only did Rothburg remember Ilona, but she had been following her story closely and taking notes, notes that would shortly become her best-selling book, *The New Holy Land*.

And as Rothburg plucked the files and keys of the most "charming" of her "charming" co-ops, condos, and penthouses, she pulled a mink coat from her closet and said, "Let's go." But Ilona didn't budge. "She just glared at me," Rothburg would explain in her book. " 'What's wrong?' I asked. 'That coat,' Ilona said pointing and glaring. 'Isn't it charming?' I asked. 'Not at all,' Ilona said, still glaring. 'What ever do you mean?' I asked, wishing immediately that I hadn't, because Ilona began a twenty-minute lecture on how I was wearing the fur of animals that had been bred, tortured, and slaughtered for my vanity. So I quickly took off the coat, not wanting to lose this sale, and told her that I would get rid of it promptly. And though I kept the coat, I never did wear it again, because the more I thought about those dead animals and Ilona's glare, the more I felt like a complete and total asshole."

And though both Ilona and Stephanie fell for a "charming" four-thousand-square-foot loft on Broome Street in SoHo with eighteen-foot ceilings and sunlight-filled rooms so large you could ride a ten speed in them, they ultimately chose a "charming" twenty-fifth-floor, three-bedroom, duplex penthouse in a new high-rise on Charles Street in the very "private," as Rothburg would say, West Village, complete with a "private" elevator and a "private" bilevel wraparound balcony that gave Ilona an unobstructed and "private" 360-degree view of the world she had come to save. And though Ilona wondered if "private" had replaced "charming" as Rothburg's favorite word, the privacy that this Charles Street apartment offered was, despite the way the word smacked on Rothburg's lips in the most materialistic of ways, something she knew she'd need, something she knew she'd want, something.

"I told Ilona the asking price was $1.8 million, but that maybe we'd be able to get the owner down to an even one-point-five," Rothburg would write. "And Ilona said, 'You can't be serious,' and asked me who owned the building. I explained that it was owned by billionaire developer Donald Trump. And she said to me, I can still hear the words as clear as day, she said to tell Mr. Trump that she would just live in the apartment for as long as she needed to, but would gladly donate the $1.8 million to a charity in Mr. Trump's name."

"My jaw dropped," Rothburg would continue. "But, What about my commission? I thought, though the words never made it out of my mouth. Instead, I found myself calling Mr. Trump and describing Ilona's offer, which he gladly accepted, 'Sounds like a splendid idea,' he said, adding that he would match the $1.8 million donation if the entire amount, the $3.6 million, could be used to build some affordable housing for the homeless.

"And the deal was done. Ilona could move in immediately, using the apartment for as long as she needed it, the $3.6 million would be used to convert a half dozen dilapidated brownstones in Alphabet City, just down the block from the Soup Kitchen, into the Trump Development Project—affordable housing for the homeless, and I learned that you just don't make commissions off God."

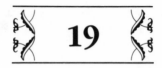

19

Promoting Kindness

"Be kind"?

"Easy to understand," Ilona had said, "No misinterpretations this time around."

&

Also easy to promote.

And in the days and weeks following the Tom Brokaw interview, "Be Kind' became the catch phrase of the day, the year, possibly the decade, even century.

Brokaw himself began ending his daily newscast by saying, "Good evening and be kind."

MTV would begin running outrageously animated promotional clips featuring the music station's logo and the words, "Be Kind." And other television and cable stations would follow, running "Kindness" public service announcements.

And soon "Be Kind" clothing and accessories would be the fashion rage. Huge white T-shirts with the words, BE KIND in huge black block letter, screaming across the front, or vice versa, huge black T's with huge white block letters. Baseball caps promoting "Be Kind" or even "Kindness" instead of some team or tractor. Pins, buttons, scarves, belts, even shoelaces, all reading BE KIND or in the case of the belts and shoelaces, BE KIND BE KIND BE KIND BE KIND BE KIND."

Next would come the "Kindness" manuals, "Be Kind" posters, stationery, and calendars, and even a cover of *Playboy* magazine featuring an overhead photograph of twenty-four nude female models, two year's worth of centerfold possibilities, spelling out the words, "Be Kind" using their bodies, arms, and legs to form the necessary letters.

And not to be outdone, *Penthouse* magazine would then feature a centerfold model whose pubic hair had been ever so carefully shaved and groomed and plucked to read, "Be Kind."

The Stouffer Foods Corporation would produce a line of frozen low-calorie vegetarian meals called "Kindness Cuisine," major cruise lines would launch "Kindness Cruises," and the Chrysler Corporation would introduce a new sports coupe—available only in *Ilona green*—known as "Peace." Its advertising slogan, "Your *kind* of car," with one hundred million dollars worth of emphasis on the "kind."

Sport stadiums would begin sponsoring "Kindness" nights, where sweatbands printed with BE KIND and some team's logo, would be given to all the fans.

And there would be a television special, "Kindness, An Abbreviated History," narrated by anchorman Dan Rather, and a Broadway play, *The Eleventh Commandment*, written by Tom Stoppard.

Even Elvis Costello would get in on the kindness trip. Looking carefully at the back cover of his *Spike* album, ". . . . be kind." can be found printed in very small type just after the copyright information and the phrase, "Printed in U.S.A."

And "Be Kind" computer and video arcade games would become all the rage, where those playing would have to outdo their opponents in acts of kindness, trying ultimately to reach the "divine level" where players would go head to head in a competition of kindness with a little computerized Ilona.

❧

But that's jumping ahead.

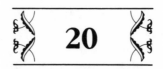

20

Commercial Breaks

And on Tuesday, Ilona and Stephanie would once again journey to Rockefeller Plaza, this time with Joaquim Magalhaes replacing Yakacen Momtaheni as "the cabbie," to tape an episode of "Late Night with David Letterman," an episode devoted entirely to the Daughter of God.

And as Letterman walked out and greeted his studio audience and Paul Shaffer and the World's Most Dangerous Band, he clapped his hands together and said, "Have we got a show for you tonight. A divine show. Wouldn't you say, Paul?"

"What's that?" Shaffer asked.

And Letterman laughed. "Divine. Tonight we have a divine program."

"Divine. Yes, very divine," Shaffer agreed in his typically cryptic manner.

"Tonight our guest is Ilona Ann Coggswater, the Daughter of God." And the audience answered with a respectable round of applause. "Y'know, Paul, I met Ms. Coggswater before the program and she is a very nice, very intelligent young woman."

"And she's here to save the world."

And again Letterman laughed. "That's right, among other things. And, y'know, she told me that this was her favorite television program."

And Letterman moved closer to the television camera and spoke directly to it. "Her favorite television program. Favorite." With extra emphasis on all the "favorites." "Do you hear that, Paul?"

"That "Late Night with David Letterman" is Ilona Ann Coggs-water's, the Daughter of God's, favorite television program?" Shaffer said.

"That's right, her favorite television program. That should be worth a rating point or two." He laughed. "Her favorite." And Letterman clapped his hands together yet again and smiled that goofy smile of his.

"By now all of you," he said, changing topics slightly, "or at least all of you who read or watch TV, know that the Coca-Cola Company has paid Ilona Ann Coggswater a cool twenty mil to be the advertising spokesperson for their diet soft drink, Tab. Well, not to be outdone, the Ayatollah Khomeini announced today that he'd also be available for commercial endorsements. But thus far only the National Rifle Association, at a loss for new spokesmodels, has expressed any interest."

And when less than a few members of the studio audience laughed at his opening joke, Letterman clapped his hands together one more time and said, "A divine show. Ilona Ann Coggswater's favorite television program will be divine tonight. Divine."

"Divine," Shaffer echoed.

"Her favorite television program," Letterman repeated.

"Her favorite program," Shaffer echoed again.

And with that Letterman gestured toward Shaffer and the band and said, "Ladies and gentlemen, Paul Shaffer," before taking his place behind his desk.

"A divine show," Letterman said once seated and holding some light blue index cards. "Y'know, Paul, we were originally planning on doing a serious program tonight in honor of our guest. A serious program."

"But we decided to be funny instead?" asked the band leader.

And Letterman stretched his mouth over his teeth as he sucked in a breath and said, "Yeah."

"Divine," said Shaffer.

"Her favorite television program," said Letterman, tapping the light blue index cards on his desk just as a phony eight hundred phone number flashed across the bottom of the television audience's screen. "1-800-555-DAVE," it read, to the studio audi- ence's and Letterman's surprise and amusement. "What the heck was that," the host said, laughing. And "Dave's Donation Hot- line" began flashing directly above and in sync with the eight hundred number. And then, "Mastercard, Visa, American Ex- press, and Diner's Club accepted."

And Letterman asked the program's director, Hal Gurnee, "What do they get for donating, Hal?"

And Gurnee's voice boomed godlike from out of nowhere, "Salvation, Dave. Salvation."

And, still laughing, Letterman said, "Oh, really." And the flash- ing stopped and the show's host yelled out, "Enough already," as he snapped back those blue index cards.

"Let's get right into it. Tonight's Top Ten List as compiled by the home office in Barcelona, Spain."

"Dave," said Shaffer.

"Yes, Paul."

"When did they move?"

"Today, I think."

"Why Spain?"

"Damn good question," Letterman said. "Hal?"

"Yes, Dave," said Gurnee, his voice still booming.

"Do you have any idea why the home office moved to Spain?"

"Yes, Dave, I do."

And Letterman laughed. "Would you mind telling us?"

"Not at all, Dave," Gurnee said. "They figure that overseas checks will take longer to clear."

"I see," said Letterman. "Now you know, Paul."

"Now I know," agreed Shaffer.

"Tonight's category," Letterman said, still laughing, at least to himself. "The Top Ten Things Jesus Christ Would Say if He Arrived in New York City Today."

Nervous laughter.

"Number ten," Letterman continued. "Anyone got a Certs?"

And when the studio audience failed to respond, he repeated- ly, loudly, "Anyone got a Certs? A divine show. Divine. Number nine: Show me your stigmata and I'll show you mine."

Some laughter, a raised eyebrow.

"Number eight: What do you mean 'Joanie Loves Chachi' was canceled? Number seven: Carpenters are making *how* much an hour? Number six: You don't actually think the Dodgers could have beat the A's without my help, now do you?"

Hoots and hollers and a round of applause.

"Number five: I never knew Jesus was such a popular name. The number four thing that Jesus Christ would say if he arrived in New York City today: A couple of ice-cold brewskies can really take the sting out of a crucifixion, if you know what I mean. Number three, number three: Blessed are *these*, buddy!"

Wild and hearty laughter.

And Letterman took it as a cue, standing and tugging only as a baseball catcher would, he yelled, "Blessed are *these*, buddy!" once again to the delight of the studio audience.

Continuing, "Number two: The *Virgin* Mary, talk about a contradiction in terms."

A few boos and one hiss.

"They're getting ugly," Letterman said. Then, without missing a beat, "And the number one thing Jesus Christ would say if he arrived in New York City today: And don't call me Jesus Coggswater."

Applause, a crescendo from Shaffer and the band and a "We'll be right back."

❧

After the commercial break, a commercial break during which Shaffer and his band played the song, "Kum-ba-yah," Letterman, tapping the light blue index cards on his desk, said, "Our guest tonight on this divine program, our only guest, Ilona Ann Coggswater, the Daughter of God whose favorite television program is none other than what, Paul?"

" 'Cosby'?"

"No. Not 'Cosby.' "

" 'Matlock'?"

"Gosh, I hope not."

"Then it must be 'Late Night with David Letterman.' "

"That's right, it must be. Her favorite television program." With yet more extra emphasis on "favorite."

And, as if on cue, which it was, out walked one of the 'Late Night' regulars, Chris Elliot, shopping bag in hand, pretending to be actor Marlon Brando.

"Oh, my word, Marlon Brando, ladies and gentlemen," said Letterman. "It's Marlon Brando."

And Elliot, doing the worst Brando imitation imaginable, sat in the chair at the right hand of Letterman, the chair that was more than excited at the proposition that the Daughter of God would soon be comfortable within its bounds and was more anxious than usual about ridding itself of Chris Elliot's butt.

"David. David. David," began Elliot. "How are you?"

"Fine, Marlon, fine," said Letterman, acting, or quite possibly not, embarrassed about Elliot's cheesy performance. "What brings you to our studio?"

"David. David. David."

"Yes, Chris. I mean, Marlon."

"I'm here to say hello to my daughter."

"Your daughter?"

"Yes, Ilonie."

"That's Ilona."

"That's what I said."

"But she isn't your daughter."

"David. David. David."

"Yes, Chris."

"I'm surprised at you."

"Why's that?"

"Am I not the Godfather?"

"But that's just a movie."

"David. David. David. I am the Godfather."

"That's nice, Chris."

"And I just want to tell Ilonie."

"Ilona."

"Whatever. Hello, I love you, and why don't you ever call? Me, your mother and your six sisters miss you a lot."

[156]

"All right. Very nice."

"I'm not finished."

"I think you are."

And as Elliot kept rambling, Letterman turned to the camera and said, "We'll be right back with Ilona Ann Coggswater," adding, "if she's still here."

༄

And after that commercial break, one during which Shaffer and his band played "Old Time Religion," Letterman gave the Daughter of God the following introduction.

"In the past week, tonight's guest has become the most recognizable person in the world, a world she has come to save. Ladies and gentlemen, the Daughter of God, the lovely and talented Ilona Ann Coggswater."

And Ilona, dressed in a simple but elegant and very long black jacket over black pants and a black top, walked out from the Green Room to a standing ovation, her first of many. And she took her seat, to the chair's delight, at the right hand of Letterman, smiling his way. And when the applause died down, as it always must, Ilona looked up and directly into the television camera and smiled ever so slightly, just as called for in television etiquette. But something happened on this first look, or more specifically, nothing happened. Again. No zooms, no watching, no directing, no hosting. Everyone present, from technician to studio audience member to director Gurnee to host Letterman, just gasped then gawked helplessly at tonight's special guest, all momentarily forgetting their responsibilities, permanently awed.

And Stephanie LaVasseur, watching the television program on a monitor in the Green Room, a waiting room of sorts for guests and their guests, couldn't help but think what she was sure so many were saying and or thinking and or both. God, is she pretty, was what Ilona's roommate thought. Then, she thought, But give her a break already.

And as Ilona looked from technician to studio audience member to director Gurnee, whom she could not see but imagined was also gawking uncontrollably, which he was, to host Letterman, she thought to herself, Stephanie, they just wanna fuck. Me, they just want to stare into my eyes and sigh, but smiled and said, "I'm very excited about being here."

And the technicians and studio audience members and director Gurnee and host Letterman eventually snapped to with a lot of fervish zooming and watching and directing and hosting, and Letterman saying, "It's our pleasure, believe you me."

And though Ilona made no verbal comment about Letterman's last three words, she looked, just for a moment, a split second, into the television camera through a confusing tangle of cables and out the Green Room television monitor, directly at Stephanie, who was laughing heartily. And Stephanie nodded a knowing roommate nod at the Green Room television monitor that she knew Ilona could only feel. But it was enough.

"So, how you doin'?" Letterman asked.

"Fine," said Ilona, feeling nervous, a bit human. This was, after all, her favorite television program.

"So, is the world safe yet?"

"Afraid not."

"Didn't think so."

"I've got a big job ahead of me."

"Where are you going to start? I mean, if you don't mind me asking."

"Not at all. I'll begin by meeting with world leaders," Ilona explained, "Presidents, premiers, dictators, secretary generals, and you, Dave."

And laughing, Letterman said, "Yeah, right. World leader, David Letterman."

And the audience encouraged Letterman with some more of those hoots and hollers.

"World leaders," he continued, "don't get speeding tickets." And he laughed and asked Ilona. "So, is this really your favorite television program?"

"Yup."

"You heard it, ladies and gentlemen," said Letterman, standing, raising his fist triumphantly.

And Ilona smiled.

"And I owe it to the Professor," she said, waving a small wave to her former employer who she knew had to be watching.

"The Professor?" Letterman said, sitting back down, "Sounds like a Chris Elliot character."

"He owns a record store in Cooperstown," Ilona explained. "Cheapskate Records on Main Street. He turned me on to your show."

"So, he's got a good shot at being canonized?"

"Something like that."

"Now, where were we?" asked Letterman.

"Talking about how I was going to save the world."

"That's right. Please continue."

"Well, first on my agenda is the environment."

"The environment?"

"You know, pollution, the greenhouse effect, endangered species, saving the rain forests."

"The whole gamut."

"Basically."

"And that should take you, what, maybe a day or two? And then what?"

"I wish it were going to be that easy."

"Do you know for certain it won't be?"

"You mean, can I predict the future?"

"More or less. Like, will this program be canceled anytime soon?"

"This is my favorite television program. I'd never allow it."

"She said it again. Her favorite television program. And thank you for the compliment. But getting back, you're the Daughter of God, won't world leaders just listen and do whatever you say?"

"It's doubtful."

"That must disturb you deeply."

"I'm prepared for it."

"Okay, so you save the planet, then what?"

"I'll work on humanity, human rights, animal rights."

"Why the environment before, say, human rights?"

"What use would it be to save the people when they'll have no planet to live on?"

"Good point."

And Ilona just shrugged in a cute sort of way, a shrug that threw Letterman off guard and made him think for a moment, This girl is a doll, and made him wonder for slightly more than a moment, Jeez, I wonder what it would be like to sleep with the Daughter of God?, and then made him realize quite bluntly, That could seriously jeopardize my career. I mean, what if she has a protective Father? and he dropped the idea all together.

"So, you really like this show?" Letterman asked.

"Stephanie and I watch it almost every night."

"Stephanie?"

"My roommate."

And Stephanie, watching the television monitor in the Green Room, was suddenly on TV. And Ilona pointed at the studio monitor and said, "That's Stephanie." And Stephanie waved and smiled nervously.

And many male members of the studio audience whistled and even Letterman commented, "That's a very beautiful roommate you have there."

"She's a great friend."

"I've been looking for a roommate like that for quite some time."

And again we saw Stephanie in the Green Room.

"You two must make quite a pair when you're out on the town," Letterman said.

"We've turned a few heads."

"I'll bet."

And the audience whooped and Letterman said, "Now cut that out!"

And Ilona, beginning to relax, asked, "Can I tell a joke? It's one of Dad's favorites."

And Letterman laughed. "Dad?"

"Yeah."

"Of course." And he turned and warned his studio audience. "Remember this is one of God's favorite jokes. Laugh, or spend eternity burning in hell."

"Absolutely," said Ilona.

And Letterman shot her a cautious look.

"I'm only joking," she said. "Well, here goes. What does it take to make a fundamentalist cry?"

"I don't know," said Letterman. "What does it take to make a fundamentalist cry?"

"Nothing."

And Letterman looked at Ilona and bit his bottom lip. "Yeah," he said.

And Ilona shrugged in that same cute sort of way. "It kills Dad," she said.

"You sure one of our staff writers didn't come up with that?"

"Yup."

And "1-800-555-DAVE" began flashing on the screen, followed by "Dave's Donation Hotline" and Letterman flung one of the light blue index cards at a television camera, "Now cut that out!"

And changing the subject altogether Letterman said, "So, tell me about this deal with Tab?"

"Well, I needed money to survive."

"The Daughter of God can't exactly be an overnight cashier at 7-Eleven."

"Exactly. So Stephanie suggested that I do a commercial."

And once again Stephanie could be seen on the studio monitors.

"I could make all the money I would possibly ever need at one time and could then concentrate on what has to be done."

"Twenty million, huh?"

"Yup."

"Well, it just so happens that we've got copies of the Tab commercials and they're going to make their world premiere tonight, right here on your favorite television program."

"Oh, my God," said Ilona.

[161]

And Letterman laughed. "That's pretty funny coming from you."

"Stephanie was in one of the commercials with me."

And yet again Stephanie could be seen on the television monitors.

"Why don't we bring her out," suggested Letterman. "Can we do that, Hal?"

"Whatever you want, Dave," said director Gurnee from out of nowhere.

"Stephanie, get out here."

And we cut to Stephanie exiting the Green Room and making her way to Letterman's set. And as soon as she, in a short, tight, black mini-dress, was glimpsed by the studio audience, another collection of hoots erupted from the males present. And Stephanie took a seat to the right hand of Ilona and was introduced to host Letterman.

"This is Stephanie LaVasseur," said Ilona.

"A pleasure to meet you," said Letterman. Adding, "You are a stunning young woman."

"Thank you," said Stephanie.

"Have you guys seen the commercial yet?"

"No," said Ilona.

"Then roll the video, Hal."

"Anything you say, Dave," said director Gurnee.

And the viewers and all present were treated to the "two very expensive thirty-second commercials" for the diet soda known as Tab.

And the response from the studio audience and home television viewers was overwhelming, in that most every member of that audience and every home television viewer immediately felt a burning desire for Tab. A desire that would continue burning until quenched by a gulp of this soon-to-be-popular-again soft drink. And even at twenty million, the Coca-Cola Company representatives watching, and they all were, realized that this was the bargain of their Coca-Cola Company lives.

And even Letterman, reaching for a cup of something or other after viewing the commercials, was disappointed to find simply something or other in his cup and not Tab. I wonder if I can get her to do some promos for the show, he thought to himself as he heard himself saying, "Those were great, didn't you think so, Paul?"

"Fabulous," said Shaffer.

"We have to cut for a commercial break," Letterman said, "but we'll be right back with Ilona and Stephanie."

❧

And when they returned from the commercial break, one during which Shaffer and his band played "You Can't Hurry God (He's Right On Time)," Letterman said, "We're speaking with the Daughter of God, Ilona Ann Coggswater, and her lovely roommate and friend, Stephanie LaVasseur. So, tell me, has anyone else approached you about commercial endorsement?"

"That was my one and only. I'm retiring from the commercial endorsement business. But Stephanie's available."

"If the price is right," said Stephanie.

"I'll bet you're a killer in tight jeans," said Letterman.

"Nothing comes between me and my Calvins," said Stephanie.

"Could I?" asked Letterman.

A round of hoots.

And though Stephanie smiled, Letterman was embarrassed. I can't believe I just said that in front of the Daughter of God, he thought to himself.

"Don't worry. I'm pretty liberal-minded," said Ilona, as if she could read his mind.

"So, tell me. Have you had a chance to spend any of that twenty mil yet? Y'know, a Ferrari, a yacht, diamond earrings, things like that? I know it'd be burning a hole in my pocket."

"We found a new apartment," Ilona said.

"We needed more room," explained Stephanie.

"In New York?" asked Letterman.

"Yup."

"And she went on an art spree this morning," said Stephanie.

"An art spree?"

"We've got lots of wall space."

"So you picked up some paintings."

"More or less. Lots of off-beat street stuff."

"No Rembrandts?"

"No, but I got a great Terninko."

"Who?"

"August Terninko. He sells his paintings in front of a boarded-up building on West Broadway," Ilona explained, "Down in SoHo."

"Oh," Letterman said.

"They're really stressed-out, painful."

"Oh," said Letterman, "I prefer soothing tapestries. Y'know, of mountains and lakes. Stuff like that, preferably on black velvet."

"Paintings of Dad's art."

"Yeah," said Letterman, shaking his head slightly, "I guess."

"Always remember," Ilona said, not really knowing why, "only art survives."

"Then I'm in real trouble," Letterman said.

"We all are."

☙❧

"Ladies and gentlemen," Letterman said after yet another commercial break, one during which Shaffer and his band played "Guilty as Judas," "when Ilona Ann Coggswater agreed to be on our show she made one simple request. And here now is a fulfillment of that request. Wanna roll the tape, Hal?"

"Yes, sir, Mr. Letterman," said director Gurnee, cutting to a tape of Ilona and Letterman walking down a deserted alleyway.

"I've always dreamed of doing this," said Ilona just as she and Letterman entered a darkened doorway of what appeared to be an abandoned building.

"Understandably so," said Letterman with eyebrows cocked.

And as the camera followed Ilona and Letterman up six flights of treacherous stairs, Letterman asked, "But is this really appropriate behavior for the Daughter of God?"

"We all have to go wild sometimes," she answered, sprinting up the stairs ahead of him.

But before taking off after her, Letterman said to the camera, "I'm getting all tingly inside."

Next we saw Ilona walking onto the roof of the building and an out-of-breath Letterman eventually joining her.

"Are you sure you want to do this?" he asked.

"Only if you're up to it," she answered, sprinting to the roof's edge.

Again, hamming it up, Letterman shook his head at the camera and took a deep breath before joining Ilona at the roof's edge.

"Where do you want to start?" Letterman asked.

"I guess with the Big Mac," said Ilona, picking up one of the giant hamburgers.

"Now didn't you originally want to throw the entire McDonald's Corporation off the roof?"

"Yup."

"Why is that?"

"Rain forest beef, for starters, not to mention those Styrofoam containers."

"Well, of course."

"Here goes."

And Ilona Ann Coggswater, the Daughter of God, dropped the Big Mac off the top of the six-story building upon which she and Letterman stood and a camera followed its path to its utterly disgusting demise on the concrete below.

"Tasty," was Letterman's comment. "What's next?"

And Ilona lifted a ceramic bust of the Reverend Jerry Falwell, leader of the Moral Majority.

"Jerry Falwell, leader of the so-called Moral Majority," she said, obviously enjoying herself.

"Let him fly."

And she did, and the camera recorded that bust smashing into countless pieces, more or less on top of the ex-Big Mac.

"This is fun," said Ilona, smiling wildly. "Next is a National Rifle Association lifetime membership card."

"But that's not really gonna break and make a disgusting mess when it hits the ground, now is it?"

"Not by itself," she said, "but when I wrap it in a list of the two thousand, one hundred fifty-three people who were killed by guns in this country during the month of November, drench that list in gasoline and light it, it should provide an interesting three or four seconds of viewing pleasure."

"That's what we're here for, three or four seconds of viewing pleasure," said Letterman. Adding directly to the camera, "Yours, not ours."

And Ilona dropped the National Rifle Association lifetime membership card wrapped in a list of the two thousand, one hundred fifty-three persons who were killed in this country by guns during the month of November, drenched in gasoline and set on fire, and sure enough, it provided an interesting three or four seconds of viewing pleasure.

"Next," she said, lifting a case of AquaNet hairspray in large aerosol spray cans and heaving them over the edge of the rooftop.

And the camera watched as the cans exploded upon contact with the concrete below, adding insult and injury to the ex-Big Mac, what was left of the Falwell bust, and the more than charred National Rifle Association lifetime membership card.

"Whoa," Letterman screamed. "Now *that's* entertainment!"

"That was for the ozone," Ilona said, rubbing her hands together.

"What's next?"

"The Rambo videotape collection," she said, holding video-cassette copies of the films *First Blood, Rambo, First Blood II* and *Rambo III* up for Letterman's inspection and amusement.

And Letterman spoke to the camera, raising his eyebrows high, "Ladies and Gentlemen, Ilona Ann Coggswater, Daughter of God, movie critic"

And soon the tapes had joined the sloppy concoction below.

"And this one's for the homeless," said Ilona, smiling and waving her hand to the side in a manner quite similar to that of a game show hostess, "a BMW 5351."

And we saw a seemingly new, bright red BMW 5351 hanging from a crane just over the rooftop's edge.

[166]

"That car looks exceedingly familiar," said Letterman, with a nervous laugh.

"It's yours," explained Ilona.

"Oh, gosh," said Letterman. "Is this covered by my insurance?"

"Nope. Unless your policy has an Act of God clause," said Ilona. Adding, "Just think of your ratings."

"Uh-huh," mumbled Letterman. "My ratings. My ratings. I'm thinking about my ratings, Ilona, but y'know, I still can't get the image of my BMW hanging from that crane out of my head."

"You ready?" asked Ilona.

"Do I have a choice?" said Letterman.

"Ultimately, no," said Ilona.

"Then let her rip," said Letterman. Adding, "I'm afraid to look."

And Ilona gave the signal to whomever it was controlling the crane that held the BMW 535i suspended in midair, and down it went, smashing quite nicely into the mess below.

"Okay," said Letterman, with extra emphasis and breath on both syllables. "And for the grand finale? Or should I ask?"

"Well, originally I wanted to dangle Randall Terry over the edge. He's the leader of Operation Rescue, the Right to Life group that blocks the entrances to family-planning clinics."

"But that wouldn't exactly be setting a kind example, now would it?"

"Some people need to be forced into kindness."

"I see," Letterman said, clearing his throat. "So, what happened?"

"Your producer explained that it wasn't in your budget."

"But my BMW was?" Letterman said.

And Ilona shrugged, which made Letterman laugh.

"Well, maybe you can dangle Randall Terry when you do Carson," Letterman said.

"That's what your producer said."

"So, what did you decide on instead?"

"This," said Ilona, lifting a huge jar of greenish/brownish gook.

"Should I ask?" said Letterman.

"It's a sampling of water I took from a river that runs adjacent to a schoolyard in New Jersey."

"That's river water?"

"That's river water."

And she let if fly. And when that jar of greenish/brownish/gookish water hit the sloppy concoction below, it exploded. Not an explosion of the nuclear variety, but an explosion nonetheless and, as everyone watching knew, water is not supposed to explode, even if it is crashing into a slop heap that includes an ex-BMW 535i.

And as Ilona and Letterman descended the six flights of stairs we saw a slow-motion replay of the six drops in all their gratuitous glory. And next we saw Ilona and Letterman exiting the darkened doorway.

"That was fun," she said.

And Letterman, panting from the six flights, just took another deep breath, looked into the camera, and said, "Yeah, fun, fun, *fun*!"

And the scene cut back to the studio and the wild applause of the studio audience and Letterman's face.

"We'll be right back," he said.

❧

And after the commercial break, one during which Shaffer and his band played "Can't Nobody Do Me Like Jesus," the conversation turned to Ilona's meeting with the pope and "What about this kindness thing? I mean, do I have to be nice to Bryant Gumbel?"

"I think we can make an exception in his case," Ilona said.

"And George Steinbrenner? Do we have to be nice to him?"

"Only if he sells the Yankees."

And the talk continued, the Brokaw interview, whether or not Stephanie had a boyfriend, Ilona's wardrobe, "I'm a blonde and I look best in black," she explained. "What else can I say?"

And Letterman ended by saying, "You're a remarkable, intelligent, and beautiful young woman and I wish both you and Stephanie the best. Thank you for spending some time with us."

❦

And after the commercial break, the last commercial break, one during which Shaffer and his band played "What a Friend We Have in Jesus," with the applause just beginning to die down, as it always must, Letterman said, "Ladies and gentlemen, Ilona has left the building. Good night, God bless, and be kind."

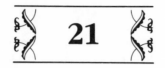

21

And the Right-to-Lifer Cried

And on Wednesday, Ilona and Stephanie began packing their belongings to the beat of their usual noontime entertainment, CNN's "Sonya Live."

Sonya's guest on this Wednesday was none other than Randall Terry, leader of Operation Rescue, whom Ilona had wanted so badly to dangle from that sixth-floor rooftop. Terry was reacting not only to Ilona's appearance on "Late Night with David Letterman" but to the recent disclosure that Ilona would be donating what he felt should be the IRS's five million, forty thousand dollars to five charities, among them Planned Parenthood, in the name of the U.S. government.

"She's a murderer," Terry exclaimed. "She's condoning the murder of unborn children. God's children."

And Sonya argued back with what had become a daily ritual, "But Ilona Ann Coggswater is God."

"But what right does that give her to kill unborn babies?"

"The Lord giveth and the Lord taketh away," said Sonya.

"Jesus was the Lord. She's just his kid sister. An eighteen-year-old girl. A teenager. What could she possibly know about being a God?"

"More than you, one might argue," said Sonya.

And Ilona, watching, said, "Sonya's cool. Maybe I should go on her show."

"Why don't you give her a call?" suggested Stephanie.

"Hmmm," went Ilona, thinking momentarily, wrapping a glass in that day's *New York Times*, whose headline read, "Reagan Opposes Ilona's Donations." The *Times* article explained how then-President Reagan, a staunch right-to-life, a staunch supporter of the right to bear arms, a staunch antienvironmentalist, disapproved of Ilona's donations in the government's name. The piece also contained Ilona's one-word comment on Reagan's opposition. "Tough," was all she said.

And Sonya took a call. "We have Jill from Amarillo, Texas, on the line," said Sonya. "Hello, Jill."

"I just want to tell Mr. Terry that I support what he is doing," said Jill from Amarillo, Texas, before she began to sob. "I'm sorry," she said. "I just can't stop crying when I think about all those dead little children."

"And that's exactly what they are," said Terry. "Dead little boys and girls."

"She's the devil, I'm telling you," said Jill from Amarillo, Texas. Adding, "The Daughter of God wouldn't dish out soup to drug addicts and rapists. And, and," and her sobbing became almost hysterical as she spit out the next five syllables, "homosexuals."

"Very good point," said Terry. "An excellent point."

"God bless you," said Jill from Amarillo, Texas.

"God," interrupted Sonya, "wants to drop you from a six-story building."

"I assure you, Dr. Friedman, God is on my side," said Terry.

"What God might that be?" asked Sonya.

And Stephanie said, "I got the number for you."

"What's that?" Ilona asked.

"They just flashed Sonya's number. Give her a call."

And Ilona did. And as she dialed and waited for Sonya to get to her call, Ilona heard what the program's other callers, those who had dialed ahead of her, had to say.

And Louis from Brooklyn, New York, came on the line. "I'm sitting here listening to your program and I just had to call. How dare Mr. Terry make such blasphemous statements about Ilona. She is God. And to insult her is to insult everything that is sacred and wonderful."

And Sonya smiled a slight but potent smile as Louis from Brooklyn, New York, continued. "Mr. Terry is nothing but a second-rate terrorist."

"I'm a terrorist in the name of the Lord," Terry interrupted.

"You're a terrorist in the name of Randall Terry," snapped Louis from Brooklyn, New York. "The gospel according to Randall Terry. Everything according to Randall Terry. God is among us, trying to show us the way. And your overinflated ego won't let you realize that you've been on the wrong track all along."

"Show us the way?" yelled Terry, growing impatient with Louis from Brooklyn, New York. "What way?"

"The way out," the caller answered.

"The way out of what?" asked Terry.

"Out of the cesspool man has created for himself."

And Sonya interrupted. "Thank you for the call."

"It's unbelievers like that who are destroying the moral fiber of this great country," said Terry.

"Is it possible that you are the unbeliever?" Sonya asked before taking the next call.

And Michelle from Hamden, Connecticut, came on and echoed the sentiments of Louis from Brooklyn, New York. "Ilona's here to save the world," this caller said. "Shouldn't we listen?"

And the next caller and the next and the one after that all agreed with Louis from Brooklyn, New York. And though Terry remained firm in his stance, he wondered where were his crying fundamentalist supporters, where were his teary-eyed right-to-lifers, where were his Jills from Amarillo, Texas.

But the Jills from Amarillo, Texas, were nowhere to be heard. Their calls never came. Instead there was Ted from Asheville, North Carolina, who said, "Ilona has given the world hope," and Lee Ann from Hawthorne, New York, who called Terry an "ignorant, narcissistic, evil man," and Laurie from Santa Monica, California, Robert from Jackson, Mississippi, and Cindy from Hutchinson, Kansas, who all said they "loved" Ilona. And other callers from other places who all in one way or other seemed to agree with Louis from Brooklyn, New York. "What about abused children?" they asked. "Teach birth control in the schools," they demanded. "Overpopulation?" "The homeless?" "Back alley abortions?" But Terry's answers and statements were the usual fundamentalist bumper-sticker slogans, no more, usually less. He fumed. Sonya smiled. The calls continued.

And Ilona watched and smiled. Accomplishment. Not grand accomplishment, but satisfying accomplishment. She had reached the Louises of Brooklyn, New York, the Michelles of Hamden, Connecticut, the Lee Anns of Hawthorne, New York, and all the others. Ilona hung up the telephone receiver that she had gripped so tightly in her hand and she stared at the television, through the television. Stephanie caught a glimpse of Ilona's reflection in the set. That intense, wide-eyed, green-eyed gaze atop the image of Randall Terry and the voices of Ilona's supporters.

"Are you okay?" Stephanie asked.

"It's working," Ilona said, "I'm getting through."

"I never doubted you would," Stephanie said, squeezing her roommate's hand. "Never for a moment."

And Ilona hugged Stephanie. A warm hug of friendship, trust, and love. A hug that concealed the single tear that somehow escaped one of those wide-eyed green eyes and was now rolling down Ilona's cheek. A tear that Ilona wanted no one, not even Stephanie, to see.

ॐ

But on that same day while Ilona and Stephanie and filmmaker Walker were eating a late and quite vegetarian dinner at an open-all-night and reasonably quiet Village eatery, there were those expressing their views to whom Ilona had not gotten through. The those were John Charlton Hanley, national vice president of the National Rifle Association, Bill Martelli, general in command of the Born Again Army for Christ, Reverend Donald Wildmon, head of the Coalition of Christian Leaders for Responsible Television, and E. Morgan King, president of the Second Amendment Society. And these those were expressing their not-gotten-through-to views on "The Morton Downey, Jr., Show," a syndicated late-night screamfest where intelligence took a backseat to one's ability for loud and insulting repartee. And these those were pissed.

King was pissed at God for "sending a girl to do a man's job"; Hanley was pissed at Ilona for dropping an NRA lifetime membership card from a six-story building on "Late Night with David Letterman", King, Hanley, and Martelli were pissed at the thought that their God-given right to own guns and shoot innocent animals might be threatened; Martelli was pissed at King because King called the Born Again Army for Christ a lunatic fringe group; Hanley was pissed at both King and Martelli and called them "idiots"; even Downey was pissed at Ilona for donating one million, eight thousand dollars to Handgun Control, Incorporated; and Wildmon was pissed at everything and everyone, including King, Hanley, Martelli, God, Ilona, Letterman, and apparently even Morton Downey, Jr., for reasons he, like most fundamentalists, never quite made clear.

But despite all the confusion about who was pissed at whom or what, one thing was certain: Ilona was not about to, at least easily, take away the handguns and rifles that these those held so near and dear to them. Not that she ever said she wanted to. It's just that her recent droppings and donations proved worrisome.

And with all the screaming, screaming, and more screaming, all doubt, if any indeed existed, that King and Martelli were idiots, was eliminated. And all doubt, if any indeed existed, that Wildmon and Downey were too simpleminded to be called idiots, likewise vanished from public opinion.

But John Charlton Hanley, national vice president of the National Rifle Association, stood out, as in the end did his anger. He was a forty-nine-year-old, Shreveport, Louisiana–born, single, well-spoken, well-educated, hardnose conservative who had fought for nine years in Vietnam and now was second in command at the most powerful lobbying group this country had ever known. He believed in the United States, its Constitution and its Second Amendment, an amendment he had spent the last eighteen years of his life, since his return from military service in hell on September 15, 1970, defending. And he was pissed.

[174]

But Ilona and Stephanie and filmmaker Walker would graciously miss that evening's "Morton Downey, Jr., Show," not that it was on any of their must-watch lists or that they indeed ever gave the program any thought, but because their after-dinner conversation turned to "only art survives." A thought that pressed on in Ilona's mind as surely as protecting the Second Amendment controlled John Charlton Hanley's.

"The Constitution of the United States of America," said Hanley, to anyone who'd listen, as this episode of "The Morton Downey, Jr., Show" came to a close.

"Explain," Ilona said to filmmaker Walker.

"The Second Amendment," Hanley screamed over something or other screamed by Morton Downey, Jr.

"Even the most ignorant of men have this strange reverence for art," explained filmmaker Walker.

"A well-regulated militia," said Hanley, as a fight broke out in the Morton Downey, Jr., studio audience.

"Paintings?" asked Stephanie, listening intently to the conversation between her lover and her best friend.

"Being necessary to the security of a free State," Hanley continued.

"All art forms. Painting, literature, sculpture, photography," said filmmaker Walker.

"The right of the people to keep and bear arms," Hanley said, standing.

"Film?" asked the Daughter of God.

"Shall not be infringed," concluded Hanley, more pissed than ever, not only at Ilona, but at the buffoons who were ignoring his words of inspiration.

"Which brings me to," said filmmaker Walker, nodding.

"That's it for tonight," screamed Morton Downey, Jr. "Tomorrow night's guest will be Randall Terry."

"The documentary," said Ilona, finishing filmmaker Walker's sentence.

[175]

And Hanley sat down in desperation and shook his head in disgust.

And filmmaker Walker nodded his with hope while Ilona shook hers, dashing it.

"Goodnight," screamed Downey, "and God bless you all."

And filmmaker Walker said, "You can't blame me for trying."

And the credits rolled on "The Morton Downey, Jr., Show."

And Ilona said, "I thank you for asking."

And John Charlton Hanley left the studio determined.

And Ilona Ann Coggswater changed the subject, period.

22

Not Everyone

And on Thursday, Ilona would grant an hour-long interview to popular CNN talk-show host Larry King.

And after the usual gasping and gawking, those watching, an estimated seventy-eight million in this country alone, approximately twenty-one times King's usual viewership, got to see Ilona at her most relaxed and personable yet.

And after the usual questions about the usual subjects were out of the way, King allowed his viewing audience the right to call in and speak with the Daughter of God.

And the first call was from a very-young-sounding Fred from Boston, Massachusetts, who asked Ilona, "What's it like being the Daughter of God?"

And Ilona asked Fred from Boston, Massachusetts, "How old are you, Fred?"

And Fred from Boston, Massachusetts, answered, "Eleven."

And Ilona smiled. "It's scary. Because there's so much that I have to undo. And even though I'm the Daughter of God, I can't do it alone. I need your help. I need the help of all your friends and family."

"I'll help you," shrieked the eleven-year-old. "What can I do?"

"Well, how about if you and your friends all get together and clean up your neighborhood. Make it spotless, no litter anywhere. Make it an example that the other neighborhoods of the world can follow."

"Does that mean I have to clean up my room?"

"Yes," Ilona answered, laughing. "Will you do that?"

"I'll try," Fred from Boston, Massachusetts, said. Adding, "I love you, Ilona."

"And I love you, too, Fred."

And next Lillian from Somerset, Kentucky, asked, "Does Satan walk among us?"

"No, he'd have too much competition," Ilona answered. Adding, "But he was here for a good part of Charlie's life."

"During Charlie Chaplin's life Satan walked the Earth?" asked King.

"Yes," she said as if she were shocked that no one knew, which in fact she was, "Adolf Hitler."

"Hitler was Satan?" said King.

"The Son of Satan," said Ilona.

"My word," said King. "But Satan isn't on Earth today?"

"I promise."

"How can you be so sure."

"My Dad and he have kept the lines of communications open."

"This is all so incredible," said King. "But it just occurred to me that Chaplin wasn't crucified by Hitler."

"That's right. He was crucified by the American public, specifically Attorney General James McGranery."

"Was McGranery also related to Satan?"

"No, McGranery was just an idiot."

And Ilona said hello to Marianne from St. Augustine, Florida.

"Ilona," Marianne from St. Augustine, Florida, said, as she started to cry. Just "Ilona."

And though Larry King expected the worst, one of Sonya's crying fundamentalists, Ilona knew better.

"Everything will be okay," Ilona said.

"I don't know how," said Marianne from St. Augustine, Florida. "I don't know what to do."

"I'm here to listen," said Ilona.

"I'm so afraid."

And Ilona was silent.

"I got," said Marianne from St. Augustine, Florida, "I'm pregnant."

And Ilona was silent.

[178]

"And my parents found out. I don't know how. But they want me to have the baby. I'm only seventeen, Ilona. I know I made a mistake. But," said Marianne from St. Augustine, Florida, crying, "I can't."

And Ilona said nothing.

"Please. Please tell me what I should do."

"Marianne," Ilona said, slowly, very slowly, "do what you feel you should do, what you know in your heart you must do."

"But," Marianne from St. Augustine, Florida, slowly, just as slowly, "I don't want to get an abortion. I have to."

"Then do as you must," Ilona said.

"But my mother is calling me a murderer and telling me I'll burn in hell."

"Tell your mother to stop quoting Randall Terry."

"But am I a murderer?"

"Have you ever killed?" Ilona asked.

"No, I've never killed anything," Marianne from St. Augustine, Florida, said, adding, "or anyone."

And Ilona closed her eyes and concentrated, listening for the screams. Marianne's was there, among the others, all the others, so many others. So was her face, her seventeen-year-old face. A face full of such promise and excitement, such intelligence and innocence. A face full of such fear, such doubt.

"Then, Marianne," Ilona said, "you are not a murderer."

"But my mother."

"It's your life, your future," extra emphasis on the *yours*, both of them. "You'll make the right decision. I know you will."

"Thank you," said Marianne from St. Augustine, Florida. "Thank you."

And the next caller was John from Washington, D.C. And his voice, that voice, was a voice Ilona recognized, immediately.

"Hello, Ilona, this is John," that voice said. "I've left you a number of messages but this is the first chance I've had to actually speak with you."

"Hello, John," Ilona said, thinking of her answering machine, his messages, something about destiny. "What can I do for you?"

"Explain."

"Explain?"

"What you're doing."

"I'm here to stop the self-destruction."

"That's very noble," said John from Washington, D.C., a slight laugh, more like a snort. "Very noble, indeed."

"Do you have a question you'd like to ask Ilona?" asked Larry King protectively.

"I just want her to know how badly I want to meet her, how badly I want to look into her eyes," said John from Washington, D.C.

"One day, you will," Ilona said.

"Yes," said John from Washington, D.C. "It's our destiny."

✌

And in his Washington, D.C., penthouse, John from Washington, D.C.—John Charlton Hanley from Washington, D.C.—hung up his phone and smiled. Standing, he walked past the racks of rifles and handguns—his prized possessions, the only art he understood—to his well-stocked bar and poured himself a half tumbler of high-quality scotch, and, downing it, he returned to the overstuffed leather chair and Ilona's image on his television screen.

✌

Next on the line was Kristine from Plymouth, Connecticut, who asked, "Who turns you on?"

And Ilona blushed. It was the first time the world would see its Savior blush. It would not be the last.

"Excuse me," Ilona said, caught off guard and embarrassed, though she knew she shouldn't be.

"Who do you find sexy? Who turns the Daughter of God on?"

And laughing, Ilona said, "Oh, my God!"

"An interesting question," said Larry King, "Who is attractive by God's standards?"

And Ilona wanted to speak, but couldn't.

"We're putting you on the spot," said King.

"You can say that again."

[180]

"Well?" said Kristine from Plymouth, Connecticut.

"Bobby Ojeda," Ilona said, a gulp.

"Pitcher for the New York Mets," King explained.

"Anyone else?"

"Well, Paul Westerberg, I guess."

"An athlete and a rock star," said Kristine from Plymouth, Connecticut. "Any movie stars?"

"If I had to pick one, I'd say Mel Gibson."

"Nothing wrong with that," said Kristine from Plymouth, Connecticut.

"Why?" asked King.

"I don't know," said Ilona, "there's just something about them."

"Like what?" said King, teasing. "It's it a physical attraction, or maybe something spiritual?"

"No, definitely physical."

"The human side?"

"That has nothing to do with it," Ilona explained. "Gods can be horny too."

And next came Tom from Torrance, California, who asked, "Is there life on other planets?"

And Ilona said, "Absolutely."

"Are they more advanced than we are?"

"Some are light years ahead, many seem light years behind."

And Larry King interrupted, "That's astounding."

And Tom from Torrance, California asked, "Have they ever visited this planet?"

"I believe so. But we really don't keep track of who goes where."

"What are they like?" asked King.

"A lot like Earth's creatures, with the same problems, the same lack of solutions," Ilona explained. Adding sadly, "Pain is universal."

"Unfortunately," said King.

"Unfortunately," agreed Ilona.

"And are you also their God?"

"I'm everyone's God."

And Louis from Brooklyn, New York, came on the line and said, "Ilona, I watched 'The Morton Downey, Jr., Show' last night and found it very upsetting to hear people doubting your word. Is there anything you can do about people like that, people like Hanley from the NRA or Randall Terry?"

"I can only hope to make them believers. But, like you and me, they, too, must follow their conscience, their destinies."

"I find it hard to believe that these people have a conscience," said Louis from Brooklyn, New York.

"They do," Ilona explained. "It's just been obscured by ignorance and hypocrisy."

And Louis from Brooklyn, New York, paused for a second and said, "I wanted to thank you on behalf of, well, everybody, I guess. We really need someone like you right now."

"Thank you for the support," Ilona said, adding, "and also for the comments you made on 'Sonya Live.' "

"You heard my call?" exclaimed Louis from Brooklyn, New York.

"Heard it? It gave me a much needed boost of confidence. You helped me see that I was getting through."

"You are. Everyone loves you."

"Not everyone," Ilona said, shaking her head ever so slightly.

And Larry King added, "Yet."

And Ilona repeated, "Not everyone."

She knew.

৩৩

And soon the hour-long program was over. Larry King graciously thanked his guest and seventy-seven million viewers switched channels, almost simultaneously, except Hanley, who had long since fallen asleep to dreams of destiny. His destiny, Ilona's destiny.

23

Blessed Are Those Who Wear Mustaches . . .

Ilona's comment about Adolf Hitler would elicit the usual barrage of books, articles, and even a made-for-TV movie, *Portrait of Hitler, Son of Satan*, starring an unknown-and-bound-to-remain-that-way German actor in the title role.

Hitler's evil was evaluated, reevaluated, and evaluated again. Every murder, every comment, every strategy, every look, every everything. It was all so hopelessly confounding.

And though the Daughter of God would be questioned and questioned again at length about Hitler, she would usually insist that nothing more need be said about the man or his deeds.

"Are you blind?" she would ask, thinking the proverbial, Or what?

☙

In his book, *The Great Mustache*, facial-hair expert Montague LeDuc would spend close to one thousand pages examining the mustache style shared by Hitler and Chaplin's Tramp character and point out that the only other noted historical figure to wear such a mustache was Swiss religious reformer Ulrich Zwingli, who died in 1531. But being an expert on facial hair and not religion, LeDuc would not and could not make a connection.

But in the book, *The Zwingli Mustache*, theologian Emuna Steinnagel would explain that Zwingli had spent many years trying to form a religious colony whose members, including all women and children, would wear a mustache similar to his. But branded, "a bonehead," Zwingli would be forced into exile where he wrote what is today considered a visionary master-piece, *Jesus Christ Is Coming and He'll Be Sporting a Mustache Just Like Mine.*

✧

And then there was outer space.

Life on other planets!

ALIENS!!

Why did I have to open my big mouth? Ilona would think, saying instead, "Let the scientists figure it out."

"But."

"But."

"But."

"What if?"

"Where from?"

"Who could?"

"When will?"

"And why?"

"GIVE ME A BREAK ALREADY!"

✧

But that's jumping ahead.

24

All For the Glory of God

And on Friday, Ilona and Stephanie would spend the afternoon, gasps and gawks aside, modeling affordable, all black fashions for a *Vogue* magazine photo spread titled, "Kindness in Basic Black." The spread would appear in the March 1989 issue with Ilona and Stephanie making their debuts as *Vogue* cover models.

And part-time actress/model and part-time business management student Stephanie LaVasseur would drop the part-times altogether and this dazzling young woman whose figure—a landscape of silk and goosebumps, slopes and dales, a collection of pinks, the pink scale—defied mathematical equations, would become a full-time model and within a week would sign a long-term contract with the Elite Modeling Agency and be chosen as one of eight models to appear in *Sports Illustrated*'s 25th anniversary swimsuit issue, on whose cover she would seduce the world dressed in a minuscule black bikini bottom and an exceedingly wet, white, cut-off T-shirt, where, in huge black block letters, the words BE KIND could, for the most part, be read.

And while one specific *Sports Illustrated* photograph of Stephanie in a sinfully skimpy, moderately transparent and not-as-wet, light green bikini caused many a mom to cancel their husband's or son's subscriptions, and many fundamentalist types to write letters about "the moral disintegration of our world," etc., etc., ad nauseam, it would also force a certain Dave from Danbury, Connecticut, to write, "Stephanie LaVasseur makes me believe beyond any doubt that God exists, because from only God's hand could come a creature so exquisite."

"Wanna switch places?" Ilona would ask.

"Not in a million years," Stephanie would answer.

❦

And this *Vogue* Magazine Friday would become Comic Book Saturday, but not before Ilona would visit her friends at the Soup Kitchen.

"Miss Ilona, what'ya doin' here so early on a Saturday mornin'?" asked Flatcake Al.

A shrug. "I missed you guys."

"So how goes the struggle?" he asked.

"How goes yours?"

"Life ain't a struggle no more," he said, "Not since you showed up."

And Ilona, bowing her head, smiled, just slightly.

"There's that smile," Billie said.

And Ilona's slight smile grew and beamed as she looked at Flatcake Al and Billie, Tiny and Indian Jack and their huge toothless grins.

And Tiny asked, "You meet with that president of ours yet?"

"Not yet."

"Well, when you do, give him a kick in the butt for me."

"Give him one for me, too," said Billie.

"And me, too."

"And me, too."

"Hold on," said Ilona, laughing. "I want him to listen. I don't want to kick him to death."

"He'll listen," said Tiny, "When you get through with kicking him."

And Ilona headed home for her meeting with illustrator Stanlee, that's L-E-E, not L-E-Y, Grunch and, quite pleased with Grunch's sketches, humor, and honesty, granted permission for him to create a comic-book series based on her life and teachings.

The series, which would be issued monthly by Colossians Comics and whose profits would benefit the charity of Ilona's choice, was tentatively titled, *The Adventures of Ilona Ann*

Coggswater, Daughter of God. It would follow Ilona' life, meeting with Pope John Paul II, appearing on "Late Night with David Letterman" working at the Soup Kitchen, speaking to the president, even hanging out with Stephanie, and would always, according to Grunch, "stress kindness and humanity."

Grunch's only concern was that he would never be able to capture the power of that intense, wide-eyed, green-eyed gaze on the pages of a comic book, to which Ilona insisted, "The message works without the eyes."

And the initial press run of thirty-five thousand copies of book one would sell out almost immediately, and by the fifth book, Colossians would be printing eight million, five hundred thousand copies and selling them in seventeen countries worldwide.

ॐ

And later that afternoon Ilona, Stephanie, and filmmaker Walker would bargain hunt lower Manhattan for things to fill that "charming" twenty-fifth-floor, three-bedroom, duplex penthouse in a new high-rise on Charles Street in the very "private" West Village.

Not that the furnishings from their "safe" one-bedroom, sixth-floor walkup with working fireplace on East 10th Street in Greenwich Village wouldn't also find space in their new space, it's just that their new space had so much more new space to fill.

And while they oohed and aahed at this end table for that sofa or those chairs, filmmaker Walker couldn't help but ask, "Why a comic book and not a documentary?"

"Because," Ilona answered, "your documentary would rob me of my last bit of privacy." And she joined Stephanie at the foot of this "relatively inexpensive," but "ultimately cool" king-size bed that Stephanie felt Ilona had to have.

And filmmaker Walker would just nod and understand and join Ilona and Stephanie at the foot of that king-size bed. What else could he do?

And all the furniture from all the stores would be delivered promptly, so promptly in fact, that most of the delivery men and even most of the stores themselves were shocked at their prompt service. And though they couldn't believe the words coming from their mouths, most of the salemen from most of these stores for which most of the delivery men delivered said, "Would you like it delivered today?" To which Ilona would always reply, "Monday'll be fine." And thus the usual minimum delivery time of three to four or more weeks became a continuous echo of, "No problem. It'll be there on Monday."

"Being the Daughter of God," Stephanie said, "can sure have its advantages."

"Sometimes," Ilona said.

"What do you mean?" asked filmmaker Walker.

But Ilona didn't explain.

She knew she shouldn't.

ℰℐ

And Saturday begot Sunday. A beautiful mid-December Leisure Sunday, sunny, in the high fifties, a perfect day off for the Daughter of God.

And exiting their "safe" one-bedroom, sixth-floor walkup with working fireplace on East 10th Street in Greenwich Village, for what both Ilona and Stephanie knew would be one of the last times, they headed toward that quiet restaurant on Bleecker Street, the NoHo Star, where they had arranged to meet filmmaker Walker.

"So, what are we doing?" he asked.

"You decide," Ilona said.

With Stephanie adding, "And make it good. The Daughter of God doesn't get many days off, y'know!"

"That's right," agreed Ilona, laughing, looking over the brunch menu.

ℰℐ

And so it would be that Ilona would spend her Leisure Sunday, her last Leisure Sunday for some time to come, in the company of Stephanie and filmmaker Walker, in the pursuit of "art," Häagen Dazs Ice cream, and all the seems-interestings that might come along.

And as they walked through SoHo and the Village, filmmaker Walker took note of a miracle Ilona and Stephanie had taken for granted, that Ilona Ann Coggswater, quite possibly the news story of the year if not the decade or the century or *of all time*, was walking the New York City streets without being pestered by reporters and photographers and others whose job it is to pester those famous, and occasionally even those not so famous.

"It's not like the press to respect privacy," commented filmmaker Walker.

"I'm just lucky," said Ilona with a shrug and a smile and a twinkle in that intense, wide-eyed, green-eyed gaze, "I guess."

"And she's got better connections," added Stephanie.

And turning onto West Broadway, they noticed a crowd, a circle of spectators gathered around what was usually the place where August Terninko sold his paintings.

And walking to that circle and that place, Ilona noticed Terninko, painting away to the delight of his audience.

"He seems to be doing well," said Stephanie.

"As endorsed by Ilona Ann Coggswater, the Daughter of God," said filmmaker Walker.

And Ilona watched. Terninko had no paintings to sell. Sold out, she thought. Sold out, she knew. "Let's go," she said, smiling, pleased, as yet unnoticed by the spectators.

And turning into Washington Square Park after making a Häagen Dazs pit stop, Ilona, Stephanie, and filmmaker Walker sat on one of the park's benches and absorbed the ice cream and sunshine.

"I once had a dream," Ilona said. "A black-and-white dream."

"Most dreams are," said filmmaker Walker, "in black and white, that is." Adding and asking, "Aren't they?"

"Not mine," said Stephanie. "Mine are in living color."

"But this was a different kind of black and white," Ilona continued. "Sort of like, wide-screen, Cinemascope black and white."

"You're starting to talk like Walker."

"Sorry," Ilona joked. "Can't let that happen." And after a pause, "Anyway. I'm walking down a street, just walking, mind-ing my own, when a girl across the street, no one I knew or had ever even seen before, points at me, screams at the top of her lungs, and takes off in my direction."

And Stephanie began to laugh. "Is this some sort of lesbian paranoia?"

"No," said Ilona, laughing. "Listen. So, I take off. I don't know what this girl wants and I'm not about to stick around to find out. So, I'm running down this same street, as fast as I can, and I pass these two guys who do the same thing, point, scream, and take off after me. Now I've got three people chasing me. And I keep running, in no certain direction, other than away. Running."

"Orgy paranoia, maybe?" suggested Stephanie.

"And every person I pass points, screams, and joins in the chase, until I have this mob of thirty, maybe more, people chasing me."

"Definitely orgy paranoia."

"And I see this alley. This way! I remember thinking, This way! Wrong. Know what I found at the end of that alley?"

And both Stephanie and filmmaker Walker shrugged.

"A solid brick wall!" exclaimed Ilona.

"That wouldn't have been my guess."

"No doors, no windows, not even a fire escape to climb up. No way out, I'm trapped. And I see the mob coming toward me. But they're not running now. They're just creeping toward me, silent and slow. I'm terrified. Totally. They keep getting closer and closer and I have nowhere to hide. And when the mob is just a few feet away, I scream out, 'What? What do you want?' And this guy, a heavy-metal kind of guy in leather and studs, reaches into his jacket pocket. I'm a goner. I thought. I knew it. I was going to be slashed and left for dead. But instead of a switch-blade, he pulls out a pencil and some paper and asks if I'll give him an autograph. And soon I hear a chorus of, 'Can I please have an autograph, too.'"

"More like *A Hard Day's Night* paranoia," said filmmaker Walker, "if you ask me."

"But it's not over," said Ilona. "I work my way through the

crowd, giving them my autograph, and when I get down to the last person, the girl who first pointed and screamed and started it all, she reaches into her pocketbook, but instead of pulling out something to write with, she pulls out a gun and says, 'I didn't want your autograph,' and shoots me. Bang."

And they were silent for a moment, a long moment, until Stephanie stood and took her roommate's hand.

"C'mon," Stephanie said. "You need a beer."

❧

And as their Leisure Sunday cinematic treat, filmmaker Walker suggested Ingmar Bergman's *The Seventh Seal*, which was playing a double bill with Werner Herzog's *Every Man for Himself and God Against All* at a revival house on 12th Street. And though this partially divine trinity would decide against the Herzog offering, they would make the six fifteen showing of what filmmaker Walker called, "my favorite film."

"An allegory on man's search for meaning," filmmaker Walker explained as they took their seats.

"Not a romantic comedy?" Stephanie asked, smiling.

"Not a romantic comedy," filmmaker Walker said, returning the smile.

And the lights dimmed, and the projector whirred, and the adventure began.

" 'All for the glory of God,' " Ilona read aloud from the subtitles. Adding, "All for the glory of man."

And when a crucifix flashed on the screen, the most grotesque crucifix Ilona had ever seen, so full of pain, doubt, fear, she cried, unable to hold back the tears, unable to hold back the fears, for once unable. She cried for her Brother who had felt that pain, doubt, and fear. She cried for the artist who had carved such pain, doubt, and fear. She cried for the knight, Antonius Block, who delayed the end of his pain-filled, doubt-filled, fear-filled existence by playing a game of chess with Death.

And, as the mob in the movie, the Slaves of Sin as they were called, marched by, flagellating themselves, carrying that agonizing crucifix, Ilona felt her hands pulse and swell, and then a pop.

[191]

And holding back a gasp, a gasp of pain, physical pain, she clasped her hands together, tight, ever so tight. How did he withstand the pain? she thought. How? And as the Slaves of Sin screamed and moaned, those screams and moans reverberated in Ilona's head, bouncing around as if in a gigantic echo chamber, only getting louder instead of softer. And though she wanted to cover her ears, she kept her hands together, squeezing them so she thought they'd never come apart, almost hoping that they would never come apart. Ilona didn't need to see the blood, her stigmata were real.

And when the adventure was over, and the projector no longer whirred, and the lights were on, Ilona eased the clasp. Her hands were numb, so numb. Slowly she separated them and, looking at her palms, at the spots where she had felt the pop, Ilona saw the two small wounds, bullet-size, she thought, star-shaped wounds covered with freshly dried blood. Trickles of blood. Her blood.

"Are you okay?" Stephanie asked.

And startled, Ilona said, "What?" then, "I'm fine," fading away, lost in a Savior's hell.

"You can always count on Walker for a little stimulation," Stephanie said, for lack of anything better, sensing a problem, some problem.

"Intellectual or otherwise," filmmaker Walker said, sensing nothing, still blinded by Bergman's television.

And exiting onto 12th Street, filmmaker Walker repeated the questions that had haunted Antonius Block so.

"Is it so hard to conceive God with one's senses?" he said softly. "Why should He hide in a mist of half-spoken promises? Can we have faith in those who believe when we don't have faith in ourselves? What is going to happen to those of us who want to believe, but aren't able? And what of those who neither want to nor are capable of believing? Why can't I kill God within me? Why does He live on in this painful and humiliating way even though I curse Him and want to tear Him out of my heart? Why, in spite of all is He a baffling reality that I can't shake off? I want knowledge, not faith, not supposition, but knowledge. I want

God to stretch out His hand to me, reveal Himself and speak to me."

And Ilona took filmmaker Walker's hands into her own, felt his pulse, his heartbeat, his very life, against her still fresh wounds, looked into his eyes with that intense, wide-eyed, green-eyed gaze and said, "I who speak to you am She."

And a few loose tears formed in filmmaker Walker's eyes as he said, "I know."

But how could he?

❧

And back at their "safe" one-bedroom, sixth-floor walkup with working fireplace on East 10th Street, alone, Stephanie asked, "Earlier," with a pause, "what was wrong?"

And Ilona was silent.

"At the movie?"

And Ilona began to cry.

"Don't," Stephanie said, softly. But instead of saying anything else, she put her arms around her roommate and held her dearly.

"It hurt so bad," Ilona said, finally.

"What? What hurt so bad?"

"My hands."

And Ilona pulled away, just slightly from Stephanie, and held our her hands, palms upward. And Stephanie touched some fingertips to her lips as she saw the wounds.

"But," she said, not knowing what to say, "how?"

And Ilona cried softly.

"I don't understand. Was it the movie?"

"It was a reminder."

"Of what?"

"Of what I have to do."

And both women were silent.

"There's something," Ilona began.

"What?" said Stephanie, tears forming in her eyes, not knowing what to expect but expecting the worst. "What?"

"Give me your hands."

And Stephanie held out her hands and when Ilona touched

[193]

them, Stephanie looked down, into the eyes of her roommate, her shocking blue eyes comforting, or at least trying to, Ilona's tired green-eyed gaze.

You look so tired, Stephanie thought, but said nothing.

And Ilona said, "Close your eyes."

And as she did, Stephanie heard the screams. And she gasped. And the screams grew louder, the cries, the howls. She saw the faces, the bodies, the hands and paws and claws all reaching out, out to her. She felt the pain. How she felt the pain. And she cried, not for those who screamed, not because of their pain, but for Ilona, her roommate and friend.

And Ilona, once again, began to cry, softly at first, then a hard, steady, childlike sob.

And Stephanie leaned forward and placed her arms back around the Daughter of God, held and rocked her gently.

"It'll be okay," Stephanie promised. "It'll be okay."

&

And that night, as Stephanie curled up under her covers, her thoughts turned back to the screams and the pain and to Ilona.

Why? she thought, as she cried herself to sleep. Just Why?

But Stephanie had no answer. She didn't know.

How could she?

&

And that night, as Ilona curled up under her covers, her thoughts turned back to Antonius Block and all the Antonius Blocks in the world. Could she step forth from the mist of half-spoken promises and provide the knowledge that they longed for? That they cried for? That they screamed for? She knew she would have to. She believed she could.

"But why?" she asked herself. "Why must I? Why should I?"

And Ilona laughed, it felt good to be able to laugh. She laughed and acknowledged her Father's ego.

"All for the glory of God."

25

Holy Freight

In his book, *How I Moved Ilona*, Erik Utke, of Three Guys Who Move, described how he and his two partners, Quintin White and younger brother Dane Utke, "carefully and meticulously" moved the Daughter of God.

In four hundred pages Utke, who at best had a passable grasp of the English language, explained in painstaking detail, how each and every "thing" was carried, loaded, transported, unloaded, and delivered.

"When I arrived at the East 10th Street apartment," Utke wrote, "I asked Ilona why she had hired Three Guys Who Move. She explained to me that she liked our name because it sounded like a dance troupe. While I didn't really understand, she laughed, and figuring that she had made a joke, I laughed also. I did not want to offend the Daughter of God."

ʘʘ

And that evening as Ilona and Stephanie unpacked, arranged, placed, put, set, organized, and generally straightened up all of their "things," as the taller roommate would call them, that taller roommate asked, seemingly out of nowhere, "Am I in your way?"

"What are you talking about?" asked Ilona, straightening a rather large painting, a rather large August Terninko painting, for the seventh or eighth time, "You're clear on the other side of the room."

"That's not what I mean," Stephanie said, tears coming to her eyes. "Am I, well, a bother? Do I get in your way? In the way of what you have to do?"

"Stephanie," Ilona said.

"What?" Stephanie said, sitting on the floor, those first few tears leading to some uncontrollable sobs. "It's just that you've got so much to do and all," she said, her chest heaving. "Those screams and your hands and, well, I mean, I don't know what I mean. It's just that saving the world's gotta have its problems. And I just don't want to get in your way."

How she sobbed.

"And I don't want you to be in pain."

And now on the floor by her side, Ilona put her arms around her roommate—it was Stephanie's turn to be rocked gently—and said, "I couldn't do it without you."

"What do you mean?" said Stephanie, all sniffles and tears.

And though Ilona couldn't help but smile at the "I Love Lucy"-ness of Stephanie's wall, she said, "You help me keep everything light and in its place."

"Huh?"

"You give me a fresh perspective on things. You're down to earth."

"I'm not God," said Stephanie, more sniffles, lots of tears.

"You're my friend. You keep me company."

"Is that enough?"

"It's enough for me. And besides, you make me laugh."

"I do?"

"Yup. And you've really helped out a lot. I would have never gotten the Tab commercial without you."

"You wouldn't have?"

"It was your idea, remember?"

"Oh, yeah," said Stephanie. Adding "I love you, Ilona."

"And, I love you."

And looking into Ilona's intense, wide-eyed, green-eyed gaze, Stephanie thought, Your eyes look better today, but just sobbed some more and said, finally, "I worry about you."

"I'll be okay."

"You sure?"

[196]

"Yup."

"Yup?"

"Yup."

"Promise?"

"I promise."

"Okay."

"Want a beer?"

"Okay."

And together Ilona and Stephanie shared "a couple of six-packs of ice-cold Rolling Rock" on this cold Monday evening as they continued unpacking, arranging, placing, putting, setting, organizing, and generally straightening up all those "things."

❦

"Gorbachev is visiting this week."

"I'll be there."

"You planning on meeting with him alone?"

"No, I'd like to get him, Reagan, and Bush, all at one time."

"Three birds with one stone?"

"So to speak. Where should I put this?"

"How 'bout on that wall."

"Good enough. And besides, promises are less likely broken when there are witnesses."

"Not that you don't trust politicians."

"Heavens no, it isn't that at all."

"Heavens?"

"Did I say 'heavens'?"

"You said 'heavens'."

"Didn't mean to."

"And what about Dan Quayle?"

"What about him?"

"Aren't you going to meet with him, too?"

"I'm here to save the world, not babysit."

"Let's be nice. Remember kindness and all that."

"How does this look?"

"It's okay, but that one over there is still crooked."

"No, it isn't."

"Uh-huh. Look at it."

"I spent an hour getting that just so."

"Well, it isn't. Just so, that is. Unless just so to you is defined as crooked."

"Then you straighten it."

"Naw. Leave it. Imperfection excites me."

"Want another?"

"Why not? I don't have to drive."

"Have you ever had a car?"

"My parents bought me a Fiat Spider when I graduated high school. It was a white convertible. It looked great on me."

"What doesn't?"

"Well, this looked especially great."

"Where is it now?"

"Don't know. I sold it when I moved to the City. You ever own one?"

"A car?"

A nod.

"I don't even know how to drive."

"No way!"

A shrug.

"The Daughter of God can't drive."

"It's not that big a deal."

"Yes, it is. It makes you more human."

"In what way?"

"There's something I can do that you can't. Like you can turn water into Tab and stuff like that, but *you can't drive*."

"But I can walk on water."

"No way!"

"Yup."

"You've tried it?"

"When I was nine. We had just moved to our house on Susquehanna Avenue right near the Susquehanna River."

"Know it well."

"Right. So one night, I sneaked out of the house and went down to the river. I remember the sky was really clear, and still, and the moon, a full moon, lit up the river."

"Sounds romantic."

"Nothing's romantic to a nine-year-old."

"Depends on the nine-year-old."

"Umm."

"It does."

"Anyway, I walked down the bank to the water and stood there for a few minutes. I was scared, but I thought, If Jesus can do it, then so can I. So, I concentrated real hard, closed my eyes, and stepped out onto the river. I could feel the cold of the water just splashing at my feet and going between my toes. There were fish in the Susquehanna River back then, and I felt one press up against the bottom of my feet. Back and forth it swam, brushing up against my feet. It tickled, sort of, and I got so excited that I opened my eyes and fell in."

Laughter.

"So, here I was in the middle of the night, sopping wet, and more determined than ever."

More laughter.

"But this time I didn't close my eyes. I just concentrated, really concentrated, and stepped out onto the water."

"And?"

"And it worked. I walked clear across to the bank on the other side."

"Cool."

"I was proud of myself."

"Did you ever try it again?"

"No, once was enough. But after that, I was always afraid every time my Mom took me to the beach that I wouldn't be able to get into the water and swim. That I would just be stuck forever walking on it."

"So you can walk on water but you can't drive."

"We all have our limitations."

"Speaking of which, what are you gonna wear to the Gorby, Ronnie, Poppy meeting?"

"Speaking of? What does that have to do with limitations?"

"They're gonna be talking about arms limitations, aren't they?"

"Probably."

[199]

"Well, there ya go."

"Right."

"So, what are you gonna wear?"

"Basic black, I guess."

"I know that. But how basic? I mean, you don't want to look like a Russian peasant."

"I don't know. Does it really matter?"

"Of course it matters."

"Well, then, what would you suggest?"

"I suggest we go shopping."

"When in doubt, shop?"

"Something like that."

"Umm. Want another?"

"There's some left?"

"Plenty."

"Sure. I don't have to drive."

"Let's not start that again."

"Start what?"

"Never mind."

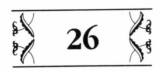

26

Photo Opportunities

And it came to pass that by week's end—a week that included being interviewed by *Time* magazine, being interviewed on Armed Forces Radio, and a few refreshing visits to the Soup Kitchen—as her roommate packed this or that to go pose this way or that in this bathing suit or that on this Mexican beach or that, Ilona Ann Coggswater, Daughter of God, would sit down with arguably the world's most powerful men, Mikhail Sinéad Gorbachev, secretary general of the Union of Soviet Socialist Republics, Ronald Wilson Reagan, president of the United States of America, and George Herbert Walker Bush, vice president and president-elect of the United States of America. She would sit down and talk.

And on this cold Friday in December, December 16, 1988, to be precise, in a special meeting room arranged on the thirty-second floor of the southern tower of the World Trade Center—a meeting room with grand windows overlooking Ellis Island and the lower Hudson River with the Statue of Liberty cautiously peering in, watching, listening, hoping—Ilona, arriving alone, entered silently to find Reagan, Bush, Gorbachev and his Russian/English translator, a dry, balding man in his early thirties named Ioakim Sabovik, standing by those grand windows discussing the fine art of fishing. Salmon versus trout fishing, to, again, be precise.

And Ilona said, "Hello," startling them.

"Hello," they all more or less said, turning.

"Ilona Ann Coggswater," she said, extending her hand.

"Mikhail Gorbachev," he said, seizing her hand and the opportunity.

And as he grasped her hand, Ilona took her opportunity to gaze that intense, wide-eyed, green-eyed gaze into the Russian leader's own green eyes. And he gasped and gawked and mumbled something in Russian that Sabovik either could not or would not translate or did not completely hear.

And Ilona left the gawking Gorbachev and moved on to Reagan, who, aside from the gasping and gawking, clasped his hand to his chest. And though it occurred to Ilona that her gaze might be giving the president of the United States a heart attack, Reagan quickly issued a small burp and said, "Pardon me. Too many onions in the salad," and he smiled and Ilona smiled and he nodded and Ilona nodded and moved on.

And as she grasped Bush's hand and looked into his tired brown eyes she felt such compassion for this man as he gasped and gawked. She knew much better than he the true task that lay ahead. God help us both, she said silently, just mouthing the words. She knew he would if he had to.

And they took their seats, their respective and thoroughly thought out, by this or that thoroughly overpaid political seating expert, places, around the oval mahogany table in this special meeting room. This is all so just so, Ilona thought to herself, smiling only slightly.

And Ilona said, "Let me tell you a story."

And Gorbachev leaned forward, placing his elbows on the oval table.

And Bush leaned back and touched a hand thoughtfully to his lips.

And Reagan sat still and sighed, barely.

"In the late 1960s," Ilona began, "the Tennessee Valley Authority began work on the Tellico Development Project in the valley of the Little Tennessee River in eastern Tennessee. The valley was an extremely productive farming area and the river was widely known as the best trout stream in eastern Tennessee."

Bush, especially, seemed to perk up upon hearing the word "trout."

"The Tellico Development Project included a dam," Ilona continued. "The TVA's plan was to turn the valley, nearly half of which would be flooded by the dam, into a flourishing recreational area. That is, until the discovery of the snail darter, a previously unknown member of the perch family, which fed on snails and made its home in the waters of the Little Tennessee above the dam sight. This tan, three-inch-long fish would have been made extinct by the completion of the Tellico dam."

And Reagan sighed again, barely.

"Because of suits from the Environmental Defense Fund and citizens' groups and the passing of the Endangered Species Act, the building of the dam was in jeopardy, all because of this little fish. Then in 1978 an amendment to the Endangered Species Act was passed that created an Endangered Species Committee, a group that became known as the God Committee because it could grant exemptions to the Endangered Species Act and spell life or extinction for an endangered species. The first case to be reviewed by the God Committee was the Tellico project, who surprisingly ruled in favor of the snail darter."

And Gorbachev poured himself a glass of water, never once taking his eyes off Ilona or spilling a drop.

"There would be no dam; the fish was granted a reprieve. For a short while, anyway. Then in June 1979, a Tennessee congressman, a staunch proponent of the dam, added an amendment to the annual ten-billion-dollar water projects appropriation bill. The amendment was never read out loud, and never discussed, and only a few members of the House were even in attendance. But this amendment exempted the Tellico project from the Endangered Species Act. And though the Senate tried unsuccessfully to kill the Tellico amendment, it was ultimately signed by President Carter in September 1979. Within twelve hours the dam builders were at work in Tennessee. And, as predicted, with the dam came the extinction of the snail darter."

And Ilona paused for a second to pour herself a glass of water.

And Gorbachev leaned back, folding his hands together over his chest.

And Bush leaned forward, resting his right elbow on the oval table and resting his chin on the back of that right hand.

And Reagan moved only slightly, sat still, and sighed, heavily.

"I'm not quite sure what you're getting at," Bush said, quietly.

"That's not the end of the story," Ilona said. "With the snail darter gone, two things happened. First, the snail population exploded. And this proliferation of snails consumed all the algae and small aquatic plants, totally throwing the area's food web out of balance. Secondly, and more important, especially to the Tellico people, the trout, which had fed upon the snail darter, now had nothing to eat."

And Ilona spoke the next five words slowly, enunciating each syllable, so that even Reagan would get the message, "*No snail darter, no trout.* And no trout, no sport fishing, and without fishing there was little to do in the way of recreation. So, with the farmers gone because their farmland had been flooded by the dam, and the fisherman gone because there were no trout, there was an extreme loss of revenue to the surrounding communities, which led to unemployment, bankruptcies, even homelessness and suicide. The quality of life just kept on diminishing and the once thriving Little Tennessee River valley became a virtual ghost town. So much for that flourishing recreational community. So much for the Tellico Development Project. So much for the dam. Too bad about the snail darter."

And Ilona sat back and sipped her water.

And Reagan closed his eyes and thought to himself how he hadn't had escargots in quite some time and how he really enjoyed them prepared in a little garlic butter and how he would make sure he ordered them that evening at dinner.

And Gorbachev, looking at Ilona, stared directly into that intense, wide-eyed, green-eyed gaze and asked, "But what can we do? Where can we start?"

"Anywhere and everywhere," answered Ilona.

"Give us an example," said Bush.

"Reclassify the elephant from its current listing as a threatened species to that of an endangered species."

"But legislation like that takes time," said Reagan.

"There is no time," snapped Ilona. Then, speaking calmly, "Humankind is destroying almost one hundred different species every day, making virtually every species an endangered species. One hundred examples of my Father's work being forced into extinction because of what?"

"Greed," said Bush, quietly.

"What?" demanded Ilona.

"Greed," said Bush, ashamed.

"Greed," agreed Ilona.

"What else?" asked Gorbachev.

"Pick up a newspaper and just read the headlines. It's all there, the rain forests, ocean dumping, whaling, toxic waste. You're intelligent men, you know what I'm talking about."

And Ilona took another sip of water as the three world leaders shifted nervously.

"Jesus Christ," she said, raising her voice as Gorbachev, Reagan, and Bush collectively raised their eyebrows, "start in your own backyards and start today. Take care of this Earth, and protect all of its inhabitants. It's the only place you've got."

And, taking just one last sip, more for effect than thirst, Ilona concluded firmly, sadly, irrevocably, "And this is your last chance."

❧

And Gorbachev, Reagan, and Bush promised Ilona they would move quickly and do what they could.

"I plan on being known as the environmental president," said Bush.

And Ilona just nodded sadly and forced a small smile.

And Bush looked at Ilona and thought of how she frightened him, how she expected too much of him, how he would ultimately fail and spend eternity burning in hell, most likely with Dan Quayle by his side.

And Gorbachev looked at Ilona and thought that she was a remarkable young woman, but dressed in that simple black dress, the dress that she and Stephanie had picked out specifically for this occasion, she resembled a Russian peasant. Not at all fitting for the Daughter of God.

And Reagan looked at Ilona and sighed. He was tired and glad that his presidency was coming to an end. And he thought, Let George deal with her, I've got my autobiography to have written and other things to worry about. I just hope I can have escargots tonight.

And after the meeting they posed for photographs, Gorby and the Daughter of God, Ronnie and the Daughter of God, Poppy and the Daughter of God, all three and the Daughter of God.

And some reporter from ABC News asked what was accomplished.

And all three leaders said that they would begin immediately to reform this, clean up that, or put a halt to something else.

And Ilona did her best to smile and force an occasional nod before quietly disappearing into the crowd without having to answer any questions.

27

Trouble in Paradise

"You look like you could use a beer."

"And a back rub. And a vacation. And a break."

"Bad day for the Daughter of God, huh?"

"Did you watch it on TV?"

"I saw you guys posing for pictures."

"Photo-ops. Thanks."

A sip, a sigh.

"About that back rub."

"Sit down."

"That feels good."

"You're so God-damn tense."

"You sure you don't wanna switch places?"

"Not in a million years."

"So, where are you off to?"

"Cancun. But I should be back next Wednesday."

A pause.

"If you need me, I won't go."

"Don't be silly."

"You sure?"

A nod.

"You okay?"

"No, but the beer helps."

Another pause.

"And so does the back rub."

"Gonna miss me?"

Another nod.

"A lot."

"Can I use one of those black suitcases?"

Another.

"And you can borrow Walker if you need to."

Half-choking laughter.

"I beg your pardon. I lend you an overnight bag, you lend me your boyfriend?"

"You could use a good . . ."

"Stephanie!"

"It would relax you."

"He's your boyfriend."

"But I'm willing to share."

"Thanks, anyway."

"Well, if you change your mind."

"Right."

❧

And that night, shortly after Stephanie left to catch the beginning of her career at Kennedy Airport, Ilona sat down to the evening news. And after wading through all those Gorby/Ronnie/Poppy/Ilona photo-ops, the newscaster, in this case, NBC's Sue Simmons, said, "And on a lighter note, the first song about Ilona Ann Coggswater has been released by Genesis Records, an independent record label based here in Manhattan. And here now with that story, Andrea Dailey."

And Ilona stared at the television set expecting the worst. Which was exactly what she got.

A heavy-metal song that began with some searing guitar licks to a heavy backbeat. Soon a bass line was established, followed by a screeching high-pitched voice singing:

> The world comes a crumblin' down,
> Crumblin' down, crumbling down,
> At our feet today.
>
> Racism, drug addiction,
> Homelessness and more,
> There's got to be a better way.

> It was time,
> Time, time, time,
> God knew it was time,
> Time, time, time,
> Time for Ilona to lead the way.

"They're called the Killer Nuns," Andrea Dailey said, mercifully drowning out the music. "And the song is called 'It's Time for Ilona.' "

The song continued:

> Gay bashing, flag trashing,
> Environmental sleaze,
> And then there's the big disease.

And just as Noah Zark, lead vocalist for the Killer Nuns, was about to explain his inspiration for writing "It's Time for Ilona," the Daughter of God flipped channels, landing on MTV, where John Cleese was walking silly on some episode of "Monty Python's Flying Circus."

Something completely different, she thought to herself, smiling.

And though she watched the rest of this British comedy, Ilona shut off the television altogether before MTV got back to what MTV was best known for, in honest-to-God fear of seeing a music video for "It's Time for Ilona."

☙

And that Sunday afternoon, a Sunday afternoon that followed a much needed Soup Kitchen Saturday, as Stephanie was posing in that sinfully skimpy, moderately transparent and not-as-wet, light green bikini, Ilona herself caught an airplane to catch what was left of the future, our future, an airplane that would take her to another kind of tropical paradise, an airplane that would take her to Brasilia, the capital of Brazil, where she would meet with José Sarney, president of the Brazilian government.

And, for the next two days, they, with countless other Brazilian politicians and the Brazilian press, toured by boat some of the untouched rain forests of the Amazon Basin. And often, Ilona would step from the boat onto the fertile soil and raise a finger to her lips to silence both the boat's engines and the endless babbling of Brazilian politicians to Brazilian reporters. Not that she needed to silence anyone, for the screams and cries and howls had never been louder, more distinct, than here in Brazil. The screams of millions of species all pleading for their lives. And she would close her eyes and see the little faces, the eyes, the paws and claws. Faces she had never seen before of creatures even she did not know existed. Beautiful creatures, exotic creatures, bizarre creatures. My Father's art, she thought as she gasped at the beauty and cried at the pain. And she would look at the Brazilian politicians. And the immediate hatred was suffocating, more suffocating even than the screams and cries and howls. More suffocating because these politicians were within reach, ready to be snuffed out with the crack of a lightning bolt. But would that make the screams stop, even for a moment? she thought. Would the screaming creatures at least take some time out from their suffering to smile? And Ilona would shake her head, ever so slightly, reboard the boat, and remain silent as their journey continued up or down the river.

And as often, Ilona would step from the boat and walk quickly, very quickly into the forest, and though the politicians and press would try to keep up, they could only catch up to find Ilona standing near a tree or in a clearing holding her hand out to some as yet unnamed creature who would reach out its paw to touch the Daughter of God. And Ilona would smile at the creature, who would look up into her intense, wide-eyed, green-eyed gaze, It'll be okay, that gaze would say, and the creature would try to believe. And some politician would warn that "those" have been known to "bite" or "attack," and some guard just catching up to the politicians would raise his rifle and aim its sights at the creature and Ilona would turn and stare at the guard, a stare that ordered the guard to lower his weapon. And the guard would, for justified fear of his life.

And when Ilona asked to see the other side, the miles of forest that had been burned and destroyed, Sarney laughed and said, "Think of the press."

And Ilona said, "Take me there, or I'll go by myself. And believe me, your beloved press will follow."

And by helicopter Ilona toured the destruction. Hundreds of miles upon hundreds of miles of destruction. Death and destruction. No screams. There was nothing left that *could* scream. Just silence. Dead silence.

"And for what?" she said to no one.

"Greed," she heard President-elect Bush acknowledging.

And she nodded to herself and quietly held back the tears.

And on Tuesday evening, back at Brasilla's grossly ornate Planalto Palace, after that day's photo opportunities had ended, Ilona met with Sarney, privately, at yet another oval mahogany meeting table. And though she thought for a moment about how many trees could be saved if there were fewer meeting tables, if politicians would stop talking and begin acting—the parable of the meeting table?—she decided against parables, meeting table, snail darter, or otherwise, and instead, very simply, explained her concern for all of her Father's creatures. She explained her concern for our planet and the very air that we breathe. And she demanded that the destruction be stopped.

And President Sarney assured the Daughter of God that the Brazilian government was initiating this program and that to regulate this or that and help save the Amazon Basin.

"Bullshit," Ilona said.

"I beg your pardon," said the very surprised president.

"Bullshit," she said. "I don't want to hear about your programs and regulations."

"What then do you want to hear?" said Sarney, frightened at what he felt might be the wrath of God.

Little did he know.

And Ilona stood and turned her back on the Brazilian president. And she spoke, firmly, almost threateningly, "That the destruction and killing will stop. Now."

"Governments do not work that way," Sarney said, with a nervous little laugh.

And after a long pause, a pause that seemed even longer to Sarney, Ilona asked, "And what of that Japanese-backed highway that would link your western state of Acre to Peru?"

And she turned and shot that intense, wide-eyed, green-eyed gaze at Sarney, nailing him to his seat.

"What about it?" he said, not knowing what else to say.

And Ilona slammed a fist into the table. And Sarney jumped back, seemingly for his life.

"It's Japan's idea," he said, quickly. "They need the wood. You'll have to talk to them about it."

"It's totally out of your hands, isn't it," Ilona said, biting her lip, drawing blood.

And President Sarney nodded, quickly.

And Ilona shook her head, slowly.

❧

And that night Ilona caught a red-eye to Tokyo for an impromptu meeting the following afternoon with Japanese Prime Minister Noboru Takeshita. And as unplanned and awkward as the meeting was, Takeshita was gracious and honest.

"The highway of which you speak is very important to the Japanese economy," he explained.

"The Japanese economy is not what I came to save."

"And these creatures that you care so much about. They mean nothing to us here in Japan."

"You're missing the point."

"No, I'm afraid it is you, Ilona Ann Coggswater, who is missing the point."

And Ilona was silent.

"We cannot interrupt our economic system, or any economic system for that matter," the prime minister continued, "to save the nameless creatures or the trees of South America that no one will ever see."

"No, Prime Minister, it is you who are missing the point,

because eventually there will be no more creatures, nameless or otherwise. Eventually there will be no more trees."

"But for now both are in abundance."

"So what are you telling me, that you'll begin to worry as the last tree is being cut down?"

And Takeshita stood. "Ms. Coggswater, I understand who you are and what you say but I cannot help you."

"You will not help me."

"I cannot help you. The people would not stand for it."

"Don't you mean, the economy would not stand for it?"

"Our economy and people are one in the same," he said. "Now, if you please. The press corps is waiting to take some photographs. Please follow me."

And Ilona was silent as she stood by Prime Minister Take-shita's side and the photographers snapped away.

☙

And flying back to the United States, Ilona watched those around her, in the airport, on the plane, they were familiar, some more than others, but, in one way or another, all familiar, too familiar. She had seen them all scream, cry out, howl even.

"Pain is universal," she heard herself saying.

"Excuse me," said the person sitting next to her.

And startled, Ilona looked at that person. Yet another familiar face.

"Were you speaking to me?" asked that familiar face.

"No," Ilona said, quietly, her thoughts fading back, back to pain and screams and cries, back to the faces. Every face she saw, seemingly every face she would see, had a scream or cry, some pain, that went with it.

"You're Ilona?" asked the familiar face sitting next to her. "Aren't you?"

A nod.

"I can't tell you how comforting it is to have you on this flight."

And Ilona smiled slightly, she knew she was expected to, she knew she had to.

[213]

And headphones were passed out. Ilona needed none. The headphones from the Walkman given to her by Mariam what seemed like so, but wasn't barely that, long ago, would work quite nicely. And though she thought that maybe a dose of Replacements—to sing along to "Here Comes a Regular" or "I Don't Know"—would be just what the proverbial doctor ordered, she knew her off-key sing-along would draw unwanted attention. So, instead, Ilona plugged in and tried to concentrate on the in-flight movie, as she watched the actors and actresses act, she realized that they, too, were familiar. Familiar, but not because of their fame or their success or their talent, not because of magazine covers, "Entertainment Tonight," or stars on Hollywood Boulevard's Walk of Fame, but familiar because of their screams.

And Ilona couldn't help but smile. She thought of the Soup Kitchen and Flatcake Al and Billie. They'd be laughing out loud, laughing out loud if only they knew.

"If only they knew. . . ."

And she laughed, just a slight laugh, Ilona at herself, because Flatcake Al and Billie and all the others knew, knew all too well, and understood, that even the rich and famous scream.

⁊

And though Ilona Ann Coggswater had been invited to dine with President and Mrs. Reagan and others that Thursday evening at the annual White House Christmas dinner, she was forced to decline because Mrs. Reagan refused to alter the traditional turkey offering to satisfy Ilona's all-vegetarian request.

"We'd be glad to make up a large salad or a cheese sandwich or something like that," offered the first lady. "Whatever she wants. But the president and I really love our Christmas turkey."

And a close Reagan aide was said to have overheard the president confess that he was relieved that the Daughter of God would not be attending the Christmas dinner because, to quote Reagan, "She's the worst storyteller I've ever heard. And besides, I'm really looking forward to a nice escargot appetizer."

"You look like you could use a beer."
"And a back rub. And a vacation. And a break."
"Bad day for the Daughter of God, huh?"
"Bad week."

ℰℐ

She knew.

28

Only Three Dots

And that Saturday morning, December 24, a Christmas Eve Saturday morning that followed a Stay-in-Bed Friday, Ilona received a preview issue of that following week's *Time* magazine, an issue whose cover featured a rather flattering Robert Mapplethorpe portrait of the Daughter of God under the heading, "Savior of the Year."

In it, the publishers and editors and all involved explained that Ilona was a unanimous, "hands down" choice for their annual Man of the Year issue. "But," explained one senior editor, "we struggled over whether to call her 'God of the Year' or simply 'Woman of the Year.' The argument went on for about two hours until an electrician who was checking for an electrical short in our meeting room overheard us talking about his 'savior.' We all just sort of looked at each other with this why-didn't-I-think-of-that look. And the argument was over."

A photograph of that electrician, Louis from Brooklyn, New York, appeared on the magazine's Letter from the Publisher page, giving Louis credit where credit was obviously due.

The magazine praised Ilona for everything, from her Mother to her wardrobe to her roommate to her sense of humor. It included an abridged account of all Ilona had said and done since that fateful meeting with the pope over Thanksgiving weekend, along with charts and graphs illustrating how violent crime in the country had decreased some thirty-four percent, nonviolent crime had suffered a forty-one percent decrease, gun sales were down by a solid sixty-five percent, nonreligious charitable donations were up by seventy-three percent, religious charitable donations had been cut in half, environmental action and cleanup had just about doubled, illegal dumping had virtually ceased, illegal drug use was down by nineteen percent while Tab sales had increased by roughly six thousand, four hundred percent, just in the four weeks since Ilona had made her presence known. The issue also contained more photographs than one could imagine, a list of Ilona's favorite bands, foods, and pastimes, and even a pull-out poster of the rather flattering Mapplethorpe photograph.

Ilona laughed when she pulled the poster from the magazine.

"Ilona Ann Coggswater," she said, "superstar."

She laughed and tossed the poster and the magazine aside. Oh, how she laughed.

What else could she do?

❧

And later on that Christmas Eve Saturday afternoon, over "a couple of six-packs of ice-cold Rolling Rock," Ilona, Stephanie and filmmaker Walker bought and decorated the "biggest Christmas tree," as Stephanie would call it, they could find and baked and decorated the "tastiest Christmas cookies," as Ilona would call them, "ever made."

And as Ilona was placing a giant sparkly star atop the tree, filmmaker Walker asked, "Are you celebrating the birth of Christ or mourning the death of Chaplin?"

"A question for every occasion," said Stephanie.

A question that, or so it seemed, like many of filmmaker Walker's too many questions, Ilona did not answer.

❧

And that evening, as midnight and gift-opening time approached, the three friends drank and laughed and joked and munched on those "tastiest Christmas cookies ever made."

And Stephanie gave in first, "I can't wait any longer." And

handing a beautifully wrapped package to Ilona, said, "This is for you."

And Ilona smiled and shook the meticulously wrapped, in black paper with a black bow, shirt-size box with curious passion, a quizzical look taking over as the shaking progressed.

"There's nothing in here," said the Daughter of God.

"Yes there is," said Stephanie as she took a seat on the floor, in front of the place on their huge sofa where filmmaker Walker sat, and leaned back against his legs.

And Ilona shook the box just a bit more before ripping off the wrapping in one savage swipe. And pulling open the box, Ilona found an envelope. A white envelope. And the quizzical look pressed on.

"Just open it," Stephanie said.

And Ilona did, laughing as she read aloud what the contents of the envelope said, "This certificate entitles Ilona Ann Coggswater," she read, "to driving lessons at any authorized Sears Driving School." And smiling, she flashed that intense, wide-eyed, green-eyed gaze at Stephanie and said, "Thank you." Then, with a laugh, "I think."

And reaching under the tree, Ilona grasped a small box wrapped in red paper, just red paper, and handed it to Stephanie, who slowly began unwrapping the package, seemingly trying not to rip any of that red paper.

And as Stephanie exposed the side of the small box that read SONY WALKMAN, she issued an "oh, wow" and accelerated her unwrapping process to get to that Walkman. "How did you know I wanted one of these?" she said.

"I know everything, remember," Ilona said. "And I thought it would keep you entertained on all those boring flights to all those boring locations."

"Cool," Stephanie said, showing the gadget to filmmaker Walker.

And handing Stephanie another red-paper-wrapped package, Ilona said, "These kinda go with it."

And Stephanie bit down on her lower lip and ripped open the

present exposing a half dozen cassettes and a package of batteries.

"I never heard of half these bands," said filmmaker Walker as he read the side of the six cassettes, smiling.

"I bought what I thought you'd like." Ilona shrugged.

"And I do," Stephanie said, crawling over to Ilona, hugging her. "I love it." And, taking a seat next to her friend, "Thank you."

"You're welcome," Ilona said. "Now, how 'bout one for Walker?"

"Does he deserve it?" asked Stephanie.

"You're his girlfriend, you tell me."

And Stephanie made a face, a yucky face. "I guess so," she said without much enthusiasm.

And Ilona reached over and grabbed a medium-size box wrapped in green paper, just green paper, and handed it to filmmaker Walker.

And taking it he said, "Only if I can give you yours." And he reached beneath the tree and handed Ilona a box wrapped in a brightly patterned paper complete with Santa Clauses and reindeer.

"Ready? Set? Go!" said Stephanie, and Ilona and filmmaker Walker simultaneously ripped away at the wrapping, exposing their respective and probably not surprisingly similar presents.

And filmmaker Walker read aloud the note that was attached to the now exposed collection of videotapes. "If only art survives. . . ." he read. "Dot, dot, dot, dot."

And Ilona read aloud the note attached to her new collection of tapes. "The art most likely to . . ." she read. "Dot, dot, dot."

"The Kid," continued filmmaker Walker, reading the title off the first videotape box.

"Eight and a Half," continued Ilona, reading from the first tape in her new video collection.

"The Gold Rush," read filmmaker Walker.

"Taxi Driver," read Ilona.

"City Lights," he read.

[219]

"Manhattan," she read.

"Monsieur Verdoux," he read.

"And *The Seventh Seal,*" she concluded, wondering if she'd ever be brave enough to watch that film again.

"Thanks be unto God for her unspeakable gift," said filmmaker Walker, reaching over and squeezing Ilona's hand.

"And thank you," Ilona said, smiling, adding softly, "really."

And Stephanie and filmmaker Walker exchanged a few presents, a kiss, a hug, and another kiss.

And Ilona placed a very large just red-paper-wrapped package in front of Stephanie, who said simply, "It's big." And, after lifting the package, "And heavy."

"Well, open it," urged Ilona.

And Stephanie did, all the while smiling. And when that red paper was peeled from the very large box, a very large box that gave no hints as to what it contained, she ripped open the cardboard top and reached in pulling out a large aluminum-and-black-rubber designer suitcase of French origin. And inside that large aluminum-and-black-rubber designer suitcase of French origin was a just slightly smaller matching aluminum-and-black-rubber designer suitcase of French origin. And so on, until Stephanie had four of those aluminum-and-black-rubber designer suitcases of French origin open at her feet.

And Stephanie just admired and touched.

"I thought you could use them," Ilona said, finally.

And Stephanie hugged her friend.

And looking over the suitcases, filmmaker Walker said, "Amazing." Then, "French designer luggage and not a trace of leather. Absolutely amazing."

"Thank you, so much," Stephanie said, again. "So much."

And Stephanie reached over and grabbed a larger-than-shirt-size box wrapped in more of that black paper, topped off with three black bows, and handed it to Ilona.

"Hope you like this," Stephanie said.

And Ilona opened the box and grinned as soon as she spotted the special blue of the New York Mets. And pulling the official

Mets satin jacket from the box she saw the number 19 on the back just under the word, OJEDA.

"Oh, my God," Ilona said, standing, running to her bedroom.

"Where are you going?" Stephanie asked.

"Be right back," Ilona promised.

And she returned, wearing the jacket and an old, well-worn but official New York Mets baseball cap, modeling both proudly.

"How do I look?" the Daughter of God asked.

"Happy," said Stephanie.

And Ilona shoved both hands into the jacket's pockets only to discover the real surprise. And pulling out a white envelope from the jacket's right-hand pocket, Ilona eyed her roommate, who eyed her right back. And they both smiled.

And Ilona opened the envelope, another envelope, much like the first but different, looked over its contents, very different, and dropped into the closest chair.

"How did you get these?" Ilona asked.

"I have my ways," said Stephanie. "Do you like it?"

"Like it? Like it? I'm fucking speechless."

"Good," said Stephanie with a satisfied grin.

"Should I ask?" said filmmaker Walker, confused, as usual.

"Season tickets," said Stephanie.

"Oh," said filmmaker Walker.

"Field box, section thirty-one, row A, seats one and two," said Ilona, shaking her head, not taking her eyes off the tickets.

And filmmaker Walker looked to Stephanie for an explanation.

"The two seats closest to the Mets' dugout," said Stephanie. Adding proudly, "Only the two best seats in the entire Shea Stadium."

"Yup," said Ilona, with a sigh, still shaking her head, still staring at the tickets.

"Right next to Richard Nixon's box," continued Stephanie with a smirk.

"So, how did you get 'em?" asked filmmaker Walker, extra emphasis on the "did."

"I just got them," said Stephanie, a wink.

"Thank you," said Ilona.

"You're welcome."

"I don't know what else to say."

"There's nothing else you have to say."

And Stephanie and filmmaker Walker exchanged the last of their presents, a kiss, a hug, and another kiss.

And the telephone rang. Mariam, from a Christmas party at Linda's Dew Drop Inn, wishing her Daughter and her friends a very Merry Christmas.

"I love you, Mom," Ilona said.

"I love you, too, dear. Merry Christmas."

And Ilona, still wearing number 19 on her back and that old, well-worn but official New York Mets baseball cap on her head, excused herself and stepped out onto that "private" bi-level wraparound balcony that gave her an unobstructed and "private" 360-degree view of the world she had come to save. And she observed and listened. Christmas in all its glory.

And after a few moments, maybe longer, Stephanie was by her side.

"We're going to bed."

"Okay."

And they hugged and exchanged more thank-yous and good nights and Merry Christmases.

And Stephanie was gone.

And Ilona beheld the Manhattan skyline, the Statue of Liberty to her right, the Empire State Building to her left. The world she had come to save.

And a cold late December breeze came seemingly out of nowhere and sent goosebumps marching under that Mets jacket.

"Dad," Ilona thought. But getting no response she shook her head and smiled.

"No," she said. Just no.

And the wind picked up and she dug her hands deep into that jacket's pockets looking for warmth, finding some.

And down on the New York streets below a police cruiser

with its sirens screaming screeched by. And then another, and another, all heading, more or less, in the direction of the Chrysler Building.

The world I came to save . . . Ilona thought. Dot, dot, dot.

And as she peered back into the still of her apartment, the wind died down, as did the sirens. And all was quiet until a Christmas song, Bing Crosby's "White Christmas," began playing in an apartment on some other floor.

And shivering, swaying to the music, hugging herself to stay warm, Ilona Ann Coggswater, Daughter of God, alone on that "private" bi-level wraparound balcony, alone now on Christmas Eve, smiled and laughed, then sang along with Bing.

ℰℐ

And Christmas Sunday morning, after breakfast, yet more thank-yous and a check of the day's headlines on CNN, Ilona explained that she would be spending at least part of the day at the Soup Kitchen.

"Want some help?" Stephanie asked.

"No," Ilona explained, "this is something I need to do alone."

And Stephanie and filmmaker Walker walked with their friend to that "private" elevator.

"What time should we expect you back?" asked Stephanie.

"I'm not sure," said Ilona. Then, "Late."

Ding.

And the elevator door opened and Ilona entered its small confines.

"Thanks again," said Stephanie.

"No, thank you," said Ilona.

"Merry Christmas," yelled Stephanie as the elevator door began to close.

"Merry Christmas," said Ilona.

Ding.

And Ilona was gone.

And directing their eyes upwards, Stephanie and filmmaker

Walker watched the elevator numbers, twenty-four, twenty-three, twenty-two, twenty-one, twenty, nineteen, which just sort of blinked and buzzed, eighteen, seventeen, sixteen, fifteen, fourteen, there was no thirteen, twelve, eleven, ten, nine, eight, seven never did light up, six, five, four, three, two, one.

Ding.

Dudley & Jerry Revisited

"Aren't you going to say anything?" Jerry asked anxiously. He was pacing. "How 'bout a drink? I've got some two-thousand-year-old bourbon I've been saving. It's got quite a bite."

But Dudley said nothing.

"Y'know, you're pushing me!" Jerry stammered. "Don't push me. I'll talk baseball. Honest I will. And I know how much you hate it when I talk baseball."

Dudley made not the slightest movement or sound.

"I'll talk pitching." Jerry said. "Fastballs, curveballs, backdoor sliders, the split-finger fastball. I'll drop names, talk for hours about the best players I've ever seen, Babe Ruth, Lou Gehrig, DiMaggio, Cy Young, Honus Wagner, Ty Cobb, Mantle, Maris, Aaron," he was yelling now, "Three fucking Finger Brown, even fucking Tinker, fucking Evers, and fucking Chance."

Jerry sighed.
Nothing.
Or so he thought.

What he hadn't noticed was the tear. The single tear that rolled down Dudley's face.

Jerry had never seen Dudley cry. He never wanted to. Because if Dudley could cry, it meant that so, too, could he. And Jerry never wanted to be able to cry. Jerry never wanted a reason to cry. Ever.

He figured, "Tears were in abundance."

And who among us would understand his?

PART THREE

29

A Single Scream

"God was pissed."
—Updated Psalm 7:11
The Next Testament

The tightest squeeze.

And though the safety, comfort, warmth, and friendship of her apartment seemed preferable, Ilona took one deep breath, another, then smiled. Smiled, because as the elevator descended, she thought about the Mets. Bobby Ojeda pitching a complete game shutout. Darryl Strawberry and Howard Johnson hitting that long ball out of the park. She couldn't wait for those hot summer days and muggy summer nights, eating peanuts and drinking beer, smiling at her favorite players as they walked back to the dugout right by those box seats. Stephanie by her side, laughing, flirting, relaxing.

At least the Mets made her smile.

But other matters pressed. The glory of God and all that.

Ding.

The elevator doors opened and Ilona stepped into the brightly decorated lobby of her apartment building. She thought of her Brother. "My God, why have you forsaken me?" And she laughed, like Father, like Son. Men. Gods. Ego.

And stepping out onto Charles Street, that cold late December breeze was back, its impact lessened only by the sun. How Ilona loved the warmth of the sun.

And turning a corner, south onto Washington Street, the Daughter of God bent to pick up what was left of a copy of Friday's *Daily News,* whose headline screamed, "Geisha Goddette," over a photo of Ilona standing with Prime Minister Takeshita, and tossed it into one of those small corner trash cans as her thoughts drifted back to the Mets. Yes, they made her smile. And she wouldn't let the team down this year, she promised. No more seventh-game wins for the Dodgers. In fact, after last year, hardly any wins for the Dodgers at all.

And halfway down the block Ilona heard someone call her name. A familiar masculine voice, though she couldn't immediately place it.

"Ilona," the voice said again.

And Ilona turned and faced the voice. "Ilona Ann Coggswater," it now said.

And she recognized the voice. That voice. John from Washington, D.C., she thought, saying nothing.

And John Charlton Hanley stepped up to the Daughter of God and smiled. She's so small and helpless, he thought to himself as he raised the .25 caliber Beretta automatic pistol that he held tightly in his right hand and aimed its barrel at her heart.

"Ilona Ann Coggswater," Hanley said again. "Meet your destiny."

And Ilona looked up and into Hanley's brown eyes, reaching into his soul, reaching into his heart, stunning him with that intense, wide-eyed, green-eyed gaze.

Hanley faltered and felt weak. He gasped, began to sweat, his right hand shaking slightly.

"Get it over with," Ilona said, her gaze locked on Hanley's now near squint. Her lack of fear frightened him.

And Hanley exhaled though his nose, his nostrils flaring. He closed his eyes, he had to. He squeezed the Beretta's "skeleton grip" hard, then harder. James Bond's gun felt good in his hand. So good. And wasn't *he* on a secret mission? A very special mission? His mind drifted to thoughts of the NRA and his right to bear arms. He thought of how this blond teenage girl had shown such utter disrespect for everything he loved, everything that mattered. He thought of how small and helpless Ilona looked at first and of the pleasure he usually, no, always, got out of killing the small and helpless.

And John Charlton Hanley pulled the trigger.

ↅↄ

Stephanie LaVasseur and filmmaker Edward Davis Walker were seated in the kitchen when they heard the thunder. Thunder so loud that it sent them running into the living room to see just what the hell was going on.

And together they watched as the sky through the windows that virtually surrounded them became fierce and dark, violent and noisy. Lightning, thunder, The wrath of God, ran through filmmaker Walker's mind. But he had no idea. "What the hell?" was all he said.

But Stephanie knew. "Ilona," she screamed, bolting for the elevator. And she watched and waited, patience lacking, as the elevator numbers, one by one, lit up in the other direction. One, two, three, four. What the fuck? Five, six, seven. Seven would not light up, it never did. Eight, nine.

"Walker," she screamed, looking for him. The sky was black now. Deadly black, she thought. "Walker," she screamed again, smashing a fist into the elevator door. Ten, eleven, twelve, thirteen, why wasn't there a thirteen? Fourteen. "C'mon, God damn you." Fifteen, sixteen, seventeen, eighteen, nineteen, which just sort of blinked and buzzed, twenty. "Walker." And he was by her side, holding her coat, trying to help her into it, already wearing his. "Fuck the coat," she said, knocking it out of his hands and to the floor, tears streaming down her face. Twenty-one, twenty-two. Stephanie pounded on the elevator door. Twenty-three, twenty-four.

Ding.

ↅↄ

"Whoosh," the bullet said.

Ilona heard it.

"Goosh," it then said, tearing into her flesh.

[231]

And Ilona heard a scream. A single scream. A pained scream. Her scream.

And John Charlton Hanley opened his eyes. But instead of feeling the triumph of his direct hit—if a hit could be more direct than point blank—Hanley felt ill. Seriously ill.

And as Ilona grew weak, faltered, and fell to the sidewalk, Hanley flung the Beretta that he still held in his right hand to the ground and ran, as fast as he could and in no certain direction other than away.

Oh, how he ran.

"Crash," the thunder said.

The whole world heard it.

❧

It was pouring by the time Stephanie and filmmaker Walker reached the lobby and ran out onto Charles Street.

Hard, deadly rain.

Pouring and hot.

Too hot for the cold late December afternoon it was supposed to be.

"The wrath of God," filmmaker Walker said, this time out loud.

And a lightning bolt crashed into that small trash can that rested on the corner of Charles and Washington, smashing it ablaze and apart.

And Stephanie ran toward what was left of that trash can, stopping when she reached the corner. Filmmaker Walker watched as she turned, raised a hand to her mouth, gasped, then disappeared around that corner.

He reached Ilona and Stephanie as a crowd, a circle of spectators, was beginning to form. A mumbling, frightened circle of spectators.

"What's happening?" someone asked.

"Isn't that Ilona?" asked someone else.

"Is she dead?" asked yet another.

Stephanie cradled her roommate's head on her lap. A pool of blood surrounded them, and like a mortal oil slick, it grew.

"It hurts . . . " Ilona said, looking into her roommate's face.

But Stephanie said nothing as she stroked the wet bangs from Ilona's face. She just cried.

"It really hurts."

And the rain and lightning and thunder and heat raged, making many in that circle of spectators scream, "It's the end of the world!" or something like that.

And Stephanie leaned forward, ignoring the circle, and kissed Ilona's forehead. And as she did, Stephanie did something that she had never done before. Ever. Stephanie prayed. Please. Don't take her away from us, she thought, hoping Dad, as Ilona had so often called him, would be listening. "Please."

But when Stephanie pulled away, those wide-eyed green eyes, Ilona's eyes, were closed.

30

Beeps and Pings

Ilona's eyes were still closed that evening when Mariam Coggswater entered the recovery room of the Saint Noah of the Divine Roman Catholic Hospital.

"I'm her mother," she said to any one of the many who were rushing around in such seeming chaos, to any one of the confused amidst the confusion.

"I'm Stephanie," said Ilona's roommate.

And Stephanie held out her hands and when Mariam touched them, Stephanie looked into the eyes of the Mother of Ilona, her swollen, tear-filled, and shocked blue eyes comforting, or seeking comfort from, Mariam's sad, green eyes, Ilona green.

You look so tired, they each thought.

"How is she?" said a salt-and-pepper-haired man standing behind Mariam.

"Oh, I'm sorry," said Mariam. Then "Stephanie, this is the Professor."

"I've heard a lot about you," Stephanie said.

The Professor nodded. "I had to come," he said.

Stephanie returned his nod.

"What's going on?" asked Mariam.

"That's her doctor," Stephanie said, pointing at one of the many. "He can explain it better than I can."

And Dr. Luther Brody, who introduced himself as being world renowned for his innovative reconstructive heart-surgery techniques, explained, more or less, to Mariam, the Professor, and once again to Stephanie, that Ilona was lucky, as lucky anyway as someone who had just gotten shot could be, that the bullet pierced this but missed that which would have been fatal. Though the this that was pierced was severely damaged, and, "She's lost a lot of blood."

"But will she be okay?"

And Dr. Brody swallowed hard and looked away from Mariam, Stephanie, and the Professor. He looked in the direction of the many who were rushing around the Daughter of God and he swallowed hard again.

"I don't know," said Dr. Brody softly as he turned back to face them. "She's slipped into a coma."

ℭℑ

And the rain continued, as did the lightning and thunder and heat. UnGodly heat for December. Eighty-two degrees that evening in New York City. That Christmas evening.

And it spread, the rain and lightning and thunder and heat, as it had been spreading since that first crack of thunder. West, south, north, east. Quick, violent, the wrath.

It was pushing ninety in Tom Brokaw's hometown of Denver as he exited a Christmas party to catch a plane to New York City to cover the assassination attempt, as it was being called.

It was in the high seventies in Minneapolis as the Replacements took the stage for a special hometown Christmas concert that Paul Westerberg dedicated to Ilona.

It was seventy-nine in Cooperstown, Ilona's hometown, as the residents of the village waited for a word, a sign, a sign other than the rain and lightning and thunder and heat.

In Montreal it was sixty-nine degrees. In Tucson, one hundred and one. In Atlanta, eighty-nine. Ninety-seven in Miami. In Mexico City, one hundred and eight. And it was raining.

Weathermen across the country screamed about record-breaking temperatures, thunderstorm warnings, and flash flooding. They were clueless, a low front here, a high front there. Who knew?

But, for whatever reason, wrath included, on this Christmas night unstoppable storms covered most of North America.

CRO

And soon a chorus of voices from the world's top reporters, reporters who had now set up camp in the lobby of Saint Noah's, could be heard.

"The Daughter of God," said one.

"Shot," said another.

"Gunman still at large," said yet another.

"Dr. Brody," said someone else.

"Lost blood," said another someone else.

"Coma," they all said, repeatedly.

"Handgun was recovered," said another.

"Many are holding vigil," said someone else.

"Reporting from Saint Noah of the Divine Roman Catholic Hospital," they all concluded.

CRO

The Saint Noah of the Divine Roman Catholic Hospital, located on Manhattan's Upper East Side, with a staff of just under eighteen hundred doctors, nurses, and others, is considered to be one of the top five hospitals in the world.

It's treated and cured some of the most famous people who have ever needed treatments and cures, including three American presidents, one Beatle, eleven New York City mayors, countless novelists, hundreds of actors and actresses, many cardinals, a few bishops, a dozen visiting foreign heads of state, plus handfuls of TV news anchors, rock stars, CEOs, and just plain millionaires. But Ilona was a first. The staff at Saint Noah had never treated a God.

CRO

"I should have gone with her."

Stephanie, Mariam, and the Professor now stood by Ilona's bedside. The rushing around had stopped and all seemed still except for the beeps and pings from the machines that were somehow connected to the Daughter of God.

"It's not your fault," Mariam said.

The Professor agreed, nodding only slightly.

Ilona seemed so peaceful, no screams, just dreams. A smile even seemed to have formed on her lips. Her blond hair was brushed back, perfectly and just so. But still those eyes, those marvelous green eyes, eyes that seemed to know the secrets of the universe, which they did, eyes that could hypnotize, startle, and blind, eyes that could soothe, seduce, and see, see all, see everything, everything that ever was and everything that ever will be, eyes that were the world's only hope, remained closed.

"Do you think she'll be okay? I mean, really okay?"

And a nurse, some nurse, told Stephanie, Mariam, and the Professor that they'd have to leave, that Ilona needed rest and that they, too, looked as if they needed a good night's sleep.

"I was just about to ask you that."

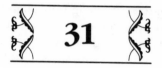

31

Hell

And Ilona dreamed.

She dreamed of when she was a little girl living in Heaven and of a field trip of sorts to Hell with her Brother, her Father, and Marilyn Monroe. Her Father would bring the actress just about anywhere and everywhere. Even God had a thing for Marilyn Monroe.

Hell was like an amusement park, a gigantic underground theme park of sorts, Satan Land, filled with people, from all walks of life, all points in time, people.

And it was hot. "Hotter than Phoenix, Arizona," Ilona heard Marilyn Monroe say.

And, as in all amusement parks, there were rides. And as Ilona and Jesus and God and Marilyn Monroe boarded the first car of a very threatening roller coaster, Ilona noticed that the man at the controls looked very much like Adolf Hitler.

"He looks just like him," Marilyn Monroe agreed.

And God explained that the Devil, or "Jerry," as God called him, awarded the cruelest people in history with one of these hellish rides, and that Hitler, or "Junior," as God called him, had free reign here in Hell. And Jesus laughed, and Marilyn Monroe oohed, and Ilona just held on, because this was one incredibly frightening roller coaster ride.

And God nodded toward the House of Horror and said, "That's Jack the Ripper selling tickets."

And as they walked past the Ferris wheel, God said, "And there's Billy the Kid."

And he continued, "That's Caligula. Attila the Hun's over there. Ed Gein is running the hot dog stand. The guy in the cape's Vlad the Impaler. That guy next to him in the three-piece suit, Al Capone."

And God waved at some robust man eating a chicken leg and working a merry-go-round and said, "Hi, Henry," and turning to Ilona, Jesus, and Marilyn Monroe, explained, "the Eighth."

And Ilona asked for some Kool-Aid as they passed a stand advertising just that.

"I don't think you want his Kool-Aid," God said.

"Why not?" said Ilona, shooting that intense, wide-eyed, green-eyed gaze at the man behind the Kool-Aid dispenser.

"That's the Reverend Jim Jones," her Father explained.

"Oh," said Ilona.

Who? thought Marilyn Monroe.

And Jesus pointed and laughed and said, "Hey, isn't that Senator Joseph McCarthy getting pies thrown in his face?"

And God said, "Yes," explained that even the Devil, or "Jerry," as God called him, had a sense of humor. Then he scolded Jesus for pointing, "How many times do I have to tell you it's not polite?"

And Ilona asked about a building that they were quickly approaching, a building without windows and with only one entrance, a door flanked by two armed guards.

"That's Jerry's museum," explained God. "In it you'll find dozens of paintings of Jerry by the greatest artists who ever lived. Let's see, there's a Degas, one by Poussin, a Titian, a Caravaggio, even a Warhol, some I can't even remember, some I don't want to. Oh, and there's a series of three small Rembrandt oils, one depicting Jerry seducing a virgin, one showing him driving a spear into my chest—he loves that one—and the last is a portrait of him impeccably dressed in a deep red suit. Even I have to admit, those Rembrandts are something else."

"But how did those artists know what Jerry, er, the Devil, looked like?" asked Marilyn Monroe.

"They didn't," said God. "But Jerry didn't care, as long as they

[239]

had good titles. You know, the Devil kills this, Satan tempts that."

And God and Ilona and Jesus and Marilyn Monroe turned a corner and walked toward a dilapidated trailer and God knocked on the dilapidated door marked OFFICE and from inside they heard, "Go away."

And God shouted, "Jerry, it's me. Open up."

And the Devil opened the door of that trailer and peered out, squinting, trying to focus his eyes on God.

"Who are you?"

"Jerry, put your glasses on," said God.

And fumbling in one of his pockets he pulled out some round wire-rimmed spectacles and fit them to his face.

"Dudley," exclaimed the Devil, his eyes lighting up with recognition. "How the hell are you?"

"Not bad. Not bad at all," said God. Adding, "Good to see you."

"Good to see you, too," said the Devil.

And Jesus looked at Ilona, who was at that moment mouthing the name "Dudley," and they both suppressed a giggle.

"Those headaches still bothering you?" asked the Devil.

"Of course," said God.

God had headaches. Bad headaches. Big headaches. And for these headaches he was always popping headache pills.

"Some things never change," said the Devil.

"Unfortunately not," said God, popping a few of those self-same pills.

"So, who do we have here?" asked the Devil.

And God introduced Ilona and Jesus and Marilyn Monroe, and the Devil winked at Ilona and shook the hand of Jesus, saying, "Sorry about the cross, kid. My people just sort of got carried away. No hard feelings, huh?"

"It's a brand-new ballgame," said Jesus.

And God rolled his eyes and thought, "Why me?"

"A baseball fan?"

"You better believe it."

"The Dodgers, right?" asked the Devil.

"How did you know?" said Jesus.

"I just knew."

"And you?"

"A Yankees fan," said the Devil.

"That explains it."

"Enough already," said God. "Baseball, always baseball."

And the Devil laughed. "Good boy you got there, Dudley," he said.

"Don't encourage him," said God.

And then the Devil noticed and just sort of stared at Marilyn Monroe.

"Pleased to meet you, Mr. Devil, sir," she said.

And the Devil whispered to God, "If only I were a few years younger."

And God, winking at Marilyn Monroe, whispered back, "C'mon, Jerry, we're ageless, remember?"

And the Devil gave God, Ilona, Jesus, and Marilyn Monroe a tour of Hell.

And while they walked and talked, Ilona couldn't help but notice how much Jerry looked like W. C. Fields. That red bulbous nose, the deep depressed eyes, the sand-and-gravel voice, the tired sarcastic manner, the shuffle.

"Attendance is way down from last season," she heard Jerry say. "I've started closing up early on Monday and Tuesday nights."

"But the weekends are still good?" she heard her Father ask.

"The weekends'll always be good."

To Ilona it seemed that Jerry had given up hope. That he just went along with the show for the hell of it. And this made her sad, because Jerry, after all, was the Devil, and without the Devil her Father would have little or nothing to do and basically be forced into early retirement. And God was too young to retire.

Dudley and Jerry continued to talk and started to reminisce and before no time at all were standing together at one of the many bars disguised as concession stands taking some on-the-house beers from Genghis Khan. "I really shouldn't," Dudley said, downing his first beer, telling Ilona, Jesus, and Marilyn to amuse themselves elsewhere.

And soon a circle of spectators had formed around God and the Devil, or "Dudley" and "Jerry" as they called each other, who to everyone's amusement were having lightning duels. A blast here from God's hand striking just at Senator McCarthy's feet, a blast there from the Devil's lighting up the sky behind the already ominous Ferris wheel. On and on and so forth.

"Wow!" said Marilyn Monroe, impressed at first.

"I wanna play, too!" exclaimed Jesus, who ran to join his Father and the Devil.

And Ilona and Marilyn Monroe stood and watched as God and the Devil and Jesus Christ downed one beer after another, lightning everywhere, laughing, as their performance, their show, their lightning and thunder, raged on over Hell.

"Men," Marilyn Monroe said to Ilona.

"Gods," Ilona said back.

"Devils," continued Marilyn Monroe.

"Ego," concluded Ilona.

A nod.

"Yup."

Ginger Ale and Vomit

"It's still raining," said Tom Brokaw, beginning his report on the front steps of Saint Noah. "And some thirty-two hours after an unknown gunman's bullet pierced her aorta, Ilona Ann Coggswater, the Daughter of God, lies in a coma, here in Manhattan's Saint Noah of the Divine Roman Catholic Hospital."

And Brokaw explained how the rain and lightning and thunder and heat had continued to spread, over the Pacific and Atlantic oceans to Europe and Asia, to South America and Africa.

"The wrath of God," he said. Everyone said. "Has man gone too far this time?"

ↁ

And John Charlton Hanley swore at Tom Brokaw, switched off the television in his cheap motel room, and threw up. He had been ill, seriously ill, violently ill, since pulling the trigger.

"The wrath of God," he said, not knowing why.

Hanley was in hiding. Not that anyone yet had the slightest clue that it was he who shot Ilona. But he was in hiding nonetheless, driving west, and taking a break in Odessa, a small town just outside of Kansas City, Missouri.

"It's too fucking hot," he said, throwing up and punching the room's air conditioner, which refused to work, injuring his hand, not the air conditioner.

"Too fucking hot."

In her book, *One Night with Hanley,* Lisa Martin, a cocktail waitress at the Sit 'n' Bull Café in Odessa, would write, "Hanley came in, immediately ran to the men's room, and threw up. But he wasn't drunk or anything like that. I brought him some ginger ale and asked if he was okay. He said that he was as good as someone who had just shot the Daughter of God could be. 'I shot her,' he said, over and over. 'I shot her. I shot her.' I told him that I believed his story and went to get him another ginger ale. But when I returned to the table he was gone, in the men's room again, throwing up."

And after hundreds of pages filled with details about Hanley's three hours of ginger ale and vomit at the Sit 'n' Bull Café, Martin would write, "I ended up spending the night with Hanley. I figured, if this guy really did shoot Ilona, I'd at least be able to say I slept with him, or something like that. But we never had sex. He couldn't get it up. All he could do was throw up. And that he did all night. It was pretty pathetic.

"The next morning I tipped off the cops. My boyfriend at the time was Deputy Sheriff Randy Bitters. And at first Randy didn't believe me. He was really pissed because I never came home the night before. But when I got it through to him that I was following the guy who shot Ilona, well, he was a bit more understanding. He started talking about how if he could catch this guy he'd be famous and get a promotion and probably, eventually get to be governor. I just remember thinking to myself, 'How do I get mixed up with these assholes?' "

❧

Hanley wasn't the only person who had been ill, seriously ill, violently ill, since the shooting. All across America people were throwing up, uncontrollably and for no apparent reason.

Bob in Jackson, Tennessee; Betty in Winston, Oregon; Jack in Madawaska, Maine; Pete in Laredo, Texas; Billy in Waycross, Georgia; and hundreds of thousands of others, were all spewing up vomit by the gallons.

And only one detail, besides vomit, linked these hundreds of thousands to Hanley. But one detail can be enough, especially in the eyes of an angry Dad. An angry Dad out to make life as uncomfortable as possible for each and every one of those hundreds of thousands of card-carrying members of the National Rifle Association.

❧

The Professor returned to Cooperstown, and to his Cheapskate Record Shop, leaving his best wishes and thoughts—"She'll be okay. I know she will."—with Stephanie and Mariam, who waited, helpless but never hopeless.

They sat by Ilona's side, speaking to her, holding her hand, wanting only a blink, a squeeze, some sign.

They read the cards that came with the flowers.

Lots of flowers.

Huge bouquets, dozens of roses, single carnations, a handful of daisies.

Three private Saint Noah rooms full of the flowers that continued to pour in from around the world.

"Hope you're feeling better real soon," wrote Paul, Tommy, Chris, and Slim, the Replacements.

"The world suffers with you. God bless," wrote Pope John Paul II.

"I don't know what to say. Just get well. We need you," wrote David Letterman and the staff from "Late Night."

"We must work together to put an end to needless violence such as this. God is on your side. Be well," wrote President-elect George Bush.

"Angels can't die," wrote Flatcake Al, Tiny, Joe, Billie, Lil' Jill, Jerome, and Indian Jack.

❧

And on the morning of December 28, on a tipoff from Lisa Martin's deputy sheriff boyfriend, members of the FBI and Washington, D.C., police broke into John Charlton Hanley's Washington, D.C., penthouse. They examined the racks of rifles and handguns, dusted here and there, moved this, lifted that, but really had to look no farther than under the rolltop of an old rolltop desk in a small office located off Hanley's bedroom.

[245]

Under that rolltop they found clippings and magazines and photos and phone numbers, all in one way or another having to do with the Daughter of God.

☙

And on that same morning, Stephanie said to Mariam, "Please come with me. There's something I'd like to show you."

And together they walked east from that "charming" penthouse on Charles Street, through the rain and lightning and thunder and heat, east to Alphabet City, east to the Soup Kitchen.

And Stephanie introduced Mariam to Flatcake Al, Tiny, and the other Soup Kitchen regulars.

"You must be mighty proud," said Tiny.

"I am," said Mariam. "I am." And tears formed in her eyes.

And Flatcake Al brought over a chair and helped Mariam sit down.

"Miss Ilona'll be okay," he said. "Angels don't die."

And Mariam put her arms around Flatcake Al and cried on his shoulders.

"Cry," he said softly. "Go ahead. These shoulders are used to tears."

☙

And the rain and lightning and thunder and heat continued. Everywhere.

Especially, or so it seemed to him, everywhere John Charlton Hanley happened to be.

Westward he continued, slow and uncertain.

He was at a diner in Boulder, Colorado, and had returned from throwing up in the bathroom when he first heard his name on television. "Police and the FBI are looking for," said a voice from a small black-and-white Zenith mounted over the cold cereal display. "All points bulletin," the voice continued.

And Hanley looked around but was not calmed by the lack of customers in the diner.

"If you have any information," the voice said.

[246]

"Fuck you," Hanley whispered as his photograph flashed on the black-and-white screen. And he would have said, "Fuck you," a second time had he not been busy throwing up on the diner floor.

"A ten-million-dollar reward," the voice added.

But Hanley was gone.

Westward.

❧

And as 1988 was about to turn into 1989, the world had little to celebrate. The "Savior of the Year" was in a coma. The man who shot her was still on the loose. And all that rain and lightning and thunder and heat was taking its toll.

Rivers were flooding, mud was sliding, trees were falling, and fundamentalist preachers were running at the mouth.

"An ark. We must build an ark," screamed the Reverend Donald Wildmon on some TV talk show or other.

"See the problems She has caused," said some other Reverend.

"She's destroying the world, not saving it," said yet another.

"The end has come," proclaimed them all.

And the kingpin of reverends, Reverend Head Honcho, the Reverend Jerry Falwell, head of the Moral Majority, summed it up, "God should have known a woman would screw up a job of this magnitude."

They didn't know.

They just claimed to.

❧

And Stephanie spent that New Year's Eve with Mariam and filmmaker Walker in that "charming" penthouse, though "charming" would have hardly been what Stephanie would have used to describe the apartment at that time. "Depressing," maybe. "Empty," for sure. "Lonely," yeah, lonely.

And Ilona's friend, her best friend, leaned against the base of the sofa and stared out into the Manhattan night cradling one of those "ice-cold Rolling Rocks" in her hands. She had been cry-

[247]

ing. Again. As had Mariam. Filmmaker Walker hadn't cried. He didn't know what to do.

"She never judged me," Stephanie said, breaking an old silence, one littered only with the opening of beer bottles, the sounds of ice cubes clinking, and the ever faithful glug of liquor flowing from a bottle.

"Never."

ᘓᘔ

Hanley spent New Year's Eve in his car at a rest stop not far from Green River, Utah.

He hadn't thrown up since leaving that Boulder, Colorado, diner. And this he saw as a good sign.

"I'm so sick of fucking throwing up," he said out loud. "So sick of it."

And Hanley closed his eyes and felt that he might finally get a good night's sleep. How he needed a good night's sleep.

"Ahh . . ." he said, relaxed at last.

"Ahh . . ." he said again, but this "Ahh . . ." was different.

"Ahh . . ." one more time. Then, "Shit!"

And John Charlton Hanley threw up.

ᘓᘔ

And in Ilona's "private" room at the Saint Noah of the Divine Roman Catholic Hospital, those wide-eyed green eyes remained closed. And again, the Daughter of God dreamed. This time of watching the seventh game of the World Series, the New York Mets versus the California Angels, and the pitcher for the Mets, a face that was blurred and not at all familiar, at least not in a New York Mets uniform, pitched a no-hitter.

And all was so quiet, except for the cheering in Ilona's mind. Very quiet, except for the beeps and pings from the machines that were somehow connected to the Daughter of God.

"Beep," one said for the seven thousand, four hundred, sixty-third time.

"Ping," another said, trying to keep up but making it only an even three thousandth time.

[248]

"Dee-deet," said some other machine, surprising even the Beeper and Pinger.

"Beep."

"Ping."

"Dee-deet."

Happy New Year.

Deaf

January 4, the first Sonya Wednesday of the new year.

Burt Uogintas didn't want to be there. He didn't at this point want to be anywhere. He just knew he had to start somewhere, and "Sonya Live" was as good a place as any.

As the president of the National Rifle Association, Uogintas had been answering a few too many questions since the shooting of Ilona Ann Coggswater, and even more since Hanley's identity had been made public.

"We condemn Hanley's act as vicious and unnecessary." Uogintas had said this so often he was beginning to believe it.

He thought of last summer's peace and quiet and comfort in his new Santa Barbara mansion. Drinking scotch, doing this blond bimbo or that, then some target practice of an altogether different sort on his personal and "private" shooting range. How he longed for last summer. "B. I.," he laughed, not wanting to. "Everything was fine. Everything was grand. Everything. Before Ilona."

"Murderer," screamed Cindy from Hutchinson, Kansas, through irate tears.

The believers were crying.

"I didn't pull the trigger," said Uogintas.

"You might as well have," said Cindy from Hutchinson, Kansas.

"I'm beginning to think you're right," said Uogintas.

☙

Bert Uogintas was a handsome, rich playboy in his late thirties who inherited his fortune and good looks from his father, Seymour, an old-time oil tycoon who died of natural causes in 1981.

And from Seymour he also inherited his love of guns.

"I learned how to shoot before I learned how to walk," he would often brag. It was barely an exaggeration.

And having little or no direction in his life other than up, in and out, and too much free time on his hands, Bert, said, "It'll be fun!," and bought himself the presidency of the NRA in 1985.

It was at this point that Bert first met John Charlton Hanley, whom he viewed as a strong-willed man, a good American, a believer in the Second Amendment, and someone you'd never want to deliberately piss off.

Bert, too, believed in the Second Amendment, he believed in the NRA, he believed in Hanley. And he couldn't wait till this Daughter of God mess passed.

$$\mathcal{C}\mathcal{D}$$

Bert Uogintas also couldn't wait to get home. Speeding up Highway 101 in his red BMW 535i, as fast as he could possibly go in the still pouring rain, he thought of Heather, the previous evening's blond bimbo. He thought of how he had had her outside, in the rain, on his rain-soaked deck, again on the floor of his living room, and again as she was tied, spread eagle and naked, oh, so very naked, on his king-size bed. Oh, Heather. Uogintas hoped she would be waiting for him.

"I shouldn't have untied her," he found himself thinking. Smiling. Laughing.

But as he entered that Santa Barbara mansion it wasn't Heather he found waiting lustfully, playfully, in his living room, but John Charlton Hanley, pathetically, nauseatingly.

The room smelled of vomit, Uogintas thought. It was a smell he had become accustomed to. Almost. It seemed that everyone he knew had been spewing for days. All of his employees and associates, most of his friends. And only he remained healthy.

Only he could keep down his breakfast. It was a curiosity he couldn't explain. One he preferred not to think about.

"John, what the hell are you doing here?" he asked.

"Throwing up," said Hanley.

"Do you have any idea what you've done?" asked Uogintas.

"I shot the Daughter of God," Hanley said, adding, "and have been throwing up since."

And Uogintas walked to his bar and poured what he felt was a much needed shot of scotch. Then another.

"Want some?" he asked, regretting it.

Hanley threw up.

"Guess not," said Uogintas.

And taking a seat as far from the stinking Hanley as possible, the NRA president asked, "Why?"

"Why the fuck do you think?"

"You didn't have to shoot her. We have more lobbying power than any other force in Washington. No one is going to take our guns away."

"More lobbying power than God?"

"More lobbying power than anyone."

"Bullshit. I did what I had to do."

"It was the only course of action?"

"Exactly."

"Bullshit."

And Hanley threw up again.

"Let me get you a bucket," said Uogintas.

"Don't bother," said Hanley.

❧

Uogintas's Santa Barbara mansion was built on a cliff overlooking the Pacific Ocean.

"A million-dollar view," the real-estate agent, Samuel Gold of Rothburg Reality, had told him, adding, "It's so charming and private." And Uogintas agreed.

Three hundred feet up. No obstructions. Just ocean and sun. A "private" ocean and a "private" sun. Very "charming" indeed.

But as Uogintas searched for a bucket suitable for Hanley's

vomit a strange thing was happening to the foundation of the mansion. It seemed that the now ten straight days of rain had eroded the ground into which the foundation was laid.

The slippage was mild at first. Uogintas hardly noticed it as he bent into a cupboard.

"Want some ginger ale?" he yelled to Hanley.

Nothing.

"How about some tomato juice?"

And as Hanley finally vomited his answer, the mansion began to shake. Really shake.

"An earthquake!" Uogintas screamed. The bucket could wait.

And Hanley vomited some more. He would have been so happy if only he could have stopped throwing up.

And the Santa Barbara mansion shook violently. Parts of the ceiling began to fall, windows cracked, dishes smashed, guns fell from their racks.

"Run for your life!" yelled Uogintas.

"What life?" said Hanley, not joking, just vomiting.

And in his run for life, Uogintas managed to grab an original Rodin sculpture of a beautiful nude female reaching one hand upward, a hand whose fingertips were touching those of a large male hand, the hand of God. A Rodin sculpture titled *Creation of Eve* that Uogintas had so recently purchased from a French collector. And, Rodin sculpture in hand, the president of the National Rifle Association leaped to one of the mansion's many doorjambs. But before he could leap again, this time to whatever safety the outside might have held, the mansion, the entire mansion, began its voyage over the cliff, and plunged three hundred feet down into the Pacific Ocean.

Uogintas held on to what was left of the door frame and screamed. Hanley rolled on the floor in his vomit, spewing up more. And the Santa Barbara mansion crashed into the Pacific, breaking apart, instantly killing both of its inhabitants, instantly and finally putting an end to Hanley's vomiting.

And the rain and lightning and thunder and heat continued. Especially the thunder.

A round of applause from God.

CᴓƆ

And as the fish that inhabited the Pacific Ocean, just under where the Uogintas mansion once so majestically stood, began to nibble away at what was left of Hanley's well-crushed body, nibble, bite, nibble, nibble, they, too, began to throw up.

Dumb

And the rain and lightning and thunder and heat continued. Everywhere.

Everywhere, that is, except for the small Caribbean island of Celeste.

Because on this tenth stormy day the sky cleared and the rains stopped and the sun shone on Celeste.

Located about 350 miles due west of St. Lucia, just north of the Lesser Antilles, Celeste was generally regarded as one of the most beautiful islands in the world. Only four miles long, and three-quarters of a mile wide at its widest point, it was a vacationer's dream come true, with sandy white beaches, the bluest and cleanest of oceans, and an average daily temperature of eighty-three degrees. Celeste was natural, relatively undeveloped, and oh, so quiet.

Very quiet.

Until a group of fundamentalist preachers determined it would be the perfect location for a theme park.

And using tax-free millions from the Social Security checks of the vulnerable and scared, these preachers bought Celeste and turned the tropical paradise into "Jesus Land."

Opened in May 1987, Jesus Land was a veritable world of fundamentalist teachings trapped in the body of an amusement park. The Golgotha 500, a race where barefoot contestants dragged huge wooden crosses down a cobblestone raceway, the Bible Hall of Fame, where that book's greatest heroes came seemingly to life, and a booth where one could be pelted by Styrofoam rocks were among the more than seventy-five rides and attractions. Employees walked around the park portraying major biblical figures. The concession stands offered Adam's Barbecued Baby Back Ribs, Eucharist Burgers, and Blood of Christ Punch, all served up by workers dressed as slaves had dressed in biblical times. There was even a twenty-four-hour church service held in a nine-thousand seat chapel, complete with retractable roof and state-of-the-art sound system.

But the centerpiece and main attraction of Jesus Land, a centerpiece and main attraction that made even nonfundamentalists and non-born-agains consider visiting the island, was a series of three small paintings by the Dutch painter Rembrandt, the first of Mary holding the baby Jesus, the second of Jesus being crucified, and the last depicting his resurrection. These three priceless oils dated back to the mid-seventeenth century and were contained in their own personal and indestructible Jesus Land museum, a small windowless building complete with two round-the-clock armed guards.

In *Time* magazine's "Savior of the Year" issue, Ilona was quoted as saying, "Jesus Land is the closest many of us will ever get to Hell."

∾

But when on this tenth day the skies cleared over Celeste, the fundamentalists knew that to be their sign. Praise the Lord. Praise Jesus. They were right. They had to be. They knew it all along.

And that weekend, the first full weekend of the new year, thousands of born-again and fundamentalist Christians and every one of their beloved preachers and leaders flocked to Celeste to bask in the sunlight, swim in the ocean, and, of course, pray.

Everyone.

Reverend Jerry Falwell, Oral Roberts, Jimmy Swaggart, Jim and Tammy Bakker, Bill Martelli, Reverend Donald Wildmon, Reverend Patrick West, and even Randall Terry along with all those who headed the right-to-life and Operation Rescue movements.

Fundamentalists for this, fundamentalists against that, born-agains for something else and against everything.

And how they preached and talked and claimed that they were the world's only salvation. They knew the answer. They were the answer.

"It's all in our hands now," they screamed.

No more sex, no more abortions, no more R- and X-rated movies, an end to pornography and teen pregnancies, or so they claimed. No more birth control, no more beer, no more *Catcher in the Rye,* the end of rock 'n' roll and teen suicide, or so they claimed. No more soap operas on television, no more annual *Sports Illustrated* swimsuit issues, no more thong-back bikinis, an end to *Playboy* and *Penthouse* along with rape and child abuse, or so they claimed. No more gay and lesbian rights, no more baseball players patting each other's butts, no more women with really short hair, an end to homosexuality and thus an end to AIDS, or so they claimed.

No more God-damn First Amendment.

No more God-damn civil rights.

Just morality, their morality. And lots of it.

"Hallelujah," they all said.

"Amen."

ॐ

And on Saturday, January 14, the twentieth day of rain and lightning and thunder and heat elsewhere, the tenth day of sun and cool sea breezes on Celeste, the tenth day of preaching an end to all that was fun, the tenth day the rest of the world, those not on Celeste, marveled and questioned the beautiful weather found on this small island, found on this small island and no where else, Mark Orsini, sitting in his monitoring station at the National Weather Service, noticed some extremely violent weather activity only a hundred miles or so due east of Celeste.

Extremely violent.

Orsini contacted the small island immediately and, after being put on hold for close to eleven minutes, eleven minutes during which the violent activity moved to within forty miles of the small island, finally got to speak with a Reverend Johnny Bower, head of CLAP ("Christians Leaders Against *Playboy*"), who told Orsini that there was nothing to worry about, that God was on their side and so was the weather.

"We're in the middle of a pray-in," said Bower. "Thousands of Christians holding hands, praying, crying. It's beautiful. We can't stop it now."

"I don't think you understand," explained Orsini, or so he tried to. "The entire planet is awash in violent storms and yet the activity heading your way is sending our computers into a frenzy."

And as Reverend Bower tried to enlighten Orsini to the fact that computers could not possibly begin to understand the way of the Lord, a tidal wave four hundred feet high and seven miles long swept over Celeste destroying Jesus Land and everything and everyone that went with it.

"God is on our," was the last thing Orsini heard Reverend Bower say before the phone line went dead and that extremely violent activity disappeared altogether from this world weather map.

And the rain and lightning and thunder and heat continued. Especially the thunder. Especially on the spot that once was Celeste.

Another round of applause from God.

❧

Hallelujah.
Amen.

35

And Blind

And though the rain and lightning and thunder and heat continued, on Tuesday, January 24, thousands would converge for the ground-breaking ceremonies for the building of that Japanese-backed highway that would link Brazil's western state of Acre to Peru.

It was always hot in Brazil and rainfall was plentiful, so the weather wasn't considered that bad.

And so Brazilian President José Sarney and Japanese Prime Minister Noboru Takeshita along with countless other Brazilian and Japanese politicians, the Brazilian and Japanese, not to mention world, press, and filmmaker Edward Davis Walker, who had finally elected to make a documentary, his documentary, on the building of this Japanese-backed highway and the environmental destruction its construction would cause, stood under huge waterproof canopies and watched as the bulldozers and tractors and cement mixers were moved into place along with thousands of Brazilian workers and hundreds of Japanese engineers.

"What a sight," thought filmmaker Walker, untouched rain forest to one side, scorched wasteland to the other.

"Working together," promised Sarney.

"Paving the way for the future," explained Takeshita.

A round of applause from the countless other Brazilian and Japanese politicians, the workers and engineers.

Another roll of film for filmmaker Walker's movie camera.

"Strengthening our economies," said Takeshita.

"Progress," said Sarney, smiling.

No one there, no one on the planet for that matter, would have expected an earthquake. The last recorded Brazilian earthquake was at the turn of the century and that was in the extreme southeastern portion of the country. This section of Brazil, to the best of everyone's knowledge, had never experienced an earthquake, not even tremors.

But the ground began to shake and the canopies fell and the two world leaders, along with the countless other politicians and reporters and those thousands of workers and hundreds of engineers, ran for their lives.

And filmmaker Walker filmed. He filmed the shaking, the falling, the running. He filmed the ground splitting open at the spot where Sarney and Takeshita had so recently stood before running for their lives. He filmed the split that began there and grew, swallowing up the fallen canopies, the bulldozers, the tractors and cement mixers. He filmed and filmed as it grew and grew and split and split—devouring in its wake the scorched wasteland, harming not one square inch of the untouched rain forest—until a canyon had formed. A sprawling canyon, an amazing canyon, a work of divine art from what was once a testament to humankind's indifference, that when finally measured would measure two thousand, one hundred thirteen miles in length, a mile and a half wide at its widest point and three-quarters of a mile deep at its deepest point.

"Wow!" said filmmaker Walker, movie camera in hand, as he stood at the edge of this canyon, a canyon so naturally beautiful in its rock formations and patterns that nothing could be done by the Brazilian government and President Sarney other than to declare the entire area a national parkland and altogether trash the idea of the Japanese-backed highway that would link Brazil's western state of Acre to Peru.

"Wow!"

What else could anyone say?

And when faced with his own death even Prime Minister Takeshita agreed that the highway probably wasn't a very good idea after all and promised that he and his family would visit this magnificent new parkland on an upcoming vacation.

And the rain and lightning and thunder and heat continued. Especially the thunder and the rain. Rain that cleansed the newly formed canyon, making many of these rock formations and patterns sparkle and shine.

Another round of applause from God.

ᏭᎧ

He was proud of this one.

36

Crash, Gurgle, Splash, Crack, Bang, Boom

The headlines:

"GOD GETS EVEN" —New York *Daily News*

"BOFFO B.O. BIZ! LET IT RAIN, MAN!" —*Variety*

"UMBRELLA STOCKS SOAR" —*Wall Street Journal*

And the rain and thunder and lightning and heat continued. Continued until the morning of Friday, February 3, 1989, exactly forty days to the hour since John Charlton Hanley shot Ilona Ann Coggswater. On this morning, on that hour, as the rain and all that accompanied it stopped, Ilona, the Daughter of God, would open those green eyes and emerge from her coma, a resurrection of sorts, finally.

And while the sky cleared, and the sun broke through—how everyone had missed the warmth of the sun—a Man dressed as a doctor, not Luther Brody, another doctor, a tall, good-looking Man of about forty, though at times this Man seemed ageless, almost timeless, with a rugged face and large hands and a masculine smell, wearing a spotless white smock over a handsome handmade Italian suit and a big gold Rolex on his left wrist, stood at the foot of Ilona's hospital bed.

That cologne, Ilona thought, but all she said was, "Dad."

And God, who, when last here on Earth in 1973, had taken the name Dr. William Smith to be with Mariam, a young woman he was admittedly in love with, and to spend some quality Earth time with his only Daughter, smiled as he popped a headache pill and asked, "How ya doin'?"

"Okay," Ilona said. "Now." She was so happy to see her Dad. So eternally happy.

And God sat on the edge of her hospital bed and picked up a get-well card that stood on the little table to the side of that bed.

"Stephanie?" God asked.

"My roommate."

And he nodded a slight all-knowing nod, then began to explain. He explained all that had been happening since the shooting, sound effects, exaggerations, though none were necessary, and all. Loud, "Crash, gurgle, gurgle, gurgle." Louder, "Splash, crack, bang." Louder still, "Boom." And he beamed, "See what a little rain can do."

"Wash away the fears."

"And the confusion and lies."

And God looked at his Daughter, his beautiful Daughter, and God began to cry. He cried because, as he looked at Ilona, a thought crossed his mind, a thought that had crossed it so very many times in the past, a simple, comforting thought, a thought that usually made him smile rather than cry, that above everything else and despite her love for the game, Ilona never spoke of baseball in his presence. How he loved her for that, that small and simplest of miracles, respect. How he loved her, period. And how he cried.

"Dad," Ilona said, She had never seen her Father cry.

"I'm sorry," God said. "I'm so eternally sorry."

"Hey," Ilona said softly, touching his face, "it's okay." Then, "I'm fine."

"Are you?"

"Yup."

"Yup?"

"Yup."

"I can't ever begin to tell you how much I missed hearing you say that."

And Ilona smiled. "Try," she said, wiping the tears from his face.

[263]

Just then there was a knock on the door to Ilona's "private" room. It opened, and a familiar voice said, "Mind if I come in?"

"Professor?" Ilona said.

And he entered, walking nervously to her bed.

"How ya feelin' kid?" the professor asked.

"A lot better," she said.

And God cleared his throat.

"Professor," Ilona said, "I'd like you to meet my Father." Then, "Dad, this is the Professor."

"Yeah," God said, extending his hand, "I know."

And after the handshake and pleased-to-meet-yous, Ilona asked, "How did you know I'd be awake?"

"It's been forty days," the Professor said, shooting a caustic glance in God's direction. "Just figured God would be consistent," then, "I guess."

And after a moment of small talk, mainly about the new Replacements album, *Don't Tell a Soul,* due out the following week, of which he had brought her a preview copy, the Professor said, "Well, I gotta be going," kissed Ilona on the forehead. Whispered, "It's really great to have you back." Then, shaking God's hand, said, "Nice to meet you," and left.

"He's a great guy," Ilona said.

God nodded.

"So, tell me," Ilona said, "what's next?"

"That depends on you," God said, still sniffling. And he, too, smiled, then laughed slightly, and looking into his Daughter's eyes said, "Feeling up to leaving this dump?"

"After all that rest, I'm ready for just about anything."

"You sure?"

And Ilona nodded. "I'm sure."

That intense, wide-eyed, green-eyed gaze was back.

"In that case," God said, "it's time to really kick some butt."

A *Brief Interlude with Dudley & Jerry*

"There's that damn glint."

"Do I look okay?" asked Dudley.

"You're acting like a schoolboy," Jerry said. Then, "You look fine." A smile, "Just straighten your tie."

"It's been a long time."

"I know it has."

"Do you think she'll be glad to see me?" Dudley asked. Then, "I mean, last time I did just sort of disappear."

"I'm sure she'll understand. That she'll take into consideration who you are."

"I don't look that much older, do I?"

"You've looked the same for as long as I've known you, for Christ's sake. Just relax."

"Okay, okay, I'm fine," Dudley said. "What about these shoes? Should I wear different shoes?"

"She isn't gonna give a damn about your shoes."

"You sure?"

"Yes. Well, no. Not totally. You know women."

"What if she's pissed about Ilona?"

"She won't blame you," Dudley said. Then, "But she might think you could have prevented it."

"Think so?"

A shrug, then, "Women are funny that way. I mean, it is her only Daughter too, y'know."

A sigh. "I need a drink."

"You don't need a drink."

"I need something."

"You know what you need."

"Yeah." A sigh.

"See what love'll do to you?"

Another sigh.

Some laughter.

Some more.

A pat on the back. "Everything'll be fine."

PART FOUR

37

Etc., Etc., and So On

> Ilona answered and said unto him, for unless one is truthful and kind, he or she cannot see the kingdom of God.
>
> —Updated John 3:3
> *The Next Testament*

No squeeze at all.

And anything was preferable.

Ilona Ann Coggswater left the Saint Noah of the Divine Roman Catholic Hospital on February 6, and in the days and weeks and months that followed, the Daughter of God would meet with each and every world leader, world leaders who now seemed more interested in what she had to say than in how she looked by their sides.

"See what a little rain can do," Ilona would say to Stephanie one night over "a couple of six-packs of ice-cold Rolling Rock."

A knowing nod.

Then out of nowhere, "Can I see your scar?"

"Why not."

Three undone buttons, a look, then a gasp, sort of.

"That's severe."

"And permanent."

"But sexy."

"Sexy?"

"Remember, imperfection excites me."

And though the rain damage by this point was also severe. Very severe.

Everywhere.

None of it would be permanent.

Except psychologically.

༄

"I hope it's not too late," President George Herbert Walker Bush would say.

"Give me your hands."

And the president held out his hands and when Ilona touched them, he would look at and lock eyes with this young woman, his warm, tired, confused, deep brown eyes versus her intense, wide-eyed, green-eyed gaze.

"Close your eyes," she would say.

And as he did, George Bush would hear the screams, as did Pope John Paul II and Stephanie LaVasseur before him. And he would begin to sweat and shake slightly. And the screams would grow louder, the cries, the howls. He would see the faces, the bodies, the hands and paws and claws all reaching out, out to him. He would feel the pain. How he would feel the pain. And President Bush would begin to cry, softly at first, then a hard, steady, childlike sob.

And Ilona would lean forward and place her arms around the president of the United States of America, hold and rock him gently.

"It'll be okay," she would promise. "It will be okay."

༄

And Mariam would be ecstatic, though confused, about seeing William Smith.

"But, I thought you were," she would say, not able to finish.

"This is my Father," Ilona would explain, a new introduction.

"You even called him Dad as a little girl," Mariam would say, smiling, still confused.

"No, Mom, you don't understand. This is my real Father. This is God."

"Oh, my."

And God would bring over a chair and help Mariam sit down.

"But," Mariam would say, looking into the eyes of William Smith a.k.a. God. Then, "Oh, my."

But Mariam would come to understand, and God alias William Smith would take her away to Hawaii, where the rain damage, psychological and all, would have been kept to a minimum, just in case God would feel the need for a quick getaway, which, as it happened, He would.

"And to think my daughter-in-law Oona could have owned all of this," God would say to Mariam as they sunned themselves on a deserted beach.

"Charlie Land," Mariam would say, smiling.

And they would kiss and make love on the beach.

This is better than immaculate conception any day, they would both think.

Mariam would be happy.

And God wouldn't have a headache.

❧

And Ilona would fly to Brazil, for a close-up examination of her Father's handiwork, the canyon, now known as Celeste Canyon and now that country's largest and most profitable tourist attraction, and to meet, yet again, with President Sarney.

And they, alone this time, would tour by boat some of the untouched rain forests of the Amazon Basin. And often, as before, Ilona would step from the boat, onto the fertile soil, and listen. But those screams, those cries and howls, those millions of species that had been begging for help, were silent. And her heart would skip a beat, for fear of their annihilation. She would close her eyes, concentrate and sigh with relief, those little faces, the eyes, the paws and claws, there, safe, scared, scarred but alive. Alive.

And at the Planalto Palace, Ilona would meet with Sarney, at his oval mahogany meeting table.

"We have put a complete and definitive stop to the burning of the rain forest," Sarney would say, proudly smiling.

And Ilona would be silent.

"Not one tree, not one leaf, not one blade of grass," Sarney would continue, desperate.

"It sounds as if you've seen the light," Ilona would say. It was her turn to smile.

"Something like that," Sarney would agree, not knowing what else to do.

"Just keep it up," Ilona would warn. "We'll be watching."

And back in New York, in the "charming" twenty-fifth-floor, three-bedroom, duplex penthouse, Stephanie would say, "You guys work like the CIA."

"What do you mean?"

"Salvation through intimidation."

"Whatever works."

And showing Stephanie the many postcards and booklets she would have bought at one of the Celeste Canyon gift shops, Ilona would say, "Talk about art that'll survive."

"And to think," Stephanie would say, "that as a kid I used to be impressed when my father built a house."

"Your dad's a carpenter?"

"Uh huh."

"I didn't know that."

"It's not really something you brag about."

"Jesus was a carpenter and that didn't stop him from bragging."

"Was he a good carpenter?"

"Not according to Dad."

"What do you mean?"

"Everything he made fell apart."

"No way. Is that why he started preaching?"

"More or less. He got into preaching by way of retail."

"I'm confused."

"Well, after Jesus got out of the carpentry biz, he got into undergarments, selling them door to door."

"And that led to preaching?"

"Yup."

"I never heard that before."

[272]

"I don't think it was the image Jesus wanted to project."

"Oh. So how did he do as a salesman?"

"Not very well. He would say things like, 'Blessed are those who wear these,' and corny stuff like that. It just didn't work."

"No way!"

"But if you ask him, he'll claim he was the greatest salesman that ever lived. That he was just ahead of his time."

"Was he?"

"Who knows. He and Dad argue about it all the time. They argue about everything."

"Gods, right?"

"And men."

"And ego."

"Yup."

"Want another Rolling Rock?"

"Yup."

ℰℐ

And more than full-time model Stephanie LaVasseur's career would begin to flourish, "The Pat Sajak Show," her own guest stint on "Late Night with David Letterman," that *Sports Illustrated* swimsuit issue, and, in the coming months, more *Vogue, Cosmopolitan, Glamour, Harper's Bazaar,* and *Mademoiselle* covers than one would or could ever expect.

"You're becoming a celebrity in your own right," Ilona would tell her roommate.

"I couldn't have done it without you," Stephanie would say.

"Yes, you could have," Ilona would insist.

"No. I don't think so," Stephanie would say.

"Wanna switch places?" Ilona would ask.

"Not in a million years," Stephanie would answer.

ℰℐ

And as her career would flourish, Stephanie's relationship with filmmaker Walker would flounder, and eventually end. No arguments, no deceit, just an amicable end.

[273]

And filmmaker Walker would become involved in a relationship of a different sort, a relationship with an editing machine on which he would complete that documentary on God's latest work of art, Celeste Canyon.

Titled *Act of God,* the film would have its premiere at the New York Film Festival in late September, where it would win rave reviews and many prestigious filmmaking awards and eventually receive an Academy Award nomination as best feature-length documentary of the year.

And after seeing his film, Ilona would send a note to filmmaker Walker that would read, "Your film will survive." And there would be a postscript, "P.S. I miss your questions."

∾

And on Wednesday, March 15, Stephanie's twentieth birthday, Ilona, herself between yet more meetings with yet more world leaders, would treat her roommate to a few days in the Caribbean sun.

And when Ilona would slip on one of Stephanie's thong-back bikinis in the privacy of their hotel room she would think to herself, These aren't as uncomfortable as they look, and, checking herself out in one of the room's full-length mirrors, I don't look that bad.

"You can wear it," Stephanie would say, surprising her. "I've got others."

"I can't go outside like this."

"Why not?"

"Because," Ilona would say, "well, because I'm the Daughter of God."

"Suit yourself. But I think you look great."

"I've got some of my mother's curves."

"Then I'm sure she'd want you to keep them as tanned as possible."

"Think so?"

"Here," Stephanie would say, handing Ilona a beer, "have a Red Stripe."

"Red Stripe," Ilona would say, examining the bottle's label, before pulling off the cap and taking a sip. "I would pick an island that doesn't have Rolling Rock."

ᔕᓭ

And later in March, in Moscow, Ilona would meet with Secretary General Gorbachev.

"Everything is changing," he would tell her.

"It had to," she would say.

And he would nod. "You have awakened the people."

And she, too, would nod. "It's about time, isn't it?"

"We have made much progress in the past few months," he would say. "And this I promise, it will continue, we will protect all the snail darters."

And he would.

Gorbachev knew he had no other choice.

ᔕᓭ

And on Monday, April 3, with Stephanie seated to her left and National Baseball League President Bill White and former Mets pitching great Tom Seaver to her right, Ilona would throw out the first ball on opening day of the New York Mets' 1989 season. A game against the St. Louis Cardinals that the Mets would win by a score of eight to five.

"Thanks again," Ilona would say to her roommate just after pitcher Dwight Gooden struck out the first St. Louis batter.

"No problem," Stephanie would answer. "Want a peanut?"

And between innings Seaver would joke, "Your first word, huh?"

"Yup."

And after the game Ilona would meet the members of her favorite team, including pitcher Bobby Ojeda, who would autograph a baseball for the Daughter of God.

"Thank you," Ilona would say.

"You're welcome," her favorite pitcher would reply.

How the Mets could make her smile.

And on Wednesday, April 26, Dr. Sonya Friedman would interview leaders of a group of religious fundamentalists known as "Ilona-ites."

According to Marci Steinberg, co-founder of the group, along with Anabela Agnossi and Rose Teetler, "We formed to see that Ilona's message, her word, if you will, is not bastardized."

"We follow in the footsteps of Ilona," Teetler would explain.

"She is our savior," Agnossi would add. "She is our Lord."

"I see," Sonya would say, shaking her head slightly, "So, essentially you're Ilona freaks?"

"Hardly," Steinberg would say.

"But you dress like Ilona," Sonya would say. "And all of you have long blond hair and are wearing green contacts."

"Ilona green," Teetler would insist.

"But it's much more than a look," Agnossi would explain. "It's a way of life."

And watching in the living room of that "charming" penthouse, Ilona would comment, "Here we go again."

"Can't you just zap 'em with a thunderbolt or something?" Stephanie would ask.

"Someone else would just take their place," Ilona would say. "Humans will never learn."

And in early May, Ilona would make her second appearance on "Late Night with David Letterman."

They would talk about the Mets, the Chaplin centennial, and Stephanie's appearance in *Sports Illustrated.*

"You approve?" Letterman would ask, pointing at a full-page photograph of Stephanie in that sinfully skimpy, moderately transparent, and not-as-wet, light green bikini. Adding quickly, "I know *I* do."

"Yup," Ilona would say, laughing along with the studio audience. "And I especially like the cover photo," referring to the shot of her roommate dressed in that minuscule black bikini bottom and an exceedingly wet, white cut-off T-shirt. "Be kind," Ilona would say, reading, for the most part, from that exceedingly wet, white cut-off T-shirt. "Be kind."

And the regulars from the Soup Kitchen would appear on the program and with Ilona hand out bowls of soup along with a roll to everyone present, the studio audience, the crew, Paul Shaffer and the World's Most Dangerous Band, director Gurnee and host Letterman.

"This is mighty tasty," Letterman would say, about to cut to a commercial break. "We'll be right back."

And Ilona and Letterman would discuss Celeste and Jesus Land, John Charlton Hanley and the Brazilian canyon.

"Dad was pissed," she would say.

"I guess so," Letterman would comment, laughing. "Whew." And he would wipe his brow and play up some mock concern. "Are you comfortable? Can I get you a pillow or something? A Tab, maybe?" And he would laugh some more and smile his goofy smile.

❧

And one night in early June, screams, screams from the other side of the world, would explode in Ilona's head, waking her, suffocating her, and oh, how she, too, would scream. A billion faces would be crying, two billion hands, reaching out, wanting, needing, demanding, pleading, chanting, "Freedom."

But before she would act, before she would even get out of bed, the screaming would stop, snuffed out, become whispers, frightened whispers, angry, desperate, now faceless whispers.

And when Ilona would turn to CNN, the horror would come alive, "Hundreds, possibly thousands, have been killed," some reporter would say. "Shot down in cold blood this evening in Beijing's Tiananmen Square."

"The world is in mourning," the CNN news anchor would say.

And so was Ilona.

❧

And on June 25, 1989, *The New York Times Book Review* would list the following as this nation's best-selling works of nonfiction.

1	**THE NEXT TESTAMENT,** by Father Theodore Karkowski
2	**CHAPLIN,** by David Robinson and Kevin Brownlow
3	**DAVE WIGGITS WAS MY GAY LOVER,** by Bill Waterworth
4	**JILTED,** by Robert Cervickas
5	**MARIAM, YOU SLUT,** by Richard Coggswater
6	**THE DIVINE CATCH,** by Alice Gaugier, In which Ilona's birth would be recalled by the nurse, the nurse-in-training, who caught the just-born Daughter of God inches from the delivery-room floor.
7	**PORTRAIT OF ILONA,** by Robert Mapplethorpe, a beautiful collection of photographs, in both black and white and color, of the Daughter of God, taken by Mapplethorpe shortly before he died of AIDS.
8	**FROM JESUS, MARY & JOSEPH TO ILONA, MARIAM & DAVE,** by George Wiggits
9	**A BRIEF HISTORY OF TIME,** by Stephen W. Hawking (A book that had nothing to do, at least on the surface, with Ilona.)
10	**KINDNESS,** by Cynthia Smythe, a three-thousand-page volume that would examine "kindness" through the ages and analyze what Ilona meant when she told everyone to "be kind."
11	**THE SECOND COMING,** by Tom Brokaw

12	**RAIN DAMAGE,** by various photographers, a 752-page large-format coffee-table book of photographs that would chronicle the worldwide nonpermanent destruction caused by the rain and lightning and thunder and heat.
13	**MY VISION,** by Adrian Lyne
14	**HOW I MOVED ILONA,** by Erik Utke
15	**BELIEVE YOU ME,** by Tony Scognamiglio

❦

And that summer, Ilona would work the inner cities, drugs, murder, prostitution, gangs, man's wrath heaped upon himself. She would visit the other soup kitchens, the clinics, the emergency rooms, the morgues. She would hold hands and calm, listen and understand, or try to. She would be there, and usually, that alone was enough.

"What's it like out there?" Stephanie would ask. "I mean, really."

"You don't want to know," she would say. "And I mean, really."

And when Ilona would close her eyes, there were no screams, just silence, cold silence, deadly silence, an evil she would have to cure, one she would barely understand, and this would frighten her, eternally.

❦

And in late July, shortly after the induction ceremonies and fiftieth-anniversary celebration of the Baseball Hall of Fame, the Ilona Ann Coggswater Museum, located on Pioneer Street in downtown Cooperstown, just around the corner from the Hall of Fame, would open its doors.

And those visiting, just slightly over two hundred thousand paid admissions in the first month alone, would get to see photos and memorabilia commemorating Ilona's life to that point.

A Mapplethorpe portrait, next to the water cooler from the Farmer's Museum where she performed her first "miracle," next to a photo of the Daughter of God standing with the regulars in front of the Soup Kitchen, next to copies of her grade-school report cards, next to an autographed copy of *The Next Testament*.

And one of the museum's two theaters would schedule daily screenings of Chaplin's films, while the other would program Ilona footage, Ilona on "Letterman," Ilona being interviewed by Tom Brokaw, Ilona posing for photographs with this politician or that, Ilona here, Ilona there, Ilona, Ilona everywhere.

And at the museum's gift shop, a visitor could purchase Ilona bumper stickers, Ilona pendants, Ilona dolls, Ilona posters, Ilona postcards, small plastic replicas of that Farmer's Museum water cooler, and all the "Be Kind" merchandise imaginable, most bearing the manufacturing seal of Crosses R Us.

And though Len Osco of Crosses R Us would plan on marketing a sterling-silver pendant replica of the handgun John Charlton Hanley used to shoot Ilona, his advisers would advise against it, and Osco would wisely heed that advice.

"Why is religion so damn tacky?" Stephanie would ask, looking over the gift-shop catalogue.

"Beats me," Ilona would say. "God never had much say as far as religions are concerned."

☙

Next Ilona would travel to Prince William Sound, Alaska, to view firsthand the death and destruction caused by the *Exxon Valdez* oil spill.

And as she would survey the miles of stained beaches, stained beaches that forty days of rain could not cleanse ("It rained harder in Alaska than anywhere else," God would have told her with a helpless shrug), Ilona would think, You should have shared a little of that wrath with the people at Exxon.

And she would visit the temporary shelters where otters and

birds and various other creatures were being cleaned, scrubbed, helped, fed, or, to put an end to their suffering, destroyed.

And this time when Ilona would close her eyes, she heard not screams, not cries, but moans, low, lifeless, agonized.

"Greed," she would hear George Bush say. "Greed."

⋐⋑

And, to celebrate Ilona's nineteenth birthday, the world would shut down and be humane, a Christmas of sorts where gifts of kindness would replace gifts of neckties, dolls, fruitcakes, etc., etc., and so on.

A good deed, a kind word, a helping hand was all that was required and, or so it seemed, everyone would pitch in.

"How?" so many would ask.

"Just be kind to each other," Ilona would say.

"But we *are* being kind to each other."

"Then, on my nineteenth birthday, be extra kind. Go out of your way to be kind. Reinvent kindness. Double your efforts. And keep that level of kindness around throughout the year. Then on my twentieth birthday, reinvent it, double it, once again."

⋐⋑

And also, to celebrate Ilona's nineteenth birthday, Stephanie would throw "a party to end all parties," inviting, among others, the four members of the Replacements, David Letterman, the Professor, Sonya Friedman, Elvis Costello, Mikhail Gorbachev, Laurie Anderson, Bobby Ojeda and all of his teammates, and Flatcake Al and all of the Soup Kitchen regulars.

And toward the middle of the evening, after speaking with Mariam and Linda, who conveyed their birthday wishes long distance from a telephone on a luxury barge cruising down the Nile River, the Daughter of God would corner Paul Westerberg and plant a huge kiss on her favorite rock star's lips.

A surprised Westerberg, not knowing what to say, would say, "I don't know what to say."

[281]

"You don't have to say anything," Ilona would explain, "That was my birthday present to myself."

And though she and Westerberg would spend, according to the next day's gossip columns, "a great deal of time" talking in one corner of that "private" bi-level wraparound balcony that gave them an unobstructed and "private" 360-degree view of the world Ilona would be saving, Westerberg would eventually go home as would the rest of his bandmates and the rest of the guests, leaving Ilona with her fantasies and her roommate.

A roommate who would ask, "Why didn't you go for it?"

"I just couldn't."

"Why not?"

"I was scared."

಄

And in mid-October, the Mets would win their third world championship, in a World Series against the California Angels decided in the seventh and final game, a game in which Bobby Ojeda would pitch a no-hitter for his New York team.

"I was only able to watch four of the games," Ilona would say.

To which most members of the sports media would comment, "Four was enough."

಄

And CNN would continue to question its viewers about Ilona in its nightly nonscientific Newsnight 900 Poll.

"Do you feel Ilona has any influence on the New York Mets winning ballgames?"

To which seventy-three percent of the callers would answer yes, while twenty-seven percent would say no.

"Do you miss watching TV preachers such as Reverend Jerry Falwell, Oral Roberts, Jimmy Swaggart, and Jim Bakker?"

To which nine percent of the callers would answer yes, while ninety-one percent would say no.

"Would you visit the Ilona Ann Coggswater Museum in Cooperstown, New York?"

To which a eighty-six percent of those calling would answer yes, while fourteen percent would say no.

"Should Ilona Ann Coggswater date Paul Westerberg of the Replacements?"

To which a full one hundred percent of those calling would answer no.

❧

And on Thursday, November 9, drained from a recent visit to Africa, where, in Kenya, she would applaud that country's near miraculous efforts to save the elephant, and in South Africa where she, on national television, would scold that country's president for his deplorable policy of apartheid—"Times are changing," she would have told him, "Not here," he would say— Ilona, now in Germany, would hear cheering, cheering from around the world, no screams on this day, not from anywhere, just celebration, celebration and hope.

And she would stand and watch and smile, witnessing the spectacle firsthand, that intense, wide-eyed, green-eyed gaze seemingly lighting up the sky.

And when a reporter would ask, "What do you think?" the Daughter of God would shrug and hug herself against the cold, and say, finally, "I think it's wonderful."

What else could she say?

What else could anyone say?

And when another reporter would question, "Is this your doing?" Ilona would reply, "It's everyone's doing."

And Ilona, the many reporters, the hundreds of thousands present, and the entire world would watch and marvel, marvel at the history, marvel at the emotion, marvel at the sight, marvel at the meaning, of the Berlin Wall tumbling down.

❧

And later that month, Ilona would take a much needed vacation.

Paris.

[283]

And though Stephanie wanted to spend the Thanksgiving holiday in New York, Ilona would convince her to come along.

"We could go wild," Ilona would plead.

"We'd only do things we'd regret in the morning," Stephanie would say.

"Yeah, but you only live once, right?" Ilona would say.

And, after a moment of silent thought, Stephanie would begin packing those aluminum-and-black-rubber designer suitcases of French origin.

"When do we leave?"

And as Ilona and Stephanie would tour the greatest of museums examining the greatest of art, one thought would haunt the Daughter of God.

"Y'know what?" Ilona would say.

"I know. I know. Only art survives."

"No."

"What then?"

"Art can be so depressing sometimes."

And without any need for thought, silent or otherwise, Stephanie would suggest, *"Une bière?"*

"Oui."

☙

And, after returning from France, while attending a late afternoon screening of just Werner Herzog's *Every Man for Himself and God Against All,* which was still playing a double bill with Ingmar Bergman's *The Seventh Seal* at a revival house on 12th Street, Ilona and Stephanie would run into filmmaker Walker, who would be seeing the Bergman film, "for the fiftieth time."

"Your golden anniversary," Stephanie would say, happy to see her former lover.

And that evening, this partially holy trinity would sip cappucino in a coffee house on Bleecker and Macdougal and talk and reminisce.

"Paris, huh?" filmmaker Walker would ask. "Go to any of the museums?"

"Virtually every one, or so it seemed."

"And?"

"I've got a thought for you," Ilona would say.

"What's that?"

"Art can be so depressing sometimes."

"Yeah. And the more depressing it is, the more it survives."

"Oh," Stephanie would say, "that explains it."

ᘓ

And a few days before Christmas, the last Christmas of the decade, and immediately after she had shared an all-vegetarian meal with President and Mrs. Bush and others at the annual White House Christmas dinner, Ilona Ann Coggswater would receive a preview issue of that following week's *Time* magazine, an issue whose cover would feature a just as flattering August Terninko painting of the Daughter of God under the heading, "God of the Decade."

Once again the publishers and editors and all involved would unanimously choose Ilona for their annual Man of the Year issue. "But," one senior editor would explain, "this year we chose to call Ilona 'God of the Decade' instead of, well, 'Savior of the Decade.' It just sounded better."

And again, once again, the issue would praise Ilona for everything, from her Mother to her wardrobe to her roommate to her sense of humor. It would include an abridged account of Ilona's shooting and everything that followed, along with those charts and graphs illustrating how violent crime in the country would have decreased by some seventy-four percent, nonviolent crime would have suffered a sixty-five percent decrease, legal handgun sales would have virtually ceased, nonreligious charitable donations would be up by six hundred fifteen percent, religious charitable donations would be down ninety-eight percent, environmental action and cleanup would have become a worldwide obsession, illegal dumping would have totally and finally stopped, illegal drug use would be off by forty percent, Tab sales would have increased by roughly sixteen hundred percent, and illiteracy, unemployment, inflation, and homelessness would, also and finally, be on the decline, all in the twelve months since Ilona had been named "Savior of the Year."

The new issue would also contain more photographs than one could ever imagine, a list of Ilona's favorite albums and movies from 1989, a piece about the dissolution of the National Rifle Association which mentioned that its members were, quite simply, sick and tired of throwing up, and even short obituaries for Bert Uogintas and Jesus Land, obituaries that would mention that the only remaining reminders of either, that original Rodin sculpture of a beautiful nude female reaching one hand upward, a hand whose fingertips were touching those of a large male hand, the hand of God, titled *Creation of Eve* and that series of three small paintings by the Dutch painter Rembrandt, the first of Mary holding the baby Jesus, the second of Jesus being crucified, and the last depicting His resurrection, had been recovered, damp though undamaged, and could now be seen and enjoyed by all at the Metropolitan Museum of Art in New York City.

∽

And early on New Years Day, 1990, seated alone in the living room of that "charming" twenty-fifth-floor, three-bedroom, duplex penthouse on Charles Street, Ilona Ann Coggswater, Daughter of God, a glass of Tab by her side, would look back at the year, happy, confident, and mostly content. The Earth, antique and crumbling as it was, would be in the process of being refurnished and refinished and most humans would have adopted kindness as a way of life. And the screams, though still there, would have diminished, not totally, but greatly, and though greatly wasn't enough, there still was time.

And the Daughter of God would smile. That wasn't so painful, now, was it?

And on the end table where she would now place her half-full glass of Tab, Ilona would pick up a book that had sat, for so long, collecting dust. A book that she had always meant to read, but.

What the hell, she would think. She hadn't read anything good in quite a while. It almost seemed as if good books weren't being published anymore. And besides, it's early. Stephanie wouldn't be up for hours.

And, opening to the first page of that tattered old copy of Vonnegut's *Cat's Cradle*, that copy given to her by the Professor, just the Professor, what seemed like so very long ago, Ilona would read.

She would begin with the inscription, "We've all got to follow our destiny. Good luck with yours, the Professor. P.S. Nothing is impossible," and flip the page.

ဪ

But that, too, is jumping ahead.

Some Final Thoughts from Dudley & Jerry

"Ha."

"What was that?"

"I said, 'Ha,' " and Dudley smiled.

"So, you won game one," Jerry said. "Remember, this is a seven-game World Series."

"Baseball. Why the fuck does everything always have to come down to baseball?"

"It's the great American pastime," Jerry said.

"I thought fucking was the great American pastime."

"Fucking isn't limited by international boundaries."

"Umm."

"Speaking of which."

"What?"

"If you despise baseball as much as you obviously do," Jerry said, with extra emphasis on the "obviously," "why Cooperstown?"

"Remember that night when you first told me to give up?" Dudley asked.

"Yeah."

"When I left here I went to the Baseball Hall of Fame."

"You." Jerry laughed. "At the Hall of Fame?"

"I wanted to see if I was missing anything," Dudley explained, himself smiling.

"And were you?"

"Hell no, it's the most boring place I've ever been to."

"And?"

"And nothing, I was sitting on a park bench in front of the Hall."

"Sulking."

"Thinking. And Mariam walked by on her way to this party."

"And the rest is history."

"Something like that," Dudley said. "So, how 'bout a drink?"

"Beer?"

"Something stronger."

"Like bourbon?"

"Like bourbon," Dudley said. "Now what was all that about a seven-game World Series?"

"Just that, it ain't over till it's over."

"God-damn you."

"Watch that."

"Couldn't you have said, 'It ain't over till the fat lady sings'?"

"I could have, I suppose, if I had been so inclined," Jerry said, handing Dudley his drink. "But I wasn't."

"This is very nice," Dudley said, sipping the bourbon.

"My private stock."

"To Earth," a solitary toast.

"You're so confident."

"And why shouldn't I be?"

"It was too easy."

[290]

"It took two thousand years, for Christ's sake."

"But what's a couple of millennia to us?"

"True," Dudley said, suddenly rubbing his temples. "So, what are you saying?"

But Jerry changed the subject. "Headache?" he asked.

"They *had* disappeared."

"Sorry."

"I'll bet."

"Just be cautious, my friend, and keep your bullpen warmed up."

And Dudley shook his head ever so slightly.

"By the way," Jerry said, "how come all the great ball players are in heaven?"

And all too frustrated, now with a blazing headache, Dudley stood and said, "I give up."

"I told you to do that twenty years ago. But did you listen? Do you ever listen?"

"No," Dudley shouted as he walked away. "Do you?"

"Listen?"

"Ever give up?"

"No." Jerry laughed. "Never."

Acknowledgments to Kathy Milani, Steve Manzi (*for the title*), my editor Dan Levy, my agent Matt Bialer, Steve Schragis, Bill, Ovie, Len, Marion, Debbie & StanLEE, Gary, Mary, Teri, Bob Dixon, Cherie (*for the snail darter*), the New York Mets, *all* the fine folk at Boppers in New Haven including but not limited to: Michelle B., Barry, Q., Stickman, Murph, Wendy & Kendra (*for all those "ice-cold Rolling Rocks"*), and lastly to Kristine (*who loves the Replacements as much as I, but for all the wrong reasons . . .*)